Deryn Lake started to write stories at the age of five, then graduated to novels but destroyed all her early work because, she says, it was hopeless. A chance meeting with one of the Getty family took her to Sutton Place and her first serious novel was born. Deryn was married to a journalist and writer, the late L. F. Lampitt, has two grown-up children, four beautiful and talented grandchildren, and one rather large cat. Deryn has lived near the famous battlefield of 1066 for the past sixteen years where she enjoys her life as a woman about town.

PRAISE FOR DERYN LAKE:

'Lake has a strong sense of history and an uncanny ability to bring it to life' – *Daily Mail*

'Ingenious and highly readable' – *The Times*

Also By Deryn Lake

Series

John Rawlings Murder Mysteries

Sutton Place Trilogy

Collection

Lovers Lost in Time

Novels

As Shadows Haunting

Banishment

Pour The Dark Wine

The Governor's Ladies

To Sleep No More

The King's Women

The Prince's Women

Deryn Lake

LUME BOOKS

First published in 2019 by Lume Books
85-87 Borough High Street,
London, SE1 1NH

ISBN 978-1-83901-161-0

www.lumebooks.co.uk

In memory of Chris Hart (actor-fellow and friend),
Charles Purle (judge and great supporter)
and Beryl Cross (poet and one-off).

Prologue

He glistened. He stood quite still in the arched entrance and knew that every eye in the room had turned in his direction. Dressed from head to foot in full Highland evening dress, the diamonds dripping at his breast scintillating in the hall of mirrors that lined the enormous room, he drew in a breath and waited. The other guests, all members of the high society of Rome, had turned to look as the newcomer made his entrance, and now they stood entranced. He was tall, lean and beautiful to behold. Very slowly, as he gauged their reaction, he bowed his elegant head. There was a ripple of applause which grew in volume, while a hundred feather fans whisked into action and cooled the cheeks of the ladies present. Smiling inwardly, though remaining totally straight-faced, the prince put forward a foot encased in a soft black buckled shoe and entered the room.

His host, the Cardinal Rohan, a swirling mass of scarlet robes, approached and held out his hand.

"Your Highness," he said, in a voice bigger than he was.

Charles Edward, contrary to custom, kissed the proffered hand.

"Your Eminence," he replied.

The cardinal was very slightly abashed; Charles Edward noted it with inner amusement though he kept his face quite straight. From his magnificent height he looked at the churchman to see what he would do next. After a moment's hesitation, Rohan raised the royal hand to his lips and gave it a kiss in return.

Charles allowed a small smile to twitch his lips as he looked up and saw the admiring glances of both men and women. He was twenty-one and this was the best, the most glamorous, the most brilliant moment of his life. A very attractive woman, well into her thirties but with all the beauty that life alone can give, was being led forward.

"May I introduce my niece, Your Highness?" asked the cardinal.

"The pleasure will be entirely mine," answered Charles Edward, bowing his head once more.

"The Princesse de Parma, sir. She is an ardent admirer of both you and your family."

The woman curtsied before him, sinking to the ground so that her skirts billowed out round her, and holding up one small, slim hand to be raised. Charles became convinced that the strange attractiveness he held for women was working its magic. He smiled, mighty pleased.

"Would madame the princesse care to dance?"

The cardinal answered for her, twinkling away in his rustling robes. "She most certainly would, sir."

Charles gave the woman a smile that radiated charm. "Then, if you would do me the honour I would be enchanted."

She rose delicately and then looked up at him. There could be no mistaking that glance. Charles Edward knew she could be his at any time he chose. But this night he was on his best behaviour as, with every person in the vast gleaming room giving him their full stare, he, the Prince of Wales, led the lady into the ballroom.

He was a superb dancer; energetic, lithe, supple, possessing everything that modern manners required. And though a great deal of his personal style had been slowly acquired, his abilities to leap round the floor with agility, or to move like a stalking cat, were natural. Bestowed upon him at birth, just like his ability to handle horses.

But the dance was over and he was being besieged by partners as all the daughters, wives and sisters of the Italian nobility pressed upon him from every side. Charles could not help himself; he laughed with pleasure before reluctantly opening his eyes.

He was in his bed, an uncomfortable great thing, in the Palazzo Muti, where he had been born some sixty-six years earlier. His daughter, Charlotte, was standing close by, looking at him, her face a little anxious.

She spoke. "You're awake, Father. You were laughing heartily in your sleep. Did you have a pleasant dream?"

He looked at her. "I was dreaming of the past, my dear. I was at a ball and dancing with a glorious creature. Have I missed anything important while I slept?"

"No, Papa. I heard you laugh, that is all. Would you like to see the Moor? He is always good company."

"Please, send him in."

Turning, she left the room giving a quiet call for Charles' favourite servant to attend him. He came quickly.

"You know I was once a great lover of women, Marcus," said that wreck of what had once been the noblest Stuart of them all.

"I am sure you were, Bonnie Prince."

"You know all about my past, don't you?"

"Yes, favoured one. But you are not allowed to speak of it. Last time you did so you became greatly upset. The Duchess of Albany, your daughter, forbids it."

The old man's voice became sad. "But I like talking of it. I was once a very great person."

"And you are still, sir. But you also need rest. After all, you are going to the theatre tonight. You must save your strength for that."

"Indeed I must, Marcus. Would you like to attend with me?"

"I would be very honoured. May I leave the room now, or do you have any further wishes?"

"No, go. I shall sleep again." And Charles Edward waved a hand.

To think that this had once been the bravest of men, the toast of Paris, the lover of many women. Just so, Marcus thought, as he bowed his way out of the room. Allah is merciful, these things happened to people, it was merely the way of the world.

*

He was moving fast as a gale, as fast as it was possible to ride, guiding his reckless horse with a spring that had surprised even him. It was a snorting dark beast, a present given for his tenth birthday, but even then Charles had not been afraid of it. He had talked to it, cajoled it, stroked its silky ears when it had leaned forward to take the apple he held out. Then, their eyes had been on a level and the boy had gazed into the luminous black orbs and spoken very softly.

"You are my horse now, so I shall respect you; but in return I require your loyalty."

They had gazed at each other for a long, deep moment and then the beast had lowered its head even further, brushing its leg with its lips before straightening up. Charles had taken this as a sign of submission and had immediately asked a groom to give him a lift up into the saddle.

But today, mere days after his fourteenth birthday, his mother had finally died. He had hardly known her and yet he felt utterly bereft.

He had vaulted into the saddle, not knowing quite how he had done so because tears were pouring down his face and half blinding him. He was weeping because he had desperately craved her love. That sad, unaffectionate, skeletal creature who had given birth to him and his brother Henry, had departed from the world.

Charles would always associate her with a slight smell of parchment, coming from the skin drawn so tightly over her face that it was possible to see the skull underneath. She had not responded to his farewell kiss, being too near the brink of life to notice anything. But then, she had never responded. Even when, as a child, he had rushed towards her, arms outstretched, she had hugged him but briefly before dropping her gaze back to her book.

When Henry was only a few months old their mother had walked out on their father, departing for a convent from which she had refused to budge. Eventually, however, she had returned, emaciated and haggard, her lips moving in silent prayer, surrounded by a bevy of dark-eyed priests. After that there had been little communication.

And now that shrunken woman was gone for good and Charles was riding as fast as he could to escape; escape from a vision of that sad, shrivelled face breathing its last; escape from his father's gloom and constant criticism; escape from his know-all younger brother giving him a sideways looks when Henry was pronounced right, as he always was.

The horse was tiring and so, at last, was its rider. Charles spoke to the animal with a voice that was full of the sadness of his mother's final parting.

"Easy there, Nighthawk," and he patted its sweating neck.

They slowed to a walk, the fourteen-year-old boy looking about him with interest as he was not familiar with the outskirts of Rome.

The Palazzo Muti in which the family lived — though *family* was perhaps too cosy a description — was an odd place to call home. Even though he had been born there, Charles had never really liked the building. Shaped like a wedge of cheese, a tight V in design, built round a measly courtyard that did little more than let in light, one could stand at the far windows and see what was going on in the apartments opposite, so confined was the space.

But the prince had ridden hard to get away from it, going northwards, actually escaping the confines of the city and presently finding himself in the countryside beyond. He breathed in deeply and had a sudden strange illusion that he could smell the sea. Yet turning to look round there was only a small brook, gurgling and giggling as it rushed over the smooth stones in its glassy depths.

He was in a dense group of trees, an early evening mist seeping down through its naked branches, the splintered fingers of which pointed ever upwards as if begging for light. The brook appeared opaque, as though it had been transformed into a stream of milk. Charles Edward felt suddenly nervous, his spine thrilling with a sense of expectancy, of *what*, he was not certain.

"Hello," said a hidden voice behind him.

He was terrified witless and believed that his skin was left behind as he dismounted in a panic and stood, shaking, to see who had addressed him. It was a small ageless creature, female, dressed in ragged clothing that looked as if it had once been the philanthropic gift of a lady of fashion, but was now so wretched with hard wear that it was barely recognisable.

The stranger chuckled. "Are you lost, young fellow?"

Charles became suddenly conscious of the fact that he was not bearing his order and that his clothes — a dull brown suit slightly too small for him — gave no hint as to his rank. He stared at the creature stupidly until the funny side of the situation began at last to creep up on him.

"Can you give me directions then, signorina?" he asked, smiling slightly.

"As to your future, do you mean?"

That had not occurred to him and Charles, peering into the grubby face, saw that a pair of brilliant dark eyes were regarding him from the deep grime.

"Yes, why not? It would be amusing, to say the least."

"How do you know that? That it will be amusing? It could be a prediction of gloom and despair."

Charles' grin widened. "If it were, I don't think you would tell me. I think you will say that I am going to marry a …"

He caught himself just in time, before saying 'princess'.

"… pretty girl and have a houseful of children."

"Give me your hands then, young fellow, and I'll tell you what's written there."

Charles squatted down and placed his long fine fingers into the gypsy's grasp. Close to her like that he could see that she was much younger than he had first thought and would have been quite pleasing to the eye, if it were not for the layers of grime on her naughty ragamuffin face. She moved one of her fingers round his thumb and the prince felt a thrill run through his entire body.

Gracious, he thought to himself, then said, "How old are you?"

"Of what interest is that to you?"

"None really. I was just wondering."

She did not answer, saying instead, "You have not had a happy childhood, signor."

He gulped, "My mother has been rather ill. I have not seen much of her."

"And she will shortly die — if she has not done so already."

The tears, which had engulfed him recently, returned. Charles gave a small swallow to cover the fact but the silent drops coursed down his cheeks nonetheless. The gypsy continued to speak.

"But you will win many hearts. Women will fall in love with you. You will have an enormous attraction for them."

She giggled wickedly and Charles could not help himself, blushing deeply at her double entendre. She glanced up and said, "And how old are you, my friend? Seventeen, eighteen?"

Charles, who was nearing six feet in height already, thought seriously about lying. In the end he said, "Almost."

The girl, looking at him closely, said, "You're tall for your age."

The wild notion that she was propositioning him ran excitingly through Charles Edward's brain. However, his father, James — son of King James II, who had been thrust from the English throne because of his Catholicism and had resided in France ever since — had taken him to one side quite recently and explained to him the facts of life. Including a very sobering thought. Not the siring of bastards, nor indeed the setting up and keeping of a mistress, but the horrid fact of disease.

"One piece of advice, my boy. Never place your cock in a tart. Follow that piece of wisdom and you won't go far wrong."

"I beg your pardon, sir?" the boy had answered, bewildered, thinking of luscious fruits and whipped cream, oozing French custard and pastry light as a childish kiss.

A smile had played round the mouth of James III, de jure king of Great Britain. "I am referring to a harlot, my son. Most of them are infected with vile diseases. Only fornicate with a woman of high rank or noble birth, preferably married to a man you trust. Or one that you know to be scrupulously free of infection."

"But how can I tell, father?"

"By the female's reputation, Charles. That will be as good a guide as any."

Somewhat bewildered, Charles Edward had taken it all very seriously. And now his father's words sang in his brain. Yet his private thoughts were letting him down. He looked at the girl's dirty face, his vivid eyes searching.

"Are you of good character, young lady?"

She laughed uproariously. "Not particularly. One lives by one's wits and whatever else one has to offer."

"Oh dear."

"What do you mean by that?"

"By sighing? I was just thinking of something my father said."

"And what might that have been?"

"Oh, it doesn't really matter."

A smile appeared on the grimy face. "No need to go on. I can guess at it. Tell you what, though. Have you ever been kissed?"

"Yes."

"By your mother and father and elderly female relatives?"

Charles Edward nodded, thinking back, recalling the faces of the several ladies of advancing years who had caressed him, and the cracks that had appeared in their mask-like maquillage as their rouged lips crinkled up prior to the embrace.

"I thought as much. Here, let me show you how it is done."

It was wonderful. Her tongue forced his mouth open and he found himself subjected to a million quivering sensations. It had been at that moment, at the tender age of barely fourteen, that Charles Edward had decided that he enjoyed the feelings aroused in him enormously and had made a mental note that he would kiss again, and kiss frequently, when he grew a little older.

The gypsy held him closely for a few delightful moments, then pushed him to arm's length, her grimy face unreadable in the fast-fading light.

"There, that's how it's done. Now, young sir, are you going to give me anything to remember you by?"

Charles fished in his pockets and came up with a coin that had almost slipped into the lining, so deeply was it buried.

"I'm afraid this is all I've got."

"That will do. Remember what I've told you today. You will be loved by many women. And you'll have a fierce courage too. You are going to be a remarkable man."

"Thank you," Charles Edward answered, his lips simmering still from that gorgeous kiss.

"Remember me," she said, and the next second was gone.

He had been fishing in his pocket to see if by chance he had a further coin on him, but on hearing her speak had looked up. The gypsy had vanished, just as if she had never been there at all. But Charles, mounting his horse and turning it in the direction of Rome, knew that she had been real enough. Her magic kiss had left him feeling older, wiser, on the brink of manhood. And then he thought of his poor, dead mother and swallowed down the great sigh of unhappiness which once more consumed him.

*

His mother had died a mere eighteen days after his fourteenth birthday but, Charles Edward considered, by contrast his thirteenth anniversary had been a simply joyous occasion. A magnificent feast had been arranged for him at the Palazzo Corsini. He had danced beautifully, eaten manfully, but — and far more importantly — had been treated with the greatest respect. The cream of English aristocracy had been present and had kissed his hand. It was on that night that there had been born in Charles Edward's heart a longing to regain the throne of England, for his father and for himself. The little matter of in what way he was going to achieve this was yet to be decided. All that the prince had known was that someday, somehow, it would come about.

He had received his taste for action a short while later. The Spanish army was waging war against the Neapolitan territories and Charles had been invited by the Duke of Liria — governing genius of the forces — to serve with him. Even as a child of six, that amazing charm which would captivate all who came into contact with it, had been evident. The little boy had won the heart of the Spanish duke and now Charles' older self did nothing to displace Liria's earlier affection. At the age of thirteen he had trotted off to war, full of exuberance and ready to beguile everyone he met.

He had been a triumph. From the common soldiery to the infante Don Carlos himself, the Prince of Wales had them eating out of his hand. Refusing to be treated as a prince he had asked — with that slow smile of his — that he be served as a distinguished incognito only. And his ease of manner had won him so much respect that Liria had commented to his ducal brother that Charles' manner of conversation was truly bewitching.

And then he, the boy hero, had come home to a sniping, jealous father; a snide, smug-faced brother; and worse, far worse, the declining health of his skeletal mother. He had wept on his fourteenth birthday when the dying woman had begged him to stay faithful to the church of Rome. He had held her against his breast when he kissed her for the last time. He had walked with bent head behind her cortège and had sat dry-eyed while her requiem was sung. But he had also been kissed by a wood nymph gypsy, and told that he would be a man beloved of many women. Sighing in his sleep, the old prince turned over and dreamed of his eventful past.

CHAPTER ONE

Jeannie

He could hear them outside, shuffling about, kicking their feet, muttering in Gaelic, nobody saying a word that he could comprehend. It was a horrible experience, a truly devastating, soul-biting loneliness. Charles Edward, de jure Prince of Wales, sat alone in a shepherd's hut, and mutely gazed at the floor. Close by was that massive sheet of water, Loch Shiel, ahead the towering and somehow frightening peaks of the Highlands. And there he was, a puny figure set against all those mighty works of nature, feeling as if the entire world was caving in on him.

With what gallantry had he sailed from France three weeks earlier, arriving in Scotland with fire in his belly and a song on his lips — but that had quickly been dowsed.

He had first set foot on what he considered his native land on the island of Eriskay. It was grey and it was raining but Charles Edward had emerged from the ship trying to look ready for anything that came his way. He had grown a beard on the journey and was wearing the disguise of a student priest at The Scots College in Rome. But this was rather lost on the natives, who spoke only Erse or Gaelic and had no idea who this religious fellow might be. His first night was spent in the most miserable of bothies, crouching over a peat fire, the only ventilation a hole in the roof. His frequent trips to the door to breathe in a lungful of air were the one thing that caused any comment at all.

But his famous charm, his bright tawny eyes, his great mastery of words, had stood him in good stead. Charles had been forced to bring them all into play over the next week or so, persuading the tough Scots clan leaders to raise their men and follow him into battle. Looking back now, as he sat alone in the shepherd's hut and realised that they had eventually thought better of it and were not going to turn up for what was to have been his finest hour, the prince felt cheapened. A sense of betrayal engulfed him. He could work his enchantment until he dropped, but none of it would ever do him any good at all.

"May I come in, sir?" said a voice outside.

At least one of them could speak English.

Charles collected himself. "Of course. Please do."

James Mor MacGregor stood in the entrance, son of the famous Rob Roy himself. Charles rose to his feet and MacGregor bowed his red head in a gesture of respect.

"They're not coming, are they?"

"It would appear that way, sir."

"But why? Why not? They gave me their word. And I can't fight the Hanoverians with the small number that you brought with you." Realising that this sounded like a criticism, Charles added quickly, "Though I thank you most sincerely for your loyalty."

His companion gave a wry smile. "A MacGregor always keeps his word."

"Indeed. Your father's famous quote. Tell me more about him. I must confess I don't know a great deal."

"He turned out to fight the English when your grandfather was forced to leave the throne. He fought bloody-handed with every muscle in him. He was a true Jacobite all his life. And do you know what he had put on his gravestone?"

Charles Edward shook his head.

"'MacGregor Despite Them.'"

The prince, temporarily forgetting the miserable circumstances in which he waited, laughed joyfully. "A true man indeed! I wish he were here now. But no, how can I say that when I have you, his son, and your clansmen? How much longer do you plan to stay?"

"Until you dismiss us, my prince. We are your bodyguard. We are ready to fight the Englishmen as we stand now."

Charles shook his head, his autumn hair gleaming in a shaft of light that came through the hut's narrow entrance.

"It would be a fool's game, MacGregor. We'd be cut to pieces where we stood. And now the gathering of the clans has proved itself to be a complete farce. My time in Scotland is over and done."

"Give it one more hour, sir. Just one more hour." And so saying, MacGregor bowed and left.

Sitting on his own, with no-one to see his shame, the prince wept silently. He had left on this fruitless expedition without his father's consent, had insisted on pressing on when worthy Scotsmen had advised him to leave and forget all about it. When someone had said bluntly, "Go home," Charles had replied, "I *am* home." That had said it all. And now, quite alone, he stared reality in the face. If ever there had been a fool's errand this was it. He was an idiot, an imbecile, an impetuous half-wit. Charles plunged his head into his hands and faced his dismal fortunes.

And then, very distantly, over the muted noise made by the men of the clan MacDonald, there came a high-pitched wailing. The prince strained his ears, wondering what it was. Whatever its source, it was getting louder.

Suddenly, Charles Edward was all attention. Was his agony coming to an end? Had somebody actually responded to his call to raise the Jacobite standard at desolate Glenfinnan? Hastily making the sign of the cross, he stepped outside. One look at the grin on the faces of the MacDonalds, seeing MacGregor put his fingers to his mouth and let out a piercing whistle, told him everything. It was the bagpipes, the clans were coming, his own personal Calvary was over.

All around him the scenery made him breathless. Behind him shimmered and glimmered the great Loch Schiel; before him the mountains had turned mauve in colour, the more distant peaks black and menacing, some covered with snow that echoed the colour of the clouds passing over their heads. To add to this dramatic panorama, the prince could see distinctly the clan Cameron snaking their way through the mountain passes, striding at their head young Lochiel, who had demanded certain guarantees from Charles Edward in return for his appearance. But he had come, and the prince had never been gladder than to see the distant but distinctive figure, marching purposefully, his pipers playing their war pibroch, seven hundred clansmen tramping behind him.

The prince momentarily turned away, dashing the tears from his eyes. His dreams were becoming reality. His father would no longer be de jure, but instead Charles would regain Britain for the royal Stuarts as the true king of England. A position to which he, Prince Charles Edward Stuart, would one day succeed.

The last of the kilted men were still threading their way towards the meeting place when there came through the clear Scots afternoon the sound of a different skirl. Another clan was approaching. Charles turned to MacGregor.

"There are more on their way. By God, man, at this rate we'll have enough for an army!"

"Aye, my prince. Just hold yourself calmly now and wait to see how many come."

But it was not to the clansmen that the prince looked with incredulity, but to the figure leading them. It was a woman. A tall, well-made woman, wearing tartan trews and a fitted jacket — a leather bag in the front — smiling as she approached. Charles judged her to be about forty years old but nonetheless thought her extremely attractive, with a mass of black curls atop of which was set a Highland bonnet at an extremely sporty angle. When the soldier woman had drawn close she curtseyed — rather a strange gesture for a figure in trousers — and then kissed Charles' hand. A pair of very pretty eyes, a deep shade like sweet sherry, gave him a mischievous glance, then looked away.

MacGregor rumbled a laugh. "So, you've come yourself, Jeannie. Was your nephew not up to the task?"

"You know very well that he is sick in the head, James Mor, that's why I came in person. Your royal Highness, may I offer up to your service three hundred men from MacDonald of Keppoch's clan?"

"You certainly may, madam," Charles answered, helping her upright and giving her his most charming smile. "And can I say how delightful you look in your warrior garb?"

She gave him a glance, which was a cross between a question and a grin. "I'm dressed for a fight, sir. For that is surely what you mean to have."

"Madam, I have left a comfortable life behind for that express purpose. I came to Scotland to restore the rightful king to the Scots and, by God, that is what I intend to do, even though I die in the attempt."

MacGregor smiled, just a trifle whimsically. "Your Highness, may I present Mrs Jeannie Cameron who, I feel certain, will obey your every command."

Charles controlled his face, wondering if there was a double meaning, and said nothing whilst Jeannie, her gaze fixed firmly on the ground, made her awkward curtsey once more.

"It is most pleasant to meet you, Mrs Cameron. Let it be hoped that we will become good friends."

The pair of sherry eyes twinkled at him briefly and then looked away. "My sword is at your command, sir."

The prince would like to have answered that so was his to hers, but thought much better of it and instead smiled and moved on.

Half an hour later the company was joined by seventy Royal Scots and with that number Charles Edward, walking amongst them, hearing the Gaelic which he would try to learn, knew that he had gathered enough men to lead into battle. The uprising of 1745 was on.

Later that day, the old Duke William of Atholl was granted the honour of unfurling the Jacobite standard of red, white and blue silk. As it fluttered in the early evening breeze Charles, standing tall and proud, heady with joy, was declared regent of Scotland. With shouts of 'huzzah' rebounding round the great hills, the prince made a short speech, cleverly phrased. Putting his hand on his heart and then projecting his voice to its best advantage, he assured the kilted clansmen that he had come to make them free from the yoke of Hanover and would restore their rightful king. Then he stepped down and immediately ordered a council of war. And when that was finished, he invited the clan leaders and other worthy men to join him for a drink of celebration.

"Not in a palace, I fear, but in a small barn in which I intend to sleep tonight."

There was much laughter and a tear or two in several ageing eyes, as the great men of Scotland crowded into the little space and raised their pewter cups to their lips.

Outside, there was a blood-red sunset. The waters of the loch shimmered like a bale of crimson silk spread out on a draper's counter, its surface broken occasionally by the leap of a silver fish. The great mountains that swept down to the water were watching, still as ebony dogs lying asleep, their heads between their somnolent paws. Above, the sky was the colour of a battlefield, dyed by the drip of dying men. And with all his guests gone to their bivouacs, Charles stepped out into that red rose evening.

From all around him came the distant sounds of a camp by night and he felt his heart leap at the thought that all this great profusion of men had come from their dwellings, however lowly or great, in support of him. For a moment he felt humbled by his surroundings, wondering how the actions of one puny man could have summoned up such a large muster of loyal people. Then, he gathered to him every ounce of energy and strength. He was determined to lead them as best he could, even if it cost him his life's blood. His heart beating fast, Charles was just about to make his way back into the barn when he heard a voice speak quietly, so close to him that he jumped with fright.

"Are you all right, Your Highness?"

In the fast-dying light, he peered to see who it was. It was Jeannie, still wearing a man's attire, her bonnet removed and her hair flowing about her shoulders.

"Yes, perfectly. I was just taking a last look around before retiring."

"As was I, sir. It's a goodly gathering you have here."

"And to think they came at my call. Why did you come, Mrs Cameron?"

"Because my father, Hugh Cameron of Glendessary, believed so strongly that your grandfather, James II of England and VII of Scotland, should never have been deposed to make way for that miserable Dutchman and his wife."

Charles grinned, he couldn't help it. William of Orange had not been exactly a casket of chuckles. However, he looked at Jeannie straight-faced.

"I'm glad to hear that you come from a loyal family."

"And I am glad to be their representative and to have brought my father's clan to your side. And I would be awfully obliged, gracious Highness, if you could call me Jeannie rather than Mrs Cameron. Because I'm not Mrs Cameron at all."

"Oh?"

"No. In fact I'm Mrs O'Neill. He was an Irish soldier I married at the age of sixteen. He used to knock me into a pulp whenever he was drunk, which was almost every day. In the end I divorced him and came home to Papa. What else was a woman to do?"

In the last remains of the day, Charles looked at her. The final rosy flush of sunset was on her face, turning it into a flower. "How old are you?" he asked.

"That is a question no gentleman should ever ask a lady."

"But I am not a gentleman. I am a prince."

"I would have hoped you were both, sir."

Charles laughed. "As you refuse to answer, I'll guess. Forty, give a year or two."

"Tell me how old you are."

"Twenty-four."

"Then I could be your mother, for I am forty-six."

Beneath the surface of their conversation Charles Edward could feel the exhilarating bubble of flirtation. He adored it.

"Age has never really bothered me. After all, it is merely a number. What I think more important is whether two people like one another or not."

The sun had gone down and it was suddenly dark. Jeannie spoke, her face hidden.

"You are the leader, sir, so naturally I will respect your judgement in everything. I wish you goodnight and bid you sleep well."

And with that she was gone, off into the shadows, while the prince, smiling a little, made his way into the barn where his camp bed awaited him.

*

The next morning, Charles gave the order to move on and the small army set forth, tramping over the mountains until they reached Achnacarry Castle, the family home of Donald Cameron of Lochiel, son of Old Lochiel, the head of the clan.

It was very much a man's house, its mighty turrets and formidable walls fit to frighten anyone who approached it. Here the menfolk liked to sit up late, raising their glasses and drinking interminable toasts. Young Lochiel, reluctant to let a woman into this masculine world, nevertheless felt a prick of conscience that a fellow clanswoman was sleeping rough and offered Jeannie a room in the maid's quarters, which she refused, very charmingly, saying that she would prefer to keep an eye on the troop of men she had brought with her. Charles was very slightly amused by this.

He was working hard on his general equilibrium. He was effortlessly delightful to everyone, contentment flowing out of him like a river. After all his childhood dreams he was actually in Scotland, in command of a sizeable army, on a mission to restore his father to the throne. Nothing and no-one was going to throw him off course.

But this euphoric paradise of dwelling amongst people who treated him with regard, who filled him with wine and bonhomie, came to its end a few days later. Orders were given by Charles himself for a general muster — the army must march south. He walked amongst them, out in the fields where they were camped, the men conversing in Gaelic, the drone of their voices mingling with the wild sounds of nature. Just for a moment, the prince had a vision that the battles were already won, that this beautiful rugged country really belonged to him. That, when his father's soul had gone on its lamented journey, he would be king of all this great conglomeration of water and mountains and could roam freely amongst its craggy passes and verdant valleys.

A voice spoke in his ear. "Good morning to you, Highness. Does all go well with you?"

Jeannie was standing beside him, looking at him with an interesting smile. Like this, close to in the bright sunshine, there was nothing to disguise the fact that she was nearing fifty, and indeed could be Charles' mother. As if she could read that thought she laid a tentative hand on his arm, knowing as she did so that she was breaking the rule of lèse-majesté but not appearing to notice. Charles decided not to notice as well.

"You sometimes have a sad air about you, my prince, almost as if you are feeling lonely. Do you miss your family? Is that it?"

Charles was used, at his considerable height, to looking down at over-friendly women, particularly those that were obviously out to charm him. But this particular woman was of above average height and was genuinely interested.

"No," he found himself answering, "hardly at all."

"Why's that?"

"My father is lukewarm about this venture, my brother — well he is just my brother."

"And your mother?"

"Is dead."

"Do you miss her?"

Charles considered. "I hardly knew her. She was remote, distant. I suppose I miss the idea of a kind, cosy being who never existed except in my dreams."

Jeannie shook her head. "My mother was caring and good to all her children but, alas, she died young."

"Would you have been a different person, had she lived to a ripe old age?"

"Probably."

"I'm certain that I would have been," Charles answered. He changed the subject. "How are all your brave clansmen?"

Jeannie pulled a slight face. "One or two are rather homesick."

"Does that mean they are going to desert?"

"What answer do you want me to give?"

"The truth."

"Then possibly. Perhaps it is something you should get used to, my prince. But for all those that leave, others will come. You're a bonny lad and quite hard to resist. There will be a lot who'll fight for Charlie."

And with that she dropped her awkward curtsy and marched off to join her troop, some of whom had been standing at a distance and watching the couple throughout their conversation.

*

The next few hours saw the small army strike camp and take off, wending its way through the mountain passes to Kinlocheil, where a runner gave the prince the news that George II had at last taken his invasion seriously and had offered £30,000 for his arrest. Charles, much amused and somewhat flattered, offered £30 for the capture of King George.

"A small sum for a tiny little man," he remarked, to the great amusement of those within earshot.

"Aye, that wee German lairdie," James Mor MacGregor had answered drily.

The following night — the army having marched for hours — the Young Pretender was offered a comfortable bed and a delectable supper by Mrs Jean Cameron, a close supporter of the Jacobite cause. Her husband, John, had been called away on business which — or so Charles suspected — was an excuse not to be openly connected with the uprising, lest there be reprisals by the Hanoverians.

Their house stood in an exquisite position, overlooking the immense sheet of glistening water which was Loch Eil. The lawns, a vivid vibrant green, swept down to an immense bed of white roses that glistened like pearls in the light of the rising moon. Beyond this, distantly, were etched the starkly beautiful shapes of the mountains.

Mrs Cameron was a rather imposing figure with a straight back and a straight front to match. She was not the type of woman that the prince could ever fancy, reminding him too much of his mother. But for all her somewhat starchy appearance, she was a kind and generous hostess and after supper suggested that Charles might like to look at the gardens before it got too dark.

As he stepped outside into the scented evening, the prince caught a breath of the heady aroma of the rose garden. Without even thinking about it, he walked in its direction. Bathed in early moonshine as he was, Mrs Jean Cameron thought of him as a silver pretender, a description that stayed with her even when she was a very old woman. Now, she followed him down the sloping lawn as quickly as her skirts would allow. Charles was standing quite still before the flower bed, absorbing it visually.

"Do you like them, sir?" she asked.

"I think they are exquisite. A glorious tribute to the gardener."

He had said the right thing. Mrs Cameron laughed, looking younger and prettier in the light thrown by the rising moon.

"I supervised the planting personally, though I cannot say that I actually dug the soil."

"Then well done, madam." The prince bent his head to sniff a bloom, looking young and vulnerable as he did so. Then he smiled up at his hostess. "It is beautiful. May I pick it?"

"Of course you can, sir. Take as many as you like."

"No, just one will suffice."

He stood, twirling the stem between his fingers, then with a laugh stuck the flower in his wig.

"D'you know, I have an idea."

"And what might that be, Highness?"

"To make a white rose the emblem of my campaign. To have cockades made out of white ribbon and wear them on our bonnets. Then wee Georgie's army will see us coming and know that we are the Jacobites, the men of the Highlands."

A tear glistened in Mrs Cameron's eye as she dropped a curtsey and replied, "It would be an honour, sir."

And Charles' answering smile gleamed in the shadowy moonlight.

*

They set off the next morning, the bagpipes blaring, the tramping of their feet echoing in the hills, marching in the direction of Perth. As Jeannie had predicted, there were some desertions on the way. But these were more than compensated for by the arrival of dozens more men. Even more importantly, great people joined the ranks — Lord Ogilvy, Lord Strathallan, Oliphant of Gask and the Duke of Perth himself — and Charles' dark and dangerous star, Lord George Murray who slipped, almost unnoticed, into the ranks. With men of their calibre swelling the mass of the Jacobite army, serious consideration was given to the fact that the Hanoverian position in Scotland was under genuine threat.

At Dalnacardoch came the most unexpected surprise. Men, women and children came running from their houses, cheering and waving anything handy, come to clap eyes on the Young Pretender. Charles blossomed. He knew that he had great charm, indeed was a charismatic figure, and he played up to it. Leaning low from his saddle he patted children lifted up by their parents and even kissed a pretty wench who threw a white rose to him. He was very much the hero of the hour.

And this feeling was endorsed when at Blair Castle — where the prince was staying for a few days — Lady Lude, who had come to organise the visit, fell on her knees in front of the prince and, seizing his hand, kissed it fervently. It was obvious that the poor woman was overcome because she babbled on, kissing wildly, until eventually Charles said in a loud voice, "Madam, you do me *too much* honour."

However, she had everything arranged very graciously within the castle itself and flew about from room to room describing the details in a welter of words that left the prince breathless. But she also insisted that Jeannie Cameron was given a small place inside, having come across her marching stolidly along in the prince's retinue.

"Oh, my dear, surely you are the acting head of one of the clans? We cannot have you camping outside. And I will not take no for an answer. You are to stay in the castle with the rest of the civilised folk."

Jeannie pulled a wry face but did as she was ordered and was led away into the castle's murky depths. Parts of the place were as old as time but it had undergone a recent overhaul and now boasted large, comfortable rooms and spacious facilities, all added on to the medieval fortress. From the exterior, it was a large and extremely strange-looking building to stare at, and it was to one of these newly-created suites that Prince Charles was now led, with Lady Lude simpering at his side, for she had not finished with him yet.

"If there is anything I can do, Highness, to make your stay comfortable — and I really do mean *anything* — hesitate not to let me know."

He bowed his head thoughtfully. "Actually, madam, there is."

"And what would that be?" she asked breathlessly.

"To arrange for me to dance a little."

"Oh. I see. Well that cannot be tonight, sir, which is to be a formal gathering. But perhaps if you would come and visit me at home, something could be arranged." She brightened. "Yes, indeed. Within my own four walls I could certainly organise a jig or two. Here, I am but the hostess for my cousin the Duke of Atholl." She gave a delicate cough. "He was called away unfortunately. But I am here, the genius loci, so to speak."

The prince nodded politely, considering that it was a pity she was such a plain little thing.

"Lady Lude, that would be incredibly kind."

"Think nothing of it, sir. It will be entirely my pleasure — yes, truly it would — to arrange such a festivity."

She fluttered in the doorway, then hesitated and ran towards him, sinking into such a deep curtsy that the prince had visions of hauling her up off the floor. But she struggled upright, saying, "Your servant, sir. Truly, your servant," before going out.

Charles crossed to the window and stared out. His room was huge, stretching from the front to the back of the castle. From this viewpoint he could see a mass of dark trees that would have been brooding, had they not been beaten back by a green sloping lawn. It was the time of year when the grass was at its most vibrant, shades of a cat's eye. Behind the house rose the brooding mountains, the one immediately to the rear shaped in a gentle curve like a woman's breast. Which reminded the prince that he had been celibate for a good month or more.

Those who considered that he had made a vow not to touch a woman until Scotland and England were won did not really know him. Ever since that first kiss from the forest gypsy, he had been eager to discover more. And this wish had been granted when he was seventeen, after an evening spent dancing at a ball at the Palazzo Fibbia. He had leapt around the ballroom until eleven at night and had promptly leapt into the bed of a high-born lady, who had had her eye on him all the evening. His initiation had been terrific and left him highly charged. And nothing had changed since then. There had been women since, but none recently. And now, relaxing in these beautiful surroundings, Charles Edward felt the first stirrings of desire.

Sitting down on the bed he quite cold-heartedly considered his options. Obviously, the first in line was the widowed Charlotte Robertson, Lady Lude. She was older than he was, though the prince had never let this stand in his way, preferring the caresses of the more experienced. But she was as unattractive as a house mouse, with a large curving forehead, mean little eyebrows, huge brown eyes that she rolled around and a long thick nose. Definitely not to his taste. But then, beggars can't be choosers — but princes can, Charles thought, with a certain cynicism that was definitely part of his many-faceted character.

And then there was Jeannie Cameron. At the very thought of her, Charles smiled. Now *there* was a very pretty woman, whose beautiful eyes could seduce any man. When she had stood close to him, laughing and toying a little, he had felt cheerful. No, more than that, he had been *joyful*. If Jeannie would have him, that was where he intended to make his play. But now there came a polite knocking on his door and Charles Edward shrugged on his jacket, which he had thrown onto the bed, and returned his mind to the present.

*

Lady Lude's ball the next night was a triumph. The besotted woman — for by now Charles was quite convinced that she was determined to inveigle him into her bedroom — had really worked her servants to the very last inch to produce a house that gleamed with polish, reflecting a million times in the dozens of candles that flamed everywhere.

As the prince entered, surrounded by his aristocratic gentlemen, a hush fell over the entire proceedings and the fiddlers fell silent. Out of the crowd of people present Charlotte Robertson, Lady Lude, detached herself and flew towards the new arrivals, her mousy face painted to outlandish proportions, her body already bent as she prepared for her usual spectacular curtsey. A barely audible whisper hummed in the air as her guests, who had never before cast eyes on the prince, all dipped or bowed a reverence to him.

Ignoring her, though she was holding his hand and once more kissing it with great enthusiasm, Charles acknowledged them with a boyish grin, then raised his love-struck hostess to her feet.

"Madam, honoured guests, pray continue with your merriment and regard me as just a fellow visitor. Fiddlers, play on."

At this, the music struck up once more and Charles, looking around, could not help but notice the wealth of fine plaids and the gleam of silken dresses amongst the assembled guests. He himself was looking absolutely splendid, like something stepped from a Scottish fairy tale, brilliant in a jacket of Robertson tartan — tailored that very day — in honour of his hostess' family. Out of the corner of his eye he saw a small clutch of females hurrying towards him.

"Musicians, play for me *This is not mine ain hoose*," he called rapidly, and bowing before Lady Lude said, "Madam, will you do me the honour?" and led the half-fainting woman on to the dance floor through a corridor of bowing guests.

The evening was a triumph. Having danced the first reel, the music was like a shot of raw alcohol. Charles could not stop. There were gasps of admiration as he elegantly stepped his way through a strathspey minuet with a pretty partner, the rest of the company standing and exclaiming at his sure-footedness. He was soaked in sweat, he was a little drunk, his wig was slightly askew but the prince did not care two tuppeny damns. He felt carefree and for once had forgotten the entire reason why he was capering in Scotland. And there was not one person in the watching room, including the fiddlers, who would not have gone out and fought for him to the death on that September night.

Charles sobered up slightly as the fresh cold air hit him on the ride home. But one thing he knew, apart from the fact that he had won every heart that evening, was that Lady Lude — of whom he now thought, naughtily, as Lady *Lewd* — would never have her wishes granted. Underneath her sugar-dropping looks and sighs there lurked quite a shrewish personality. The way she addressed her servants gave it all away. But he had other things on his mind as the extraordinary outlines of Blair Castle, etched darkly against the slumberous hills beyond, came into his line of vision.

Unfortunately, he had to ask directions from a footman to find the room in which Jeannie was lodged. And then, wandering around the recesses of the ancient castle, holding a solitary candle and hoping not only that the servant would keep his mouth shut but that nobody would see him prowling about, was extremely trying for the nerves. But the prince was no weakling and, having made his mind up, continued with his quest until at last he came to what he hoped was the right door. He knocked gently and whispered, "Jeannie."

She answered at once, her beautiful eyes alight with merriment.

"You called me, Your Highness?"

"Yes. Can I come in?"

"That depends."

"On what?"

"On what you're after."

"Now what would I be after at this hour of the night?"

"A glass of hot milk."

"Jeannie, for the love of God. Do I look like a man who drinks milk?"

"Possibly."

"If you were not female I'd call you out. Talking of which, are you going to let me in or are you going to send me away again?"

"As you are my prince I could hardly do that."

"Oh, come on. Don't bandy words with me. Please, can I enter your room?"

"If it pleases Your Highness."

She stood aside and Charles pushed his way through the narrow crack. Once within he closed the door and shot the bolt across.

"You wish to talk to me privately, sir?"

"That — and other things."

"Now, what could *they* possibly be?"

He looked down at her from his considerable height. "I want to share your bed, Jeannie. I want to make love to you."

"But you are a prince, sir. And I am just one of your loyal subjects."

"If I command you it would be insolent. If I ask you sweetly, would you consider it?"

"Of course I would, Mo Prionnsa."

"And what does that mean?"

"*My prince*, of course," she answered, and so saying pulled her night-shift over her head and stood before him, the candlelight throwing enticing shadows on her lightly tanned skin.

*

An hour before dawn, the prince made his way back to his own apartments and, throwing himself on the bed, slept deeply. It had been a spectacular night in which he had explored every inch of Jeannie's hidden secrets and had conducted himself as only a nobleman could. Actually he had made love to her like a peasant — something that they had both found totally enjoyable — and though she had protested once more that she was old enough to be his mother, Charles had answered, "Well, you're *not*, are you?"

He was fulfilled and with the promise that in future she would come to him whenever he sent her a billet-doux, they had parted company, each with their little secret wrapped around their heart.

CHAPTER TWO

Anne

The approach to Edinburgh had been surprisingly easy. After leaving Blair Castle, at which the prince had caught his first glimpse of a bowling green and tasted a fruit called pineapple — to say nothing of a finer fruit than that — Charles had marched on to Perth. Men of power in Scotland, realising that he was no strutting little toy soldier, had joined him. The Duke of Perth's regiment had come, Robertson of Struan had brought two hundred fighters, and various MacGregors — in addition to James Mor, who remained loyally close — had also joined the pack. The prince now had a sizeable army and felt confident enough to raise the standard and proclaim his father King.

The Hanoverians were sufficiently alarmed to organise a militia of their own, under the leadership of Sir John Cope, Commander in Chief of Scotland. Learning that the Whig general had ordered ships to take his forces by sea to the Firth of Forth, Charles' war council had met and decided to head straight for Edinburgh, which lay exposed and unprotected. The prince had sent a letter to the magistrates of the city demanding their surrender to avoid the spilling of blood. The city fathers were in a flurry of indecision, caught between the Stuart prince and the wrath of Cope. They filibustered unsuccessfully.

In the end it had been easier than any of the Jacobites had imagined. The Netherbow Gate — which Charles had had his eye on as being weakly defended — was left open to let a coach through, and the Jacobite army had simply marched in and hurriedly secured all the other gates. The people of Edinburgh woke up to find the prince's forces in control. The regular troops made a dash for the castle or got out of the city, fast.

So this was the moment. Charles sat on the end of his bed and mentally prepared himself for the biggest entrance of his life. Above all, he considered carefully what role he should play. Stern conqueror, unsmiling soldier, easy-going royal? But even as he shifted these thoughts through his brain, he knew the answer. He had addictive charm and tangible charisma, had proved it over and over again by persuading these hard-bitten Highlanders to risk all for him and become part of his army. Remembering how the people of Dalnacardoch had cheered and waved and blown him kisses, Charles knew the answer. The people of Edinburgh would see him play the fairy-tale prince. That would be their first glimpse of him and would live on forever in their memories. With a smile, Charles Edward Stuart stood up and dressed himself carefully.

He wore tight red velvet trousers and placed his feet into a pair of knee-length military boots. Over his shirt he put on a tartan short coat and, glittering on his chest, was the star of the Order of St Andrew. He tried on a plaid but decided against this encumbrance. Checking his chin to make sure that he had had a close shave — no ugly dark stubble for a creature of legend — the prince put on his bonnet, which was blue, decorated with gold lace, and checked the white satin cockade at the top. He was ready to meet his public.

The streets of Edinburgh were thronged with silent people as, at eleven o'clock, Lochiel, Keppoch and O'Sullivan publicly proclaimed James III to be their king. This ceremony over, the crowds then hung about, waiting to see what would happen next. At twelve noon their anticipation was finally over. Above the murmur of voices came the sound of the hooves of horses clattering over the cobbles. Every head turned, every eye stared. Slowly, sitting straight in his saddle, flanked by the Duke of Perth on one side and Lord Elcho on the other, there came a vision so charming, so young and so eager, so handsome and so downright royal, that the multitude took in an audible breath before the most tumultuous cheer broke out. High above the others, a man's voice shouted, "Prionnsa Tearlach! What a bonnie lad!" And the greeting was taken up on every side. "Bonnie Prince Charlie! Welcome, welcome!"

Only when he heard that, did Charles allow his fixed forward gaze to alter. He glanced into the crowd, saw that they were clapping and cheering, smiling, waving, giving delighted cat calls. And then, a movement above their heads had him looking up. The windows of the elegant houses were crammed with smartly-dressed women calling out joyously, "Greetings, Bonnie Prince Charlie!" And even while he watched, a cascade of handkerchiefs came flying down.

Now, he realised exactly what to do and relished the role. Taking the reins in one hand, he blew kisses to the ladies, opening his hazel eyes wide and smiling. To the men he gave nonchalant but respectful salutes, to the females who stood in little groups, throwing him a beckoning glance, he fluttered his fingers. To the women of quality who packed the balconies and windows, he gave the slightest bow of his elegant head. The arrival of the Bonnie Prince was causing a sensation — and he knew it.

But the entrance to Holyrood House, the ancestral home of the Stuarts, was the greatest triumph of all. As Charles Edward was ushered into the palace he felt history surround him like a well-worn piece of clothing. The blood of Mary, Queen of Scots, was in his veins and at last, as one of her descendants, he was claiming Scotland back for the Stuart royal family.

Alone, eventually, excusing himself, the prince sat down on the side of the great and beautiful bed, pulled off his boots, poured himself a glass of wine from a flagon glinting the colour of sunset, and considered his position. That the Stuart star was in the ascendant was beyond dispute, that he himself had enjoyed a personal victory was clear. The ladies of Edinburgh had welcomed their attractive sovereign with great enthusiasm, the gentlemen slightly less animated but still respectful. But now he must think of the future with care. He could either make love to them all — just for a moment a smile of pure amusement lit his face as he imagined a call by rota — or none of them.

He lay back on the bed and closed his eyes, thinking about Jeannie and the times they had shared, wondering how much longer the relationship could go on. Scottish women were utterly delightful, to say the least of it, but the last thing that he needed at this particular moment was to fall in love.

So it was that Charles Edward decided in that magical half-world before he fell asleep that he should favour none and instead concentrate on his image of warrior prince.

How very true it is, that the more one holds the opposite sex off, the more they try to pursue and seduce their intended victim. That evening, that very first evening, safe within the walls of Holyrood Palace, was like nothing the prince had ever lived through before. He had made his mind up whilst he was dressing, putting on his finest evening wear and making sure that the order glinted upon his chest, that he would stick to his earlier decision. So, as he made his way from the Duke of Hamilton's apartments — the King's suite being considered too disorderly to house him — Charles Edward produced the cast of features that he had decided to adopt for the rest of his sojourn. Serious but kindly, mysteriously aloof, attractively earnest, but totally unavailable.

There was a ripple of applause from the members of his court, who stood up as he entered the room. He gave a gracious smile and walked forward, passing a window as he did so. The shout that went up from outside made him jump with fright. Peering out, he could see that the outer courtyard was packed with people, currently passing a woman, who had swooned at the sight of him, over their heads.

"Good God!" he exclaimed, backing away.

James Drummond, Duke of Perth, shouted a laugh. "You'll see a great deal more of that, sir. They have us surrounded." Charles looked a little vague and Drummond continued, "Holyrood House has been encircled by hysterical women and fun-loving men. They are all in love with you."

Charles felt a grin start in his boots and work its way upwards, and his serious demeanour began to crack. Creeping forward, he peeped out of another window. Shouts of 'huzzah' and 'halloo' greeted him instantly. He couldn't help it, he smiled broadly and gave a wave of his hand before disappearing out of sight.

"And that's not all, sir," said Drummond at his elbow.

"What do you mean?"

"There are throngs of aristocratic ladies queuing to kiss your hand. We have put them in a small anteroom but they are crowding the place out. What shall we do with them?"

The prince looked blank. "I don't think we should allow them into the private rooms, do you? Shall I go down and greet them?"

"Merciful God, no. They would tear the clothes from your back."

"Whatever for?"

"As a souvenir of meeting you. No, we'll have to think of something else."

"Let them come in, but one by one," the prince answered, immensely flattered. "And with a guard, mind. I am in no mood for having my clothes removed publicly."

Drummond looked mildly surprised but bowed nonetheless. "It shall be as you wish, sir."

So that was how that magical first night in the home of Charles Edward's ancestors was spent. As the evening wore on and more and more ladies of fashion came to kiss his royal hand and gush at him, the more aloof the pretender pretended to be. But secretly he felt elated, thrilled with everything he had achieved so far. Delighted that he was cheered every time he passed a window, mesmerised by the women who drenched him with their adulation. And all the time maintaining his royal hauteur and air of detachment.

He eventually retired for the night in a great crimson-draped bed which had been made especially for his great-uncle Charles II. He slept peacefully but, had a vivid dream that a woman came and stood by the bedside, staring at him with a malevolent expression. She was stark naked and had not a hair on any part of her body but, regardless of this fact, had obviously once been not unattractive. In his dream Charles sat up and remonstrated with her angrily, but the woman had merely shaken her fist at him and gone out, waggling her hind quarters in an exaggerated manner. The next morning he mentioned the dream to James Mor MacGregor, who slept in the adjoining room as personal bodyguard.

"That was no dream, Highness. That was Bald Agnes."

"Bald who?"

"Agnes, sir. She was a midwife and healer, way back. Anyway, your grandfather, four times removed, thought she was a witch and demanded that she should be shaved of all her hair so that the devil's mark would show."

"And did they find it?"

"It is said they did, in amongst her pubes. Anyway, she was sentenced to be strangled and burnt and the old king was happy. Now she haunts Holyrood, and must have been particularly drawn to you as one of his descendants."

"You don't believe all that, do you James?"

"Indeed I do, sir. Scots people are very canny about such things."

"I see," said Charles, nodding wisely.

He stretched languidly and looked around the room with both pride and pleasure. For the first time in his life he had a sense of real achievement. He had regained Edinburgh for the Stuart dynasty, women were throwing themselves at him, if the number of notes thrust into his hand as he had bent to kiss them was anything to go by. Furthermore, men admired him. Even the tough old birds from the Highlands had rallied to his side when push came to shove.

"I'm happy," he said spontaneously.

James Mor gave him a look which contained a great deal of affection and a great deal of hope.

"I am very glad to hear it, Prionnsa Tearlach. Very glad indeed."

*

Those five weeks at Holyrood Palace turned out to be the most splendid that the prince could remember. He dined in public, gave stunning balls — to which were invited all the high society of Edinburgh — and had the palace buzzing with life and full of joy and laughter. Despite this, Charles had not changed his cool façade. Though every part of him longed to dance, he sat aside, occasionally sipping from a glass of wine, while others leaped and cavorted and yelled as the reels became hectic.

One night, when even his personal guards were up on their feet and not once glancing in his direction, he crept out, unable to bear for another second the strain of sitting still and pretending not to care.

It was a mellow night, quite unusual for Edinburgh, and as the prince entered the gardens he saw that they were lit to a marvellous silver brightness, the light of the moon enhanced by the glow coming from the palace itself. The mountains had changed to the colour of sloes, and somewhere a leaping stretch of water gurgled and swirled in the magical moonlight. The sound of the jollity from the ballroom, muted but merry, stole through the shadows like a strange echo, shattered by a voice saying, "...damnable heel. Rot the damned thing!" Charles stared towards the origins of the sound.

A small female was sitting down on the grass, her skirts spread out so that her marbled thighs were exposed above her white stockings. She held a broken shoe in one hand and was cursing like a soldier. The prince stared, highly amused, and watched her for a second or two before giving an audible cough. She looked round in alarm and pulled her skirt down to a decent length.

"Forgive me, madam. I didn't mean to startle you. I just stepped outside for a breath of air," he said.

She either did not recognise him, although the order on his chest was sparkling in the moonlight, or else affected not to do so.

"Beg pardon, sir. There was I, longing to dance, and the heel of my shoe broke off completely. I had to leave the ballroom in haste, I can tell you."

The prince approached. "May I?"

"Please do," she answered, hauling herself up somewhat inelegantly and handing him the offending item of footwear.

The heel had come away from the sole so that the shoe was irreparably ruined. The prince turned it in his hand.

"I'm afraid, my lady, that this will mean the end of dancing for tonight."

She sighed. "Well, at least I'm in good company."

"What do you mean?"

"The prince never dances. Have you not noticed? He sits through every caper staring moodily into space."

He was rocked speechless. The word 'moodily' suggested to him that she might have seen through his charade. But, more importantly, she hadn't recognised Charles for who he was. In short, she thought she was talking to a fellow guest.

The prince surreptitiously tugged at the brocade riband on his chest, attempting to cover the star of St Andrew that gleamed there. Fortunately the girl did not notice, too busy removing her good shoe.

Charles made a small bow. "May I know your name, madam?"

Her eyes shot moon beams. "Yes, if I may know yours, sir."

"Sylvester," he answered. It was true. He had received a dozen or so names at his baptism and that just happened to be one of them.

"My name is Anne Mackintosh," she replied, "though I was born Farquharson. My husband is away about his military duties at the present time, so I took the opportunity of visiting my mother-in-law at Inverness. But when I heard that the Pretender had arrived in Edinburgh, I could not resist the chance of a wee peek at him."

"And?"

"I thought him a bit of a dull fellow, sitting out all the dances like that. You see, I so love to cut a caper."

"As do I," answered Charles, without really thinking.

"Then why don't we?" He stared at her. "I mean dance, sir."

He was suddenly terribly correct. "Of course, madam. What else could you possibly have meant?"

She extended a hand. "The music has just started. Can you hear it?"

And indeed, the musicians had struck up the opening notes of a gavotte. Charles could not resist. A comely woman wanted to dance with him, a pastime that he adored. He inclined his head towards Mrs Anne Mackintosh.

"Madam, will you do me the honour?"

She curtseyed. "Gladly, sir."

And thus they danced together, she in her stockinged feet, he in his soft dark shoes; danced and danced until all the music had ended and the fiddlers were finally finished. Then Anne curtseyed and, gathering up her redundant footwear, gave him an impish grin and said, "I hope you enjoyed the dance, Highness," before turning and speeding off into the palace.

Charles stared at her retreating form, realising that she had known who he was from the start.

"Little devil," he said and then laughed softly, smiling to himself in the light of the luscious moon.

CHAPTER THREE

Murray

They had disliked each other on sight. The man who had been presented to Charles Edward had instantly filled him with a kind of distrust, a nasty creeping feeling that the newcomer lacked a sense of humour, had no style, and yet, despite that, should be treated with respect. The prince had held out his hand to be kissed. Nothing had come. There had been a blunt nod of the head, a cold smile — and that had been that.

Inwardly, Charles had seethed, but there was very little he could do about it. For this was Lord George Murray, who had come out in the 1715 and 1719 uprisings and was a committed Jacobite through and through. He was too precious a jewel to upset. Charles had given him a wintry smile and turned away to other, more interesting, things.

Yet all the time the man had been a prickle in his skin. For here was a creature born to resist the prince's glorious charm of manner. Where other Scotsmen had fallen on their knees before him, Lord George had always remained aloof, standing in the background, a small smile playing round his cynical lips. Charles Edward wanted nothing more than to go up and punch him, hard. But this would have been foolishness beyond reason. The only thing to do was to ignore the man.

Yet this was proving difficult. Lord George Murray was a military tactician of the highest order. Not popular in certain quarters, particularly with those who adored the prince and instinctively picked up on his feelings of distaste, Murray was for all that an outstanding soldier. And Charles knew that for this quality alone he must hide his deepest feelings.

This had been easy enough during the halcyon days at Holyrood, but all good things must inevitably come to an end. Sir John Cope, Commander in Chief of Scotland, was on the march against him. The time for settlement was drawing near. So it was with some reluctance that Charles Edward left Holyrood House, the place where he had watched others dance, while he had sat apart, apparently pensive and thoughtful, wistfully sipping a glass of wine.

Bolstered up by the arrival of Lord Nairne with two hundred and fifty men and, in due splendour, the grand MacLachlan of MacLachlan, bringing a hundred and fifty of his clansman with him, the prince had set out for his first confrontation. He wanted to lead his army from the front and was absolutely horrified when he was told that this was not possible.

"But why? I'm not afraid. I refuse to skulk at the back like some mincing quean."

There had been a slight silence and then Lord George Murray spoke. "It would not be wise for you to do so."

No 'Your Highness' or 'sir', Charles noticed silently.

"Why not?"

"Because your royal personage is considered too precious to be put at risk."

The prince had been about to protest again but other dissenting voices from the council of war spoke up in agreement.

"He's right, sir."

"Suppose you were shot at? It's too great a risk, Highness."

"Then I insist on addressing the troops beforehand. At least agree to that."

There had been a gruff assent, with Lord George turning to look out beyond the tent in silence.

On the morning of the twentieth of October 1745, Charles Edward, on horseback, made a brief speech. He spoke in English not Gaelic, though a clansman, fluent in both languages, was at his side. He ended very simply, unsheathing his sword and waving it in an arc over his head.

"Gentlemen, I have flung away the scabbard; with God's help I will make you a free and happy people."

The translator spoke, there was a second's silence, and then that kilted, tousled, band of wild men threw their bonnets high in the air and gave a great shout. A lone voice rose up, speaking English as best it could.

"Wha widna' fecht for Charlie?"

Charles knew what it meant, *Who would not fight for Charlie?,* and he had to brush his sleeve over his eyes to hide the hot, sudden tears that came. And then, much against his will, he watched as that army of two and a half thousand men started to trudge forward and he had to drop behind and ride in the rearguard.

All the way onwards the prince thought mutinously about his lieutenant-general, wishing that there could have been a better relationship with him. The trouble was that Lord George reminded him of his father and — to a certain extent — his beastly little brother. But ideas of anything else were swept away when he trotted up to the high ground and glimpsed his first sight of the enemy camp. So this was where they were hiding out. Charles' jaw dropped as he saw the number of them.

Sir John Cope had chosen his encampment well. It was pitched in a recently-harvested cornfield with protection on all four sides, the best of which was to the east, a sticky, deep morass criss-crossed with narrow ditches. It looked — and was — impregnable. Charles sighed and as soon as his tent was erected immediately called a meeting of the Jacobite leaders, partly glad, partly sorry, that Lord George Murray had not bothered to attend. Clearing his throat, the prince came directly to the point.

"Gentlemen, it is my belief — having studied the enemy's position carefully — that we post the Atholl men along the road to Musselburgh. In this way they can secretly observe the movement of Cope's forces."

There was a murmur of general assent.

"Is that an order or an idea, Highness?"

"An order?" Charles answered, feeling light-headed with the thought of so much power. "Yes, it is."

The tent cleared of people, and from where he sat the prince could hear scurrying feet and shouted commands. For the first time in his life he had given a military order that had been obeyed. He revelled in it.

Going out to take a look, Charles saw the Atholl brigade quietly leaving on their scouting mission. He saluted them and they responded by silently saluting back. There was a battle to be fought and his courage had never felt higher. Whistling to himself, the prince went back into the tent and poured himself a dram of whisky. Ten minutes passed and then came the sounds of a distant commotion, followed by the noise of running feet heading towards his tent.

The prince stood up. His bête noire stood in the doorway, his forehead beaded with sweat.

"Jesus Christ!" George Murray shouted, throwing his gun onto the floor with a violent thud. "I swear to God I will never draw my sword for the cause if that brigade is not brought back immediately."

"Why?" asked Charles, alarmed despite himself.

"Because it interferes with my well-laid battle plans, that's why. I intend to hold a meeting tonight, Highness . . ." That word was said with some reluctance, the prince noted. ". . . as you were shortly going to be informed. At that you will learn exactly what my strategy is. But I can assure you that nobody should make a move yet. It would be ruinous."

"You should have told me this earlier."

"That's as maybe. But the truth is there are spies out everywhere. If a whisper should reach Cope's ears first, we'll be done for."

"I see."

Charles turned to look out of the tent's opening, avoiding eye contact with his commander. He could almost hear his father speaking, that tone of reprimand never far away.

"Very well, I'll give the order for them to come back," he said, inwardly cursing Lord George's superior attitude.

"Thank you." And the Scotsman gave the slightest nod and was gone.

Like a good boy, Charles rescinded the order and was very slightly the worse for a dram or three when he attended the council of war. When he came out again he felt dubious about what he had just heard. His men were to march round the eastern end of the morass and attack the enemy flank. Open to all kinds of aggression as they did so. However, despite his gloomy thoughts, he went to his camp bed and had only been sleeping for a couple of hours when he was woken by James Mor, Rob Roy's son.

"You're to go to Lord George's tent, sir. Something of interest has come up."

"But it's the middle of the night."

"I know that. Now, where are your trews?"

"This had better be good."

It was. The son of a local laird had arrived shortly before midnight and been taken to see the commander. He had revealed that there was a narrow track through the bog which would remove entirely the necessity to march down the eastern side. Charles impulsively hugged James Mor and George had allowed himself a small, dry smile. Orders were immediately sent out that the army would march at four in the morning.

The Highland soldiers set off in the darkness. Nobody spoke a word, silence was essential. The result was that they fell upon Sir John Cope's army in the eerie half-light of dawn, savages emerging from the mist, a mud-covered figure amongst them. It was Prince Charles who had fallen attempting to leap over a ditch.

There was annihilation. The Scotsmen's blood was up, and they cut down the enemy without mercy. There were severed limbs and heads scattered all over the field. Cope fled on horseback, Murray tried to stop the wholesale slaughter, the prince called out ineffectively, "Make them prisoners, for God's sake spare them, they are my father's subjects." He ordered his surgeons to care for the dying and the injured on both sides and sent one of his followers back to Edinburgh for more medical aid. From this grew the legend of his magnanimity, his kindness, his general distress at the plight of others.

His return to Edinburgh was greeted by a multitude of cheering people hailing him as 'The good, Bonnie Prince Charlie'. To say that the entire Scots nation was won over was hardly an exaggeration. The victory at Prestonpans had made a deep impression — not only in Scotland, but also in England.

CHAPTER FOUR

The Ladies of Edinburgh

The Battle of Prestonpans had made a tremendous impact on Scotland — and an even stronger one on London. Up to that moment, Charles Edward had been considered a lightweight, a creature to be joked about in the coffee houses, an object of derision. But no more. Horrific descriptions of the battlefield had filtered through, together with tales of the prince's humanity and, as a result, his ever-growing popularity. How he sat resplendent in Holyrood House in Edinburgh, how he ruled the Scottish nation. In London the politicians were uneasy. Field Marshal Wade, the new Hanoverian Commander in Chief, was too afraid to cross the border. The Jacobite cause was growing stronger by the day.

During that delightful autumn the sun shone on the Bonnie Prince, not at all typical of Edinburgh weather in the shortening days. Because to him, even when it poured with rain, everything was glorious. He was having the time of his life. Though no women were closely involved, his return from Prestonpans had aroused a positive barrage of bare-faced propositions. If they had queued to meet him on his first arrival, now they almost physically fought to be in his presence. Females aged fifteen to fifty-five — and over! — hurled themselves at him. He had to walk hurriedly wherever he went, for fear of someone of the feminine gender curtseying in his path. In the face of this all-out assault, the prince had gone back to his earlier role of gracious detachment — which only seemed to encourage them more. Secretly, he smiled. If he had slept with but a quarter of them, he would never have come out of the bedroom.

His daily routine was to attend a council meeting, then to have a public luncheon with his fellow officers. Every time he raised a fork to his lips there was a collective murmur of admiration from the hordes of females looking on. In the afternoon he would ride out to review his troops, then — having changed for the evening into some newly-made night attire created by the delighted tailors of the city — Charles would receive his lady admirers, who would kiss, lick, tickle and gently bite his outstretched hand in their efforts to attract his attention. But the prince had chosen his role and remained aloof, yet again refusing to dance, proclaiming that he would not enter into the lighter side of life until he had won the entire kingdom for his royal father.

But there was a hidden, darker side beneath all this splendour. Though Charles Edward was receiving converts to his cause daily, there were also those who steadfastly refused to yield to his charms. What the prince wanted above all was for Louis XV of France to rally to his cause. But, as ever, there was no word from Versailles. It would seem that he must put a brave face on it, smile at all the fawning women, and await developments.

It was proving difficult to achieve. And then, on the fourteenth of October, the much hoped-for news finally arrived at Holyrood House. The Marquis d'Eguilles, envoy of the French king, had landed at Montrose. In the quiet of his own apartments, Charles dropped to his knees and uttered a silent prayer of thanks. Now, he had a weapon to use against his black devil, Lord George Murray. The invasion of England could at last begin.

If a crowd had welcomed the prince into Edinburgh, a multitude cheered his departure. Practically the entire population turned out — including all the disappointed ladies who pretended, amongst themselves, that some of them had successfully reached the young man's bedchamber, just to arouse jealousy. Charles Edward, turning to give them a final wave over his shoulder, could not help but twitch a triumphant smile. Though he had adored his stay in the capital he was itching for the victory that, he felt sure, lay ahead. And he was also quite pleased that he could drop his pose as a detached young noble and once again properly enjoy the life of a soldier.

He had argued in favour of an attack on England until he had practically run out of voice. Opposing him, drily pointing out the fact that four thousand men would have practically no chance against thirty thousand English regulars, was Lord George Murray. His features looked pale and dough-like, his eyes two pieces of glass, his monotonous voice droning on and on. As ever, Charles Edward had to fight, hard, an overwhelming urge to punch his lights out. But eventually — though the French Marquis had yet to make a firm commitment on behalf of King Louis — the vote had been taken and the ayes won. The prince fell into bed like a felled ox and had awoken with the stir of excitement in his blood.

He was leading the second division of troops. The plan was that he should appear to be heading for Newcastle, and then abruptly move off to Jedburgh to meet Lord George and his regiments, allowing the army to form up as a whole while trying to put Field-Marshal Wade off the scent. It had worked so far and Charles Edward's column made a brisk pace through the Rule valley, forded the River Esk and spent their first night in England.

It was getting chilly, November setting in, and despite the thrill of excitement as he first set foot on English soil, the prince shivered. It was deathly quiet, a mist — which had risen early from the river — was eddying round and blotting out the normal sounds of camp life. As his tent was erected, he wandered rather aimlessly through the regiments of clansmen, bravely bivouacking against the chill of the autumn air, most sitting outside, lighting little fires and in some cases getting their cooking pots ready to assemble. He greeted them as he passed and those who recognised him called back. But one voice in particular caught Charles' attention. It was more highly pitched than the others and he could have sworn that it came from a woman.

"Jeannie?" he said.

"At your feet, sir," came the quiet reply.

She was, quite literally. Sitting outside her small and somehow vulnerable tent, holding her hands out to the fire which was just beginning to spark up.

"Where have you been these last weeks? You disappeared as soon as I got to Edinburgh."

"I've been where I always am — with my clan."

"But you weren't billeted at Duddington. I know. I sometimes spent the night there. You weren't around."

"Oh, but I was. You just didn't see me."

"Why? Were you hiding?"

"Yes sir, I was."

"But why?"

"Because I wouldn't have been suitable company for you. You were a prince in your palace. I was just a member of your army."

It was true, absolutely, as Charles well knew. He smiled at her.

"So you knew the role I had to play."

"The great aloof warrior? Oh, yes, it was joked about in certain quarters."

"Good God, I didn't know that — and I thought I acted the part so well."

"Aye, you did." Jeannie stood up, her dark eyes shining with inner thoughts. "I wondered if you'd had a woman smuggled in late at night."

Charles looked down his nose. "Madam, you forget that I am a prince of the blood."

She dropped her ungainly curtsey. "I beg your pardon, Highness."

"Are you laughing or serious?"

"Which would you prefer me to be?"

"The Jeannie that I met at Glenfinnan. I could trust what *she* was saying."

They looked at each other, she almost as tall as he was.

"Have you missed me, my prince?" she asked, quietly.

"Does this answer you?" he said, and pulling her behind a tree gave her the kiss that he had been longing to give somebody — anybody — for the last month.

"Oh yes," she answered, and her naughty hand slid down his clothing and found what it was looking for.

As soon as the camp was asleep she crept to where the great trees grew thickly and Charles awaited, forgetting all about his grand status. There, he made love to her like a member of the common soldiery.

"God, I've missed this," he shouted as he climaxed within her.

And for answer Jeannie smiled in the darkness and held him tightly as she followed just after.

*

Lord George, naturally, had bad news when the prince linked up with him on the following day. There had apparently been desertions, and tents, stores and ammunition had disappeared overnight. The prince smiled grandly, muttered something like 'What can you expect?', and ordered the siege of Carlisle.

Meanwhile, Field Marshal Wade was having enormous difficulty in reaching the Jacobite troops. Held up by snowdrifts in the mountain passes, he simply did not appear at all. The prince, playing to the open-mouthed and admiring citizens, entered the vanquished border city — riven with thieves and prostitutes rough as blades — astride a white horse. George Murray promptly and pettishly resigned his commission.

"That bastard," the prince shouted at James Mor MacGregor. "That bloody little snivelling tripehound! Every move is made to upset me. I rue the moment I ever set eyes on him."

"He's well respected by the clansmen, sir."

"But not by me, by God. I swear, James, that one of these days I shall punch him so hard he'll bounce off the opposite wall. He is a mean, power-drunk, grasping, horrible arse."

"That's your opinion," MacGregor had answered under his breath. In a rage like this the prince could not bear open contradiction. Aloud MacGregor said, "He's a good commander, Mo Prionnsa ."

"If you say so."

In the end both Charles and Murray simmered down and with the help of d'Eguilles the prince managed to convince the council — against the wishes of Lord George, who was all for heading back to Scotland — that an advance on England was the only way to convince the French king that they were in earnest. So the die was cast. It was England or nothing.

Charles put on the show of his life, marching on foot at the head of his men. Sometimes he was so exhausted that he had to hold on to the shoulder belt of a nearby soldier to stop himself falling down. But he was determined and he was no puny weakling. He even found sufficient energy to make love to Jeannie — but not very often.

In Manchester he sparkled, captivated the ladies with his charm, was cheered and applauded. The prince entertained as lavishly as he could, and several titled women got to kiss his hand. It raised his spirits high and he even felt a slight warming to his erstwhile enemy. But unbeknownst to them all, their mighty antagonist, the Duke of Cumberland, one of George II's sons, had just been given command of the English army.

At that moment, though none was aware of it, Cumberland was making his first error. The Duke was puzzled when the Jacobite forces failed to appear at Stone, on the route to Wales, where he was preparing to do battle against them. Murray had successfully misled him by taking a large troop of men in that direction and then swinging them round in an arc. So, well ahead of Cumberland and his army, the prince's men had undertaken a twenty-four hour march and had finally reached Derby.

In London, when word reached their ears of the Jacobites' advance, there was total panic and disarray. George II and his family were about to sail back to their native Hanover; there was a run on the banks as everyone withdrew their money. Henry Fielding said it was 'a panic scarce to be credited.' Some high-born people fled to their country estates. But in Derby it was a very different story. The prince knew at last the power of George Murray's influence.

He entered the council meeting on the fifth of December, thinking that the only thing to discuss was how the army would line up on its march the following day. He was to be bitterly and devastatingly defeated, delivered a blow that would mark him for ever. Lord George had cut across his opening remarks.

"Sir, if I may point out the foolhardiness of such an action."

"Why? What are you saying?"

"That we have not heard a word from the English Jacobites nor has there been any promise from the French king ..."

Charles had glanced across at d'Eguilles, who had raised his beautiful French shoulders and shaken his head.

"... and without them it would be the height of folly to proceed. We have two armies coming after us — Wade's and Cumberland's — and another waiting for us at Finchley. We would be annihilated. It would be suicidal madness to go on."

There was a deathly silence during which the prince could feel his heart drop, almost, it seemed, to his feet.

"I beg your pardon?"

"I said it would be madness, sir."

"And I say that is nonsense," Charles answered, recovering himself. "One final push is all that is needed to bring the Hanoverian dynasty down to its knees. Why, if we turn back now we are playing into the enemy's hands. Cumberland is well behind us. Turn round, and we rush into his arms."

There were one or two rumblings of assent and then a voice of an irritatingly high pitch said, "But we have heard all this before, Mo Prionnsa. We have nothing in writing, have we?"

And it was true enough. Communication with the French King was difficult and so far there had been no letter stating his intentions. Nor had the English Jacobites put pen to paper.

"Unless you have received something privately, sir," someone asked.

Charles would never forget the look on George Murray's face as the man said, "Then I suggest, sir, that without such noble undertakings and in order to save Scottish life, we withdraw and turn back."

The prince knew at that moment that his dream had been shattered by the man who had started out as his supporter but who had just nailed him to the cross.

"I shall adjourn this meeting until this evening," he answered with what he hoped was a modicum of dignity. And without another word turned on his heel and left the room.

Once alone, he plunged his head into his hands. Only great oratory could save him now. Because he knew, deep in his heart, could somehow sense, the outright fear of that nasty little King George from Hanover. Felt certain that the whole of London was in a state of high alert and that the final push was all that was needed. Yet would that old misery Murray see his point of view? The answer was no. Not him, nor all his kilt-clad comrades. At that moment Charles Edward knew he was facing a losing battle.

The meeting was as dire as he feared. To compound matters, Murray had brought in an English spy, one Dudley Bradstreet. He spoke of a nine thousand strong third army, waiting at Northampton. One look at him and the prince had known that the entire story was fabrication. So much so, that he had shouted aloud, "That fellow will do me more harm than all the Elector's army!"

The assembled Scotsmen had turned ice-cold faces in Charles' direction as the spy was removed from the room.

"I call for a vote, Highness, gentlemen," said George Murray.

So this was to be the beginning of the end. The prince waited in stony silence as the word 'retreat' echoed again and again. How much he despised their craven cowardice — and how much did he want to smash his fist into the sour face of George Murray, who was now barely concealing his triumph.

"If you do not march on you will ruin, abandon and betray me," he shouted in one last ditch attempt.

"It's too late to protest, sir. It is the only sensible decision. Surely you can see that?"

"No, I can't. I tell you that the crown would have been mine for the taking!"

"Then you would have to march alone to take it, sir."

He would have agreed to anything to silence them, but at that moment the prince caught the eye of James Mor MacGregor. His friend was looking directly at him with a terribly sad expression and was, very gently, shaking his head. In that compelling glance Charles knew the game was lost and bent to adjust his shoe to hide the fact that tears had welled up in his eyes.

It was endgame.

CHAPTER FIVE

Clementina

It was a sullen prince that retreated from Derby. His appearance grew sloppy, he drank too much, he rode on horseback where formerly he had marched on foot. He hardly spoke, muttering in monosyllables, curt, rude, outwardly ugly.

Inside himself, he wept. His great hope, his great chance, had been shattered. He had very little left to achieve. To crown his abject misery he spent his twenty-fifth birthday crossing the river Esk back into Scotland. A wonderful birthday present indeed!

Jeannie tried to slip into his tent in the thick of night to comfort him, but was informed by James Mor MacGregor that the prince was not receiving, not admitting even to her that Charles was slumped drunk as a wheelbarrow and would have been no use to any woman. Somewhat slighted, she retreated to her clan and marched stolidly with them, not offering her services where plainly they were not required. It was in this way, depressed and drained of vitality and without female company, that the prince finally arrived at Douglas Castle.

Next day was Christmas Eve and the Highlanders in the army were hell-bent on enjoying themselves. They went into town and caused as much damage to women and property as they were capable of, before falling into alcoholic stupor. The prince drank wine and looked defeated. It was not a merry festive season.

But the following day, he brightened as he first set eyes on Hamilton Palace. This was one of the finest places he had ever visited. Magnificent and huge, it was to be his palatial lodging for Christmas Day. In quite a cheerful mood Charles announced to his hosts, the Duke and Duchess of Hamilton, that he would like to go hunting. And indeed they heartily agreed. The prince actually laughed with pleasure as he got on horseback and careered off at speed over the Hamilton's extensive parkland.

So it was a much happier young man who entered the city of Glasgow and moved into a large granite dwelling nearby called Bannockburn House. As he wandered from room to room he said to James Mor MacGregor, who was walking a step behind him, "I like this place. It has a certain charming solidity."

"I'm pleased to hear it, sir. Let's hope that your spirits will lift accordingly."

The prince turned on him a face that had lost its boyhood roundness and now had an indefinable expression of sadness.

"Do you know something, son of Rob Roy?"

The other man shook his head.

"When I first came to Scotland I knew what to expect from my enemies but little did I think I would get the same treatment from my friends. I realised that my army would be made up of volunteers, men who would risk their lives to see Scotland freed from the yoke of Hanover. And I expected to be their commander and lead them to glory. What a fool I was. My army is run by a committee and heaven forbid that I should have the casting vote. I am the only one with a price on his head — £30,000 of good money — but that counts for nothing with them. Repeat this last to nobody if you want to remain loyal, James Mor, but I hate George Murray with a deep and bitter loathing."

"He is the man that the clans respect, sir."

"I think you have said that to me before. And I'll grant you it is true. But nothing can replace what is in my heart, my friend."

"I'm sorry you feel like this, Highness. It must be a difficult burden."

Charles momentarily turned away, then turned on his follower a beaming smile.

"I've decided that from now on I am going to change my tactics."

"In what way, sir?"

"You will remember how in Edinburgh I sat aloof, appearing to be concentrating on military matters."

"Yes."

"Well, this time I am going to do the complete opposite. I am about to play to the gallery, as it were. I am going to put on my most elegant French clothes, dance every dance, and make eyes at all the women present."

James Mor burst out laughing and Charles shot him a look of mock severity.

"Chuckle all you like. I am determined to make some maiden fall for my charms before this stay is out."

Rob Roy's son merely bowed his head to hide the fact that he was grinning at what his royal companion was saying.

But Charles was as good as his word, cutting a neat leg at dancing, giving the women who crowded around him saucy glances, raising many a hand to his ardent lips. Then, to crown it all, on the fifth of January he could not get out of bed, complaining that he was hot and feverish.

Sir Hugh Paterson, his host at Bannockburn House, sent for a local doctor, and he also asked his granddaughter, Clementina Walkinshaw, to come and nurse the bed-ridden Charles back to health. The physician announced that the prince had a severe attack of influenza, while Clementina accepted her grandfather's request with modestly downcast eyes.

She wasn't a bad-looking girl, her best feature being her hair, which was dark brown and lustrous and worn in ringlets set back from her face, while those down-gazing eyes were blue and innocent. Her breasts were high and pert and peeped daringly over the top of her low-cut gown, almost showing the nipple, but not quite. Whether Clementina understood the effect this had on men, nobody really knew.

For the first few days of his illness, Charles was aware of very little except that someone was hovering at his bedside and administering a medicine containing cinnamon. Then, as he slowly began to recover, he noticed the breasts as their owner measured a dark fluid into a glass and raised it to his lips. He pushed himself up on one elbow.

"Madam, forgive me. I'm afraid I have caused you some bother… but perhaps it was worth being ill to be given such a charming nurse."

Clementina made a deep reverence, somewhat impeded by the bed hangings.

"Oh, Highness, thank you. I have only done what any person would, who was given the honour of helping you back to health."

Charles smiled, aware that he must be looking terrible after five days of semi consciousness.

"I'm afraid that you have seen me at my worst, Miss …?"

"Walkinshaw, sir. Clementina Walkinshaw."

"The same name as my mother."

"I was named after her, sir."

"Really? Why?"

"My father was John Walkinshaw, sir. He was out in the '15 uprising and had to escape to France to join your father."

Charles sat up straight, giving Clementina an exciting glimpse of his naked flesh.

"And he was in the escort, was he not, that brought my mother to Italy when she escaped from house arrest to marry my father? I remember now. I knew the name was familiar. Well I'm delighted to make your acquaintance, Miss Walkinshaw. Without your father's actions I might not be here at all."

She laughed delicately and so did Charles, hoping that he did not look too dishevelled with his five days' growth of beard and his red hair springing up like a forest fire on his unwigged head.

With this thought uppermost, he ran his hand over his chin. "By God, I need a shave. No hopes of a barber, I suppose?"

"I'm afraid that he only calls in the morning to attend my grandfather. But *I* could try, if you like."

The prince grinned, thinking to himself that the owner of those breasts could try anything she wanted with him. Hoping that his eyes were not revealing too much, he gave a youthful grin.

"That would be most kind of you, Miss Walkinshaw."

She curtseyed again. "It would be the least I could do to help. But I must warn you, Highness, that I am no expert at shaving gentlemen."

"I should hope not indeed," was out before he could control his words and he only just managed to curtail a wink. There was absolutely no point in his being provocative with a well brought up young woman. Earnestness must be the order of the day, he thought.

Clementina went out of the room, dropping a swift curtsey in the doorway, presumably to fetch the equipment to rid Charles of his five-day stubble. Alone, he gave a sigh of contentment and dropped back on his pillows, knowing that his energy was returning and almost feeling his old self. The door flew open once again and the prince's charming smile froze on his face as he saw standing in the entrance his arch enemy George Murray, who strode into the room giving only the curtest of bows.

"Well?" said Charles brusquely, sitting up.

"I'm here about the decision-making process. Now that you have refused to summon any more full war councils, who will make the ruling in an emergency?"

Charles put on the coldest expression he could manage in his influenza weakened state.

"I hope you realise that I am still recovering from a serious illness, Lord George."

"I do, sir. But I think this issue is too important to let mortal sickness interfere. What are we going to do?"

"You are going to have to wait until I have recovered completely and then I will give you my reply. At the moment I am too unwell even to consider the matter."

Clementina appeared in the open doorway and stood dumbfounded.

Lord George gave the prince the nearest thing to a contemptuous look, which only just stopped short of sneering.

"Of course, Highness. But think about it very carefully. Remember that it was only the collective decision to withdraw from Derby that saved our army from total destruction."

"Based on your opinion alone, Lord George. Where was your proof of the Hanoverian numbers? Solely gleaned from the word of a sordid, second-hand spy. A nine thousand strong body of men waiting for us at Northampton? I don't think so. I believe it was an entire fabrication which you leapt on as your way out. I will write you my answer shortly. Now good day to you, sir."

Murray flushed the unattractive shade of undercooked beef and stood for a moment, fulminating. Then he turned and swept through the door, thrusting Clementina to one side as he went. She turned and stared after him.

"Who was that, sir?"

"My black devil, Miss Walkinshaw. My arch enemy and, unfortunately, lieutenant general of my army."

"You don't like him?"

"I think that would be putting it very mildly indeed."

Clementina giggled and curtseyed, looking rather pretty with her arms full of shaving bowls and brushes and a cut-throat razor.

"My goodness," said the prince, giving her a glance from beneath his eyelashes, "is all that for me?"

"Indeed it is, sir. Now let me prop you up on pillows."

Charles gave himself up to enjoying the next quarter of an hour. That was until the razor started slipping over his chin in Clementina's amateurish fingers when, though he attempted nonchalance, he grew very tense indeed. However, a decent shave was produced by the end, when he ran his hand over his glossy chin and gave a slow nod of approval.

"May I have a mirror, Miss Walkinshaw — or may I call you Clementina, now that we are on such intimate terms?"

"Certainly, Highness."

"To the mirror or the name?"

"Both, sir."

Examining himself, Charles thought that he was not too bad looking a fellow. His best feature were his autumnal eyes, so tawny in colour that sometimes they could look almost green. The outer ring was brown, but the inner, round the iris, changed in the light. Today, probably because he had been laid low, they were a glinting amber. His hair was red, not carrots, not honey, but a marmalade combination of the two. Though he usually wore a peruke with flowing ringlets, this was always discarded in bed.

As to his body, the prince had no complaints. Tall, like most of the Stuarts, well-proportioned and well-hung, he was kept slim by the constant exercise of army life. Now he gave sweet Clementina a smile that was aimed at making the teapots rattle.

"When am I allowed to get up, nursey?"

"I think you should spend another day in bed, sir."

"I might indeed if you would care to join me."

Clementina put her hand to her mouth. "I hope I did not hear correctly."

"Unfortunately, sweet lady, you did. And judging by the look on your face, you rather enjoyed it."

She turned away, gave a curtsey that was as elaborate as her shaving equipment would allow, and left the room in silence.

I must go carefully with her, Charles thought. One false move and I could frighten the sweet little thing away.

*

Two days later he got up, ordered a bath to be brought to his room and washed away the unpleasant smells of illness and idleness. Then he dressed, very carefully indeed, and placed on his head his beautifully curling peruke that through its very softness made him look young and somehow vulnerable. Then he sent for Clementina.

She found him sitting alone, his head hidden in his hands, his shoulders shaking slightly. She rushed up to him, saying, "Oh Highness, what is it?"

He dashed away a tear that he had squeezed up from somewhere and looked at her, utterly crestfallen.

"My armies have been out fighting while I lay prostrate as a lily. I feel useless, Clementina. What good is a general who takes to his bed like a sickly boy?"

"But you were genuinely ill, sir. I could bear witness to it. For four days you were semi-conscious. What good would a general have been to the army in that kind of state?"

"But I shall never forgive myself," was the prince's reply and, putting his arms round her he buried his head in her adorable breasts. He couldn't help what he did next. He put his lips to the nearer one and began to kiss it. He felt Clementina's body go rigid but she did not push him away.

"What are you doing?" she whispered.

"Loving you," he answered, glancing up.

She was flushed and breathless, but her eyes were soft.

"Do you want me to stop?"

"No, but you mustn't go any further."

Charles put his hands to her waist and gently pulled her to sit beside him. Straightening himself, he looked at her, his face boyish.

"Did you not like what I did?"

Clementina looked away and he gave her his most entrancing smile. "Come now, sweetheart. Admit that you did, just a little."

"Oh, your Highness, I'm bewildered. I don't know how to answer you."

"Perhaps like this," and the prince gave her a kiss full of fire, parting her lips and flicking his tongue into her mouth.

At first rigid, Clementina finally melted beneath Charles' insistent embrace — and somewhere in his brain he smiled. He had not been in Jeannie's bed since the retreat from Derby, which had broken both his heart and his spirit, but never his desire for worldly pleasure. Slowly, very slowly, the prince slipped his hand beneath Clementina's skirts and started to caress what he found there.

She was longing for him, there could be no doubt. Charles, who had dressed very finely in French silk breeches and brightly embroidered coat, subtly began to remove them and then, for good measure, plucked off his ringleted wig so that his red hair gleamed in the afternoon sunshine as he finally slid his privy part within her and then, slowly at first, began to thrust.

Afterwards Clementina wept and laughed, held tightly against the prince's cambric shirt.

"Why are you crying, sweet girl?"

"Because I have lost my most precious jewel."

"And gained a royal lover in so doing."

She gave a wry smile. "That I have done indeed. Tell me, Highness, am I your first mistress?"

"Er ... no... not exactly."

She asked nothing further, closing her eyes, leaning against his heart, obviously in heaven. Charles, looking round the room, felt fractionally relieved when somebody knocked at the door.

"Come back in fifteen minutes," he called. "I am resting."

"Very good, Highness."

"Did you hear that, dearest? I am afraid that the time has come for us to part. Best be gone or we will be discovered."

"Oh, I could not have that," she answered anxiously, standing up and pulling her skirts back into a more respectable position. "My grandfather will have me beaten."

"I doubt it, my dear," Charles answered with a smile. "I doubt it very much indeed."

And kissing her hand in farewell, he turned his fertile mind once more to the matter of winning Scotland for his father.

CHAPTER SIX

Clementina and Colonel Anne

The Battle of Falkirk was fought in the most dire circumstances possible, not due to any weakness on the Jacobite side. In fact the ranks of followers had swollen in number so that now the prince commanded an army of some eight thousand men strong. So it was with six and a half of them at his back that he marched out to meet General Henry Hawley, known as 'The Hangman'.

Much had happened while Charles had been ill. Stirling town had surrendered but the castle still held out against the invading force — and he and Murray had had yet another falling out. No sooner had the prince re-joined his troops than Lord George had started to list a string of complaints; why couldn't the Camerons have been with him instead of remaining at Alloa? His Highness' sojourn at Bannockburn had been an unfortunate drain on forces as the troops had to do guard duty there instead of being on the front line. Charles, to his credit, had smiled and nodded and walked away, but within had come that old familiar urge to strike the puffed-up fool and tell him to mind his manners.

For once, however, he had to agree with Lord George's battle plan. The Hangman had been breathing down the Jacobites' neck too long and the time had come to face him out. Murray had suggested that they seize the higher ground outside Falkirk and the prince concurred. To disguise this manoeuvre they had sent a body of men marching down the main road to Stirling. These were soon spotted and reported back to General Hawley, alias The Hangman, who had chortled with mirth.

"Mindless bastards. Only a bunch of ham-fisted idiots, together with that pompous little princeling, could do anything so crass."

And with those words he had sat down to dinner in Callendar House. He had just started on a delicious dessert when a messenger came in.

"Excuse me interrupting you, sir, but the entire Jaccobite army is climbing the high ground. And there's 'undreds of 'em, sir."

The Hangman had sprung up, red in the face, seizing his hat then dropping it accidentally in his dinner, then sprinting to his horse. The result was that the Hanoverian army arrived a few minutes after the Jacobites, who were in full military formation. And then the heavens opened. If the prince had ever thought God might be on his side, now he metaphorically raised his hat to him. A bitter wind came up and icy rain beat directly into the faces of the Hanoverians who were still struggling up the slope. Darkness began to descend and it was difficult to see who was who in the dim light.

The Hangman was, for all his fearsome soubriquet, hopelessly incompetent. In contrast Lord George Murray — whatever his faults — had drilled his army to perfection. At four in the afternoon Hawley ordered his dragoons to attack. There were seven hundred of them and four thousand well trained clansmen, standing in silence, waiting for them.

Murray had instilled in every man that no-one was to fire until he gave the signal. So, in that deadly quiet, the cavalry came on at the trot. Waiting until they were a mere pistol shot away, Lord George finally raised his musket. The dragoons died in that dark afternoon, massacred by a devastating burst of fire. Two of the regiments turned and fled, riding over their foot soldiers in the panic. The third were brutally attacked by the clansmen, their blood lust up, rushing over the field, wielding their mighty claymores.

Discipline broke down. The MacDonalds went berserk and charged at Hawley's army with broadswords. Six front-line regiments turned and fled. And it was now so gloomy, rain slashing down like razors, that both sides were withdrawing from the battlefield in great haste. Even though the Jacobites had won the day, they had failed to clinch total victory as, sodden and mud soaked, they too left the field.

That night there was gloom in their camp. Admittedly, they had entered Falkirk and the enemy had fled, but there was no celebration. Charles despondently ate the remains of the meal that The Hangman had left and went to bed in Callendar House. Longing for someone to comfort him and tell him that everything was going to be all right, his mind turned again and again to Clementina, wishing that she was by his side.

Whether his bad night, reliving the battle, every enthralling ghastly moment of it, caused him to feel unwell the next morning it was impossible to say. Whether his illness was caused by his mental state or whether it was a physical complaint, nobody could judge. Lord George, of course, claimed that the prince was malingering. James Mor MacGregor said that it was a return of his former complaint, brought about by the appalling weather, together with the fact that young Angus Glengarry had been accidentally shot dead by a Keppoch MacDonald, who had been executed immediately. Whatever the reason, Charles — pale as death — took off for Bannockburn, surrounded by a marching bodyguard.

Clementina, hovering anxiously by the front door, cast her eyes on him and immediately insisted he went to bed, into which she secretly crept after the hour of midnight had struck. The one thing that the prince could never be was a bad lover. In illness or fighting fit, he could always please his partner, and he had to stuff a handkerchief over Clementina's mouth to drown out her loud shrieks of pleasure as she reached a delightful climax on that first exciting night together again.

In this manner, Charles whiled away a few days of delicious sexuality until he was brought back to reality by some grim news. The Duke of Cumberland, George II's youngest son and a year younger than the prince himself, had arrived in Edinburgh with three new regiments. At last the sensual young man was hauled back to reality. He immediately sent word to George Murray to prepare for battle and whistled his sudden cheerfulness about the house.

But the ebony seeds of hatred had been sown months ago and the dislike, which had been almost instantaneous between the two very different men, had bubbled away for a long, long time and had now reached boiling point. Lord George Murray convened a secret meeting with the six leading clan chieftains. He told them of the continuing daily desertions of men from all ranks, their far reduced state against Cumberland's battle-ready forces, and suggested a retreat to the Highlands would be a better way forward.

"But the idea will kill wee Charlie," said Lochgarry.

"It's either that or be killed on the battlefield," Murray answered, drily.

He was exaggerating, of course. The situation was not as black as he had painted it. Nonetheless, George Murray's view was taken seriously. So much so that the Highland chiefs solemnly signed an objection to the prince's battle orders and added their voice to the idea of retreating. This document was duly sent to Charles by messenger riding a rapid horse.

It arrived late, on the twenty-eighth of January. So late, indeed, that the prince had already retired for the night. It was read by two of his advisers who decided not to wake him, one of them riding through the night to Falkirk to try and persuade the chiefs to reverse their decision. He came back in the dawning, shaking his head. There was nothing for it but to give the news to Charles as soon as he awoke.

The scene was even more nightmarish than they could have imagined. The prince read the document in stunned silence and then, giving a shriek, dashed his head so violently against the wall that he staggered and almost fell.

"Good God!" he shouted. "Have I lived to see this? That bloody man. He is my dark devil! I shall never know a moment's happiness until he returns to the witch's womb from which he was whelped."

Then he wept and rejected even Clementina, who had come running to see what was wrong.

The retreat from Falkirk was as terrible as Charles had imagined it would be. Relations between the prince and Murray — who Charles now called 'that accursed man' — had broken down completely. Lord George tried to belittle him whenever they met. So much so that Lord Lewis Gordon made a vigorous protest and accused Murray of going mad. To add to their problems an accidental explosion of gunpowder, which Charles had been afraid might fall into Cumberland's hands, blew St. Ninian's Church sky high and also gusted Murray of Broughton's wife out of her chaise and onto the ground, where she lay unconscious.

In appalling winter conditions, the prince conducted the Jacobite army northwards into the Highlands, while Murray led his Athollmen to Perth. Charles felt that the bitter weather had entered his soul as he slowly made his way onwards, seeking a billet at which to sleep at night wherever he could find one. On the fifteenth of February he spent the dark hours at the home of Grant of Dalrachny, an unwilling host and a staunch supporter of the Whig party.

"You'll be all right tonight, sir," James Moy said the following morning as they mounted their horses.

"Why's that?"

"Surely you realise where we're bound next?"

"I know it's Moy Hall and it's the seat of the leader of Clan Mackintosh."

James More gave a chuckle. "There's something else, my prince, but I'll keep you in suspense."

"Oh come on. Tell me."

"No, you'll have to wait and see."

The prince was pleased to observe, as the small party of horsemen made their way up an impressive drive, that what appeared to be a small castle lay in front of him. And even as he thought that here he was sure of a welcome, a group of ostlers came running towards them and simultaneously the great front door was flung open by a liveried footman.

Charles stepped into a hall glowing with polished wood and then stopped short as a vision in tartan taffeta rustled towards him. She was smiling at him — quite broadly he thought, for a lady with whom he was not yet acquainted. But even as she drew nearer, the soft sheen of dark hair coiled up about her lovely face struck him as familiar. Then he started to grin and she, catching his eye in a most disrespectful manner, smiled back. He not only knew her, he had actually danced with her, and in Edinburgh at that. It was the girl with the broken shoe.

"Greetings, Highness, welcome to my home," she said, and sank into a curtsey so deep that Charles wondered if she would ever be able to get up again.

"Lady Mackintosh," he said, and held out a dignified hand for her to kiss, which she did with a certain sensuous touch of her mouth before slowly rising up in a great whisper of silken skirts.

The incredible scent overwhelmed him; every inch of her costume was perfumed with some exotic fragrance. Charles could imagine one of her servants sprinkling Otto of Arabia liberally onto the rustling material. He was quite overwhelmed and deeply attracted.

"A brandy all round," she ordered. "The gentlemen need warming up before they change for dinner."

The drink fired through the prince's system while James Mor MacGregor spoke before anyone had a chance to propose a toast.

"Just so that you are aware, sir, Lady Mackintosh raised the clan herself, her husband being somewhat faint-hearted. Rumour has it that she rode at the head of the regiment with a man's bonnet on her head, a tartan riding habit, richly laced, and pistols at her saddle-bow. Is it true, my lady?"

"It is, gentlemen, it is. And who would do less for such a Bonnie Prince?"

Charles felt humbled. It seemed that the majority of the people of Scotland loved him indeed and had turned out in their multitudes to show him how much. His mind wandered to the traitorous Murray and he wondered what could have been achieved if an entirely different man had been appointed to command the clansmen. But it was too late for that. He must go and make himself presentable and then flirt with Anne Mackintosh and whisper about their moonlit dance in Edinburgh.

He was half way up the stairs when a thought struck him. He turned to James Mor who was coming up behind him.

"Tell me, James, have you had any word of Jeannie?"

"I regret to tell you, sir, that she was wounded at the siege of Stirling. She was shot in the leg and eventually captured by the English."

"I'm so sorry. Do you have any idea where she's been taken?"

"I don't. But the dungeons at Edinburgh Castle would be my best bet."

The prince shook his head, deeply upset, but said nothing, remembering what a friend Jeannie had been to him, recalling the sensation of lying next to her and breathing in her scent, redolent of the moors and the forest. But this reminded him too vividly of his perfumed hostess, and he banished the thought as best he could and concentrated on the time ahead.

They ate dinner in the late afternoon, he and Anne sitting together at one table at which ten course settings had been laid. His aides-de-camp sat at another table with a mere eight covers. The prince's master of the household, Richard Gibb, plus his cooks, were given the night off as Anne had ordered a feast for the whole company.

Famished though he was, the prince could hardly concentrate on his food in the company of so ravishing a hostess. She was quite a tiny woman, petite almost, with sweet small hands that flew like birds when she wanted to demonstrate something. Her bosom was enthralling; not round and voluptuous like Jeannie's, not high and thrusting like Clementina's. It was small and neat and very provocative, in fact it was with difficulty that Charles stopped himself from staring at it and concentrated on her face. But it was a beautiful face, and he smiled as Anne spoke earnestly.

"I have taken the precaution of sending out the local blacksmith, Donald Fraser, in charge of four men, to watch for any suspicious movement of English troops on the Inverness road, sir."

"How very thoughtful. Do you think it was entirely necessary?"

"Indeed I do, Highness. You see, I do not trust your host of last night..."

"You mean Grant of Dalrachny?"

"Certainly. He is a committed Whig who refers to you rather casually as the Young Pretender. Furthermore, the Lord Loudon, in charge of Hanoverian troops, is longing to get his hands on you and he is — even as we speak — not far away, in Inverness. Remember, there is a price of £30,000 on your head, which his Lordship would very much like inside his pockets. So what easier than for Grant to tip Loudon the wink that you're spending the night here?"

Charles pulled a face. "He may also have passed on the information that I am travelling with a very small bodyguard."

"If he's to turn traitor he will do so in earnest."

Whatever the prince's other faults were, cowardice was not one of them. He carefully finished what was in his crystal glass, which glinted in the light of the candles, and then said, "Gentlemen, pray silence. Lady Mackintosh has some important information for you."

Anne stood up, and once more Charles was seduced by the exotic aroma that rose from her skirts, which seemed more important to him at that moment than any threat from the enemy.

And it was as well that his mind was on other things, because in nearby Inverness the noose was tightening. In a tavern in the town's centre officers of the one thousand five hundred men that had been suddenly drafted in were talking in hushed voices to one another.

"It's something to do with this pretender fellow," said one.

"Damn his eyes," came the answer. "He must be hiding nearby."

"I've heard he's at Moy Hall."

"Well, we'll have marching orders soon chaps, so drink up while you have the chance."

None of them noticed that a scrap of a child, a skinny creature with hair wild beneath a mucky mob cap but with large intelligent eyes, left her place serving behind the bar and ran as fast as she could, her bare feet rough on the frost-hardened cobbles, through the icy streets of Inverness. Her name was Mairi, her mother long dead, her father the innkeeper of the tavern in which the officers had been talking. Though she knew nothing of politics, she knew that the prince from over the water had come to save Scotland and return it to its native people, free from the English yoke. She also knew Moy Hall and that the dowager Lady Mackintosh, mother of Colonel Anne's husband, lived nearby. If anybody could save the prince — whom Mairi had never met and never likely would — it must be this sharp-witted old lady.

As the prince cast longing eyes on his elegant hostess, never dreaming that capture was so near at hand, the eyes of the older Lady Mackintosh sharpened as she heard the words that came stumbling breathlessly out of Mairi's mouth. As soon as the story became coherent, she rang a small bell that stood on a table beside her and told the answering servant to bring to her immediately a nimble youth of her household. A twelve-year-old boy came yawning from his bed, running his eyes over the waif who stood at Lady Mackintosh's elbow, both children looking frightened.

"Lachlan, I want you to run an errand for me."

"Yes, m'lady?"

"I hear you are fleet of foot and so you must be. Prince Charles — you know of whom I speak?"

"Yes, m'lady."

"He is dining at Moy Hall with my daughter-in-law this very night. He has a high price upon his head and Loudon is probably marching there already with a huge army of soldiers. I want you to run to Moy Hall — without being detected, d'ye hear — and raise the alarm. Can you do that?"

"I hope so, m'lady."

"There's no *hope* about it. You will do it and succeed, do you understand? The life of the prince is in real danger. If you do get caught make up some tale about getting home to your grieving mother. Say anything but complete your mission. The future of Scotland is in your hands."

At this dramatic statement both the children drew in a breath and burst into tears of emotion. Lady Mackintosh gave them a reproving glance and rang the bell again for a refill of sherry.

In her daughter-in-law's household, the atmosphere was calm and relaxed, the hostess beautiful and full of charm, loving the company of the glamorous prince and his entourage. Charles, slightly tipsy, was totally enamoured with Lady Mackintosh, watching her with a half-smile on his face as she prattled on.

"Of course, my husband is somewhat older than I am, though he carries his years extremely well. That was why it was this humble servant of yours, your Highness, who actually raised the Clan Chattan on your behalf. The men called me 'The Colonel', can you believe?"

"Extremely well. What a fine figure you must make, riding at their head. Do I take it that your husband's sympathies do not lie with me?"

Anne stared into her wine glass. "No, my prince, that would not be true. The Clan Chattan are Jacobite to a man. It's just that he is away on government service and so the duty fell to me."

She looked up, straight into Charles' tawny eyes. There could be no doubting the lazy expression of amused attraction that showed in them. The young Lady Mackintosh felt a slight colour rise to her cheeks. Of royal blood he might be, but there was little doubt in her mind that she could seduce him as easy as wink. She shivered delightfully.

The logs fell in the fireplace; the prince's aides-de-camp had retired to their rooms; the house was splendidly silent — and on the bleak moor, a twelve-year-old boy was shivering with fright as he lay prostrate in a ditch, watching a marching column of soldiers called to a halt.

Lachlan had slipped through the cordon of sentries easily enough, a skinny boy with the cook's black stockings and gloves on to hide his white flesh. But after that the going had not been so good. He had found himself behind the squadron of formidable marching troops and could not see any way to get past them. They completely blocked the narrow road that led down to Moy. Even in his disguise a small child running would have been spotted immediately. Now, he strained his ears. Someone with a very upper-class Scottish accent was shouting orders.

"Men, I think it is impossible to proceed down this way because of the road's poor condition. It would be more practical to take the cart track. So, company — form up."

The soldiers who had made the most of their temporary stop by relieving themselves heartily, most of them aiming at the ditch in which poor Lachlan lay, dodging the streams of piss as best he could, adjusted themselves before turning towards the other path. He heard them move off and raised his head. It was the moment and he took it. Climbing out, he ran for his life — and that of the prince — down the now deserted road.

In Moy Hall, the only sound came from the scratching of dogs, the noise made by cats sitting up, suddenly alert, when they caught the whiff of a mouse, the footman yawning as he tried to stay awake.

The prince had long since gone to his room, whispering to his hostess as he left her side.

"Good night, my lady. Thank you for your hospitality. I hope to have sweet dreams."

"I hope so too, Highness."

"If I do, they will be of you. Riding out as colonel of your clan. In your tartan riding habit."

He had kissed her hand, giving her a lingering look as he did so. He was good at those, knowing the usual effect they had on ladies — and Anne Mackintosh was no exception.

"I would be honoured to feature in your slumbers, sir."

"And to interrupt them?" This last said very softly.

"I am a married woman, Highness."

Charles had pitched a heavy sigh. "Alas."

"Yes, indeed." And with that Anne had curtsied then left him.

And now the house was totally quiet, though The Colonel lay awake, longing to go to the naughty prince but not quite having the courage to do so. She was not fully aware as yet of his joyful philandering, nor, had she been, would she have completely understood it. Being a woman and strictly brought up, she had been delighted when her husband was a man she both liked and respected. Yet all along she had these strange urges for promiscuous sexual pleasure, for wild adventure. It would have been better by far, Anne thought, if she had been born male and could have put it about as she pleased.

She sighed, blew out the candle, then immediately struck a tinder and relit it. She would go to the prince and take up his offer. Creeping on silken feet, she went out into the corridor.

She had given Charles the best bedchamber, the one used by herself and her husband, when he made one of his infrequent appearances.

Softly, she made her way towards it and opened the door a fraction. A taper flickered gently as she entered, disturbed by the change in atmosphere. From where she stood Anne could see that he slept like a child, his elegant features relaxed, his body completely at ease. To have disturbed him and offered him carnal pleasure would have been cruel. Quietly, Anne Mackintosh closed the door and went back to her own room.

*

It was five o'clock in the morning, still dark as jet, when a twelve-year-old boy who had been running throughout the night shambled, exhausted, into the courtyard of Moy House. He was shouting as loudly as he could in his state of weariness. "Help! The enemy is within a mile of us." Then the hapless child went into the kitchens and pulled at the greatcoat of Alexander Stewart, the footman who sat at the table and had fallen asleep leaning on it.

"Wake up, sir. Wake up. For God's sake go and waken the prince. The enemy are only a mile behind us."

Stewart woke abruptly, bounded up the stairs, but at that moment the door of Charles' chamber flew open and clad only in a dressing gown, shoes unbuckled on his feet and a bonnet — a soft-brimmed hat like a beret, beloved by the men of Scotland — perched on top of his nightcap, the prince appeared. Ordering Stewart to sound the alarm, he took off down the stairs at a rate of knots. Meanwhile Anne was rushing about the house, clad in her nightgown, enquiring wildly whether her royal guest was safe. Eventually, they came face to face.

"Run, Your Highness, run. Go down the side of Loch Moy. There you will find Lochiel and his Camerons. You'll be safe with them."

Charles' answer was brief. "How close are the enemy?"

"About a quarter of a mile away by now. I'll contact you as soon as it is all right."

"Take care," he answered — and was gone before Anne could speak another word, plunging into the night to save himself for what lay ahead.

CHAPTER SEVEN

Culloden

In the end the whole incident turned into a farce. Charles had to walk through a miserable bog accompanied by Richard Gibb and a handful of his aides, hating the fact that he had been forced to leave a comfortable bed in such a hurry. The members of their small party were shivering with the blistering cold and the prince, clad only in a nightshirt and dressing gown, felt physically ill with it. Eventually, when they decided they had gone far enough and the distant sound of bagpipes told them that Lochiel and his men were on their way, they decided to stop. Half an hour later a servant came running from Moy Hall.

"Lady Mackintosh says to come back, Highness. She will explain when she sees you."

It appeared that the local blacksmith, Donald Fraser, and his four stout-hearted men had succeeded in fooling Loudon's brigade completely. By firing muskets, shouting out orders to imaginary regiments to advance and cut the opposing forces to pieces, and generally making such a raucous racket, the marching men had been totally deceived and were swiftly ordered back to Inverness by the general himself. Charles did not know whether to laugh or cry.

His flight, scantily clad, across that horrible morass had left him feeling chilled to the bone and, sure enough, three days later he went down with a cold and a cough. But this time he had no Clementina to nurse him — though he had spent several days more at Moy, he had felt too poorly to regard Lady Anne as anything more than his beautiful saviour. Besides, his coughing fits made him not the most desirable male to be around.

Then on the seventeenth of February came the rallying of the troops for the attack on Inverness. Spluttering and feeling like a washed-out excuse for a man, Charles led his army into the town as the Hanoverian brigade were still staggering out. He made for Culloden House where he collapsed into bed. A doctor was called and looked serious. The Young Pretender had pneumonia.

He had several visitors — one of whom he could have done without. Lord George Murray, who had made his way from Aberdeen to Inverness through the most atrocious freezing weather — so bad that the soldiers had icicles hanging from their beards and eyebrows — finally arrived to join him. Making his way to the prince's bedside, he related a story of prisoners taken and daring raids into enemy territory. From the depths of his pillow Charles thought the man must be in a good mood and nodded his head as best he could.

He convalesced at old Lady Mackintosh's, sleeping in her grand bedroom, and was highly amused when her son — who had been taken prisoner by the Duke of Perth — was brought before him.

"Well, well, sir. Here's a to-do! Your family all support my father's cause — yet you apparently don't like the Jacobites. What am I to make of that?"

"You can make of it what you like, your Highness. The fact is that I had to work for the government and was in the wrong place at the wrong time, otherwise, be assured, I would not be standing before you." Lady Mackintosh made a little noise and her son added, "And don't you start, mother, please."

Charles gave him a cold-eyed look. He was a big fellow with a rather unkempt wig and a face of that delicate skin which would colour up in an instant. In the summer, no doubt, he would be covered with freckles. He had bright blue eyes, which were set very slightly on the squint. For absolutely no particular reason, other than the fact that Mackintosh had betrayed him, the prince found himself taking a dislike to the man.

"I could have you put in irons," he remarked, his voice harsh.

"Yes, you could," Mackintosh retorted.

Feeling definitely annoyed, Charles said, "Have you no manners? You are addressing a prince of the blood."

"My regrets, your Highness," came the unapologetic answer.

Lady Mackintosh sighed again as Charles angrily turned to the window and answered with his back averted.

"Because your family — your mother, your wife, and various servants of them both — saved my life, I am persuaded to let you go. You can return to your home and your exquisite woman. And I hope that you treat her better than you have treated me."

And he remained with his back turned until he judged by the opening and closing of the door that the Laird of Macintosh had gone. There was a solitary sigh behind him and then the old woman spoke, her voice sounding slightly hushed but other than for that, normal.

"That was kind of you, sir. But forgive him for my son has his pride and that has been deeply wounded."

"How, my lady?" Charles asked, turning.

"Because he was forced to work for them, sir, and that's the truth of it. At heart he's a Jacobite born and bred."

"Then why was he so curt and rude?"

She chuckled, a good sound. "Perhaps, sir, it was the green-eyed monster."

Charles, remembering his veiled invitation to the man's wife, did not reply, and had the good grace to feel his face deepen.

*

His health somewhat restored, the prince entertained at Culloden House that evening, throwing himself into dancing and never more pleased to see anyone than the gorgeous Anne Mackintosh, minus her husband.

"So glad that you are up and fit once more, your Highness."

"Thank you, my lady. And how is your lord and master? Well, I hope."

"I thought you had no liking for him, sir."

"Nor he for me, madam. But let it rest there. Tonight we will dance together — and this time without a broken shoe."

"So you remember?"

"It was a moment I will never forget."

Smiling at one another, they broke into a lively jig which fairly puffed the prince out.

"Don't tell anyone of my shortness of breath, Lady Anne. They will think I am growing weak," he gasped, as the rapid piece ended.

"Sir, you have only just recovered from pneumonia. 'Tis not to be wondered at."

"Thank you. Let us step outside for a moment."

The kiss that followed was inevitable between two young and healthy creatures. But whereas Anne felt more than a stab of anguish, thinking of her somewhat dour husband sitting sadly at home, the prince relished it.

He had been born with an insatiable urge for sexual activity, one that would stay with him always. Since his arrival in Scotland he had been to bed with Jeannie, followed by Clementina. Yet he felt no guilt about them whatsoever. He knew that he was the star attraction in the eyes of Jacobite women, a fact that he intended to play to the full. In short, he was a profligate man, frequently surrounded by young and eager females. It was a situation in which he had nothing to lose and everything to play for.

Unfortunately, his health gave way for the third time and most seriously in early March. He had left Inverness on the eleventh. By the thirteenth he was struck down by that most virulent of illnesses, scarlet fever. His temperature was dangerously high and the situation critical. His aides-de-camp were frantic, the physicians with their boxes of blood-sucking leeches well in hand, serious.

For forty-eight hours it was touch and go whether the Young Pretender was going to live. And though the doctors tried to persuade him to eat nothing but light broth when he finally recovered, he replied that he would rather die on horseback fighting Cumberland than in bed sipping bouillon. After that episode the prince returned to Inverness, to the blandishments of the two Ladies Mackintosh, and to dancing.

But despite his appearance of good spirits there was a prickle in Charles' spine. Since Cumberland's arrival in Scotland he had never been truly easy. Though he might seem to be on top of ill fortune it was fate which pursued him like a savage dog. Jacobite losses and failures were constantly grim, blundering and inept. It was as if he was dancing on the edge of a precipice.

On the eighth of April the youngest son of George II marched out of Aberdeen with a well provisioned army behind him. Their aim was to put the Stuart claim to the throne of England behind them once and for all. Their leader — four months younger than Prince Charles and without a hint of compassion in his Hanoverian soul — proudly rode forward to accomplish a mighty victory.

When the news first reached the prince he put a brave face on it but inwardly felt a deep and terrible shudder. It was his destiny to lead the clansmen to fight for him — but now they had dispersed back to their native lands. Calls went out for them to return as quickly as possible. But for various and varying reasons only five thousand gallant men eventually showed up for duty.

The prince spent the night of the fourteenth of April in the company of Lord George Murray. Charles had not gone to bed, instead the two men had passed the small hours drawing up battle plans for the fight which would occur next day. Or at least so the prince supposed. The fifteenth of April was the twenty-fifth birthday of the Duke of Cumberland, who surely could not let such an occasion pass without, hopefully, adding a resounding victory to his reputation. But in that supposition the prince was wrong. Nothing happened. Cumberland preferred to relax in the quiet of his encampment at Nairn. Meanwhile, those clansmen who had come to support Charles slept uncomfortably on the hill outside the big house. It was the calm before the storm.

Next day the Highlanders stood waiting with justa single biscuit each to eat at midday. They were all exhausted, some having marched over fifty miles to re-join the prince. With bellies rumbling, they were kept standing and not dismissed until late afternoon. To add to their problems, their leaders were in disarray. The animosity between Charles and George Murray had never gone away and when the prince came up with the idea of marching on Cumberland and his redcoats by night and catching them with their trousers down, he met with a somewhat frosty reply. In fact, nobody seemed to think it was a very good idea at all.

The prince called a council, determined for the plan to become reality. And eventually, he talked them round, even George Murray saying that he would admit that the scheme was feasible. But despite this, even before they started on the eight-mile march to where the Duke of Cumberland was camped, trouble broke out. The clansmen, dispirited and starving, broke ranks and headed for Inverness, looking for food. Charles, desperate, put his arm around Murray and gave him fulsome thanks for all he had done to help him. The Scotsman merely gave him an unsmiling stare, removed his bonnet and bowed, never uttering a word in return.

The night march was doomed from the very start. The Irish troops could not travel as fast as the Highlanders. George Murray, leading the van, received over a hundred messages to slow down. They were nowhere near their target and it would be dawn before they approached, thus being clearly visible. The only hope was to retreat before they were cut to ribbons. When informed of the decision the prince flew into a fury.

"Good God! Have they all gone mad? We were equal in numbers and would have blown them to the devil."

The Duke of Perth, patient and caring, drew Charles to one side.

"Your Highness, if we proceed we will reach Nairn in the daylight and we will all be wiped out. Our only chance, sir, is to retreat and fight them elsewhere."

The prince turned away and when he looked back at the older man there were tears in his eyes.

"Then so be it. But believe me, Perth, I do not regret my own loss. Instead I regret the ruin of these fine and loyal men who have stood so gallantly by me."

"Then I beg you, sir, go back to Culloden House while you still have the chance. Prepare yourself for battle."

Charles did not answer, instead giving a bitter smile before galloping off into the uncertain light of that mist-shrouded dawning.

*

His first — and only — glimpse of Cumberland was shortly after eleven o'clock in the morning of the sixteenth of April. The prince had been awoken after two hours' rest to hear that the enemy were on the move. Chaos had broken out. In order to alert the clansmen who had gone looking for food in Inverness, every conceivable noise was made. Drums, pipes and cannon all conglomerated in a great burst of sound. But not everybody came back. The Jacobites entered the fray hopelessly outnumbered.

Charles dressed very finely that day and appeared on the battlefield sporting a pair of silver-mounted pistols and a leather shield. He also carried a telescope and from his vantage point on a small hillock, peered anxiously at the opposing army. And then, all of a sudden, he saw him. The man he had never met — nor ever would — but whom he hated with a passion.

Why there was so much violent dislike even the prince himself could not say. But deep, deep down Charles was jealous of Cumberland. They were virtually the same age and in the same position. Yet Cumberland — as George II's youngest son — was infuriatingly in the place where Charles, by rights, should have been. The Bonnie Prince was only the Young Pretender, grandson of a displaced king, whereas Cumberland enjoyed all the benefits and privileges of being George II's baby boy.

"You damn dog," called Charles aloud. "If I get anywhere near you I'll break your bloody neck."

There was only one, small, consolation. Cumberland was already running to fat and had the makings of a double chin. The prince was, by far, the more handsome and definitely had a much better, slimmer physique.

The battle began at one o'clock with the tremendous boom of cannons. The shots seemed to be aimed at Charles himself, for his horse took a hit and began to bleed. Undaunted, he dismounted and took another mount, moving out of the firing line. But the die was cast.

It turned into a brutal fight. In a pall of smoke and burst of explosions the Jacobites were cut to ribbons. The prince, sensing defeat, tried to rally the remaining troops, shouting that he would lead them on foot for a final charge. He spoke in English. The Gaelic-speaking Highlanders did not understand a word he said and stared uncomprehendingly.

"You must leave the field, sir," said one of his aides.

"That I'll never do," Charles answered.

"But you're almost surrounded. You're in great personal danger."

"They won't take me alive. I'd shoot myself rather than fall into their hands."

At this someone grabbed his bridle and literally pulled his horse away. Charles turned his head and could see nothing but the utter destruction of the mighty clansmen.

"Oh no," he said. "Oh God, no."

"Do not sacrifice yourself in vain, my prince. Come."

"No, no, I won't."

But Major Kennedy, Lochiel's uncle, intervened. Seizing the bridle from the hand of the aide-de-camp, he led Charles firmly away.

"Poor Scotland," gasped the Young Pretender as the bitter tears coursed down his cheeks in an unstoppable torrent.

He was in hell, a brave and gallant man being led off the field. He cast one last look backwards and saw his army being hacked to pieces. Putting his head back, Prince Charles Edward Stuart let out a final cry of utter despair. The Jacobite dream was over.

CHAPTER EIGHT

Flora MacDonald

He was dreaming again, a dream that came to haunt him when the balance of his mind was adrift. In it he was riding, a boyhood ride, on his much-loved Nighthawk. He was heading towards the sea, then splashing through the waves that broke like frills of tattered lace on the deserted beach.

Only it wasn't an Italian beach, full of warmth, where he could bask in the loving sunshine. Instead it was a bitter stretch of sand, whipped by a vicious wind, a place where people would walk, knowing they would never see civilisation again. With a cry that came from deep within his soul, Charles Edward Stuart woke and looked around him, shrivelled with fear because he did not recognise his surroundings.

He was in a small bedroom, the walls of which showed it to be a humble dwelling. He was lying on an even more humble bed, on which he had been having a full, deep sleep for the first time in five days and nights. But this realisation brought back the memory of the savagery at Culloden, and the prince felt the familiar swell of tears behind his eyelids. He had left the battlefield weeping and the emotion had not been far away since.

The door opened a crack and John O'Sullivan, an Irishman who had sailed with Charles to Scotland and who had been a member of the small party that had left the battle with the prince, peered in.

"Oh, you're awake, Highness. You've had a good rest, I'm glad to see."

"Yes, thank you. Where exactly am I?"

"In the cottage of Donald Cameron of Glenpean. We arrived here at about two o'clock in the morning."

"Yes, it was very late. I remember now."

And indeed he could suddenly recall everything that had happened, with vivid clarity. Leaving the human agony that was Culloden behind them, the prince sobbing wildly and behaving like a lunatic, the small party had headed for Gorthlech, where he had been forced to dry his swollen eyes and sit down to supper. There had then ensued a discussion between Lord Lovat, Lord Elcho and Sir Thomas Sheridan, on which Charles could not concentrate. One side wanted him to leave immediately for France, the other to remain and fight a guerrilla war from the hills. The prince felt as if he wasn't there. Everyone was talking about him but he wasn't saying a word.

They left as soon as the terrible conversation was over and started on a journey that seemed unending to Charles. At that stage he neither cared nor worried where he was. His only aim was to escape the terrible wrath of Cumberland.

But at least the cottage owner, a Jacobite named Donald Cameron, had offered him a decent night's sleep, and before he left the cottage in Glenpean, Charles had received news that Lochiel — whom the prince had seen fall at the battle of Culloden — was still alive, although wounded in both legs. So it was with a slightly lighter heart that he set off with his few companions, into the wilds of Scotland.

Never before had he truly appreciated the majesty of the great country of which his father was the rightful king. The towering mountains that changed colour from slate to damson, depending on whether the sun was shining on their majestic heads or whether they were wreathed in magical, mysterious mist. The lochs that glittered as brilliantly as a jewelled sword or glowered as a dark, depressing sheet of unfriendly depths. The sound of the bagpipes, a high resonant lament that fell on the ear and conjured up the whole ethos of the Scots personality.

The journey that he undertook would have finished a lesser man. But by now Cumberland's army was out in force, looking for him everywhere. The reward of £30,000 on his head had never been more dangerous — yet no-one betrayed him. Rich and poor alike kept silent. People whispered in the dark, there were nods and winks, muttered phrases, but eventually the tattered, tired young man arrived in Borrodale, situated on the north shore of the great sea loch, nan Uamh. Here, at last, he had a chance to recuperate.

The horrors perpetrated by Cumberland after Culloden had fuelled his feelings of guilt and despair. No quarter had been given to those unlucky enough to stay alive after that terrible battle. Bonfires were built and onto them the living wounded had been thrown, the men who had marched fifty miles to join the prince, and then slept through exhaustion, were sabred where they slept, any living being who had fought for the Young Pretender was hacked or stabbed to death by the Redcoat army. Cumberland himself had been given the nickname of Butcher, which he richly deserved. It was only when he reached Borrodale that the prince began to recover from a period of self-loathing for leaving the battlefield and a hatred for Cumberland that knew no bounds.

Despite the fact he slept on a pallet of straw, Charles chose to spend his nights in a cottage some small distance away from the house of a loyal Jacobite, Ranald MacDonald Borrodale, one of that extraordinary chain of people who would rather have died than reveal the whereabouts of the Bonnie Prince. But in the day time he ate well with his host and lost some of the gaunt appearance that had haunted him since Culloden. He also now made serious plans for escaping to France.

His loathing of George Murray was solidified by a letter he received from the man, accusing him of betraying them all from the moment he arrived in Scotland, and being responsible for the shambles of Culloden. Charles' determination to return to France and raise an army became almost overwhelming from that moment on. An army that in no circumstances would contain that ghastly man.

The means for his escape were presented to him by Donald Macleod, a seventy-year-old loch seaman, who nonetheless argued with him about the advisability of sailing to the Isle of Skye, Charles' first idea.

"You'll excuse me saying so, sir, but the chieftains there will deliver you straight up to the Hanoverians. Better by far to let me take you to the Outer Hebrides where you'll pick up a boat destined for somewhere or other abroad."

Charles thought for a moment or two, then answered, "I think that's probably a better plan. When can we sail?"

"You're impatient to leave, my prince."

"Wouldn't you be if you had the entire Hanoverian army searching for you?"

"I would indeed. But don't you worry. We'll get you out of here fast."

The boat appeared a few days later, complete with a rowing crew of seven. It was stoutly-built and clearly seaworthy. After dark on the twenty-sixth of April, Charles, O'Sullivan and a few other followers clambered aboard against the wishes of Macleod, who said he could sniff a storm coming up.

"Oh, don't be such an old woman. I'd rather face that than the Redcoats any day. Let's be off."

Charles lived to regret those breezy words. He crouched over the side of the boat, green in the face and spewing up his guts. He had never felt so ill in his entire life. All around him he could hear the others shouting to one another over the roar of the wind and the huge claps of thunder. Overhead, lightning was cutting the sky in half. It was like a scene from Dante's *Inferno* with the principal player looking ghastly and vomiting.

There was a sickening crack as the bowsprit broke and — storm finally over — the boat now plunged on in pitch darkness.

"Why don't we put in at Skye for the night?" suggested Donald Macleod, who was gallantly steering the vessel as best he could in the lashing wind.

A groan came from the figure lying flat in the bilge.

"No, no. They will betray me. We must reach the Long Island."

This was the local name for the Outer Hebrides and Macleod understood the instruction, meanwhile cursing beneath his breath. But eventually, as dawn's rosy finger dyed the mist pink, the island of Benbecula reared before them. The prince, who had by now recovered from the terrible sickness, also recovered his spirits and helped the sailors and others heave the boat on to the shore. Indeed, he felt so much better that he had a fit of giggling joyousness when the cooking pot — old and abandoned in a decrepit hut — had to be stuffed with rags before it could be used.

But this was to be one glorious, hysterical moment in a plethora of future tragedies. For the first time, the prince experienced the full horror of going from place to place seeking shelter. The militia men were closing in, the Royal Navy was relentlessly patrolling the entire area, there seemed to be nowhere to hide. After some ghastly misadventures he felt that he and his body were finally tired of living.

He had been lying in a hovel on the island of South Uist, so small that he had to crawl on his belly to get inside it. His mind was weak, without hope, and he thought that death might be preferable to this experience. He had endured hours of standing in the rain, had been pursued by HMS *Furnace* to within an inch of capture, had eaten little and slept less. Now was surely the time to put a gun to his head. He could have wept except that it was too much effort to do so. Charles closed his eyes and wished that the whole terrible experience was over and done. But after a few minutes he heard the raised voices of his companions and then the familiar boom of someone speaking to them. Weak though he was, the prince recognised the tones of the chieftain of Clanranald, a branch of the large MacDonald clan. He listened.

"Well, my friends, how have you been faring?" Somebody murmured a reply and Clanranald went on, "I'm sorry to hear that. Anyway I've brought some food and wine to cheer your spirits up."

At this good news, Charles decided to go on living and wormed his way out of the tunnel, appearing dirty-faced and red-haired — wig long since abandoned — in the entrance. He forgot all about protocol and threw his arms round Old Clanranald in greeting.

"Well, sir, I'm glad to see you're alive and well, though — if you'll forgive my saying so — in need of a good wash."

The prince had the energy to smile, though words of gratitude stuck in his throat. Clanranald, realising, pulled the top off a bottle of wine.

"Have a wee dram, sir. You look as if you've been to the ends of the earth and back."

Charles put the bottle to his lips and felt his energy slowly return.

"Thank you. We've been existing on the remains of a duck, so there hasn't been a lot to go round."

"I've brought you a salmon and some biscuits. And more bottles to be going on with. But best of all, my prince, I've found you a hideout in Corradale, in the north of the island. It's a crofter's cottage built in an inlet on an extremely rocky coast. You won't find any Redcoats there."

Tears welled up once more in Charles' eyes. "Then perhaps I should stay alive after all."

He and his friends set off on foot in the darkness of a northern night and arrived at their destination the following evening. The little house was welcoming and the prince felt as if it had always wanted him to live in it. From that day forward he lived the life of a simple man, recovering from the recent horror, quite untroubled by so much as a glimpse of a military patrol. He felt as happy as was possible in the circumstances, and after a week or so's rest his naughty thoughts began to rove towards the female sex. If he could just have some feminine company, life would be a perfect paradise, he thought.

But the world and its cruelty could not leave him to dream for much longer. Reports came in that the search for him had been intensified. Cumberland was in full demonic flow. 'Apprehending the Young Pretender seems to be a thing much wished for just now,' wrote one of Cumberland's officials in a letter to the Duke of Newcastle. Meanwhile, the navy's presence was strengthened by nine ships, their orders to scour the Scottish coast, telescopes trained.

As the prince learned of the ever-increasing hunt, he decided that it was time to leave his peaceful little haven. His enemy's troops were closing in with a pincer movement. He had to move on — but where to?

The agony started again. Harried from place to place, starving hungry, knowing that the Hanoverian net was drawing tighter, the prince and his few companions dismissed the boat and slept in fields, covered only by the sails which they had begged from their former crew. Charles, by now, was in a terrible physical state. Bitten half to death by midges, attacks of the bloody flux coming to plague him, all he could think about was how to escape the Redcoats, who were approaching from the south, and the Blackcoats who were coming from the north.

He decided that he and Captain Felix O'Neill, together with Neal MacEachin to act as guide, would go north and risk being spotted by one of the naval vessels. After that they would make their way inland and try to get help from some of the MacDonald sympathisers. If there were any left.

As it happened there was one — though clandestinely so. His name was Hugh MacDonald, and as he was in command of the soldiers in South Uist it was imperative that his name be kept out of the plot. Despite this he had got word through to Charles that he must escape to Skye in the company of MacDonald's stepdaughter, Flora.

Though later she denied having any fore knowledge of the prince's plans, Flora MacDonald obeyed her stepfather's order and went to her brother's sheiling — a hut built for those herding cattle — and waited there alone until, late one evening, there came a knock at the door. She answered it and found that Captain Felix O'Neill was standing in the moonlight.

"You startled me. What is it you want, sir?"

"Gentle lady, please don't be afraid. I am here on behalf of one in dire need of help."

"I don't know who you are talking about, sir. Is he a friend of mine?"

"Perhaps your stepfather has mentioned him to you."

She was not giving a thing away, only too aware that the man could be a spy for the Hanoverians.

"What is this all about?"

The Captain stared at her, mentally weighing her up. She wasn't a bad looking woman, yet lacked that sparky attractiveness which he often found so compelling. Still she was female — a species that had been in wretchedly small supply since this incredible journey began.

Flora had dark hair swept back from rather a protuberant forehead, a pair of deep set eyes and a nose that dominated the rest. But beyond her physical appearance, Felix was looking for something indefinable, a traitor's face. A slight narrowing of the eye sockets, an indefinable curl of the lip. Flora had none of those characteristics.

"If you know nought of the person about whom I am speaking, why are you here alone in this good for nothing shack?"

She twitched her mouth. "I like to come here in the summer months."

Felix laughed, a somewhat hollow sound. "Alone? Not nervous then?"

"No, I am not."

"Then why don't you invite me in?"

"How do I know who you actually are?"

"I am Captain Felix O'Neill and I have the honour to serve the son of our most gracious king — James Stuart."

It was a gamble, but the Irish captain felt pretty certain it would come off. The face looking at his relaxed and a slow smile dawned on the face of Miss MacDonald.

"Then enter, sir, and allow me to bid you welcome."

*

An hour later, Charles had come from his hiding place in the hills and was turning the full force of his charm upon Flora, with little effect. It had gone through his mind that he looked such a regular ruffian that he was no longer attractive to the opposite sex. Still, tired and hungry though he was, he gallantly made the effort — but he was in poor shape and he knew it. To add to all his other problems he was aware of the fact that he stank, not having washed in the last two days.

"But I don't know that it will work. Forgive me, Highness, but I don't see how you could pass yourself off as a woman."

He looked at her wearily. "Why not?"

"Well, you're terribly tall. None of my clothes would fit you."

Charles shook his tired head. "Miss MacDonald, if you won't help me then I am a dead man. I am being harried from every quarter. I must escape from this island or my number is up. I am begging you to assist me."

He could not turn on her a compelling look; the prince felt so exhausted that he could not even raise himself to do so. Instead he put his face into his hands so that no-one could see his expression of despair. Felix looked at Flora MacDonald intently, but said nothing. She stood up and gazed at Charles with something approaching kindness, softening her somewhat severe expression.

"I'll do what I can, Highness. I'll get some clothes for you. We'll make it to Skye somehow or other."

He said nothing, shaking his head from side to side for a minute or two. Then he finally rose to his feet and taking her fingers held them in silence before finally drawing them to his lips.

"My life is in your hands, Miss MacDonald. I cannot thank you enough."

She turned to Felix. "Will you be joining us?"

"Hopefully, yes."

Later that evening they parted company, O'Neill gallantly escorting Miss Macdonald back to her brother's house and Charles Edward plodding wearily back to his hiding place in the hills.

*

It took her several days to organise the clothes for the 'serving woman' who was to accompany Flora on her journey. Though Lady Clanranald threw herself into the secret affair with zest, it was hard to find dresses that were long enough for her. But eventually something was created — a length being sewn onto an existing gown, while other bits were made up from left-overs.

Meanwhile, Charles and his two supporters lived as best they could off the food they were able to purloin from the sheilings, sleeping rough under rocks, occasionally on a stone floor, the subjects of the charity of some cattle men who gave them shelter in a bothy — anywhere away from the sight of the vast quantities of militia who swarmed the island looking for them.

Secretly, they crossed by boat in the uncertain light of an early dawning to the isle of Benbecula, only to find themselves cut off by the tide from the mainland. Later, they had to walk through the teeming rain over a muddy terrain to the arranged rendezvous with the two ladies, neither of whom showed up.

The next day was one of the worst in the prince's life. He sheltered from the driving rain under a small rock which gave him hardly any protection but was a haven for biting midges. Eventually the agony of being bitten half to death came to an end, and they were called back to the bothy where they had spent the night, to sit before a peat fire. Charles stripped off and sat in his undershirt, feeling positively cheerful that his ordeal was ended.

Finally, word came that the two Jacobite women would meet him next day. The prince slept through the message, unconscious on the floor, wrapped in his plaid, a large piece of tartan wrapped around the waist and worn forward over the shoulder.

The next morning two members of the clan MacDonald arrived with a boat, and he was ferried to Rossinish to rendezvous with Flora.

At once he felt a rise in his spirits, a rekindling of his interest in life. For the first time since he had left the little cottage on the craggy shore he experienced a definite surge of something approaching cheerfulness. He once more had to charm members of the female sex. Present himself washed and beautiful, back on his old form, a handsome prince ready to kiss hands and make small talk. With a surge of his youthful enthusiasm the Young Pretender went to the sheiling to prepare for the supper party he would host for the two ladies that evening.

In the event the gathering increased in size. Lady Clanranald brought her daughter Peggy, and Flora, her brother Angus. Captain O'Neill, making sheep's eyes at Flora, together with the two MacDonald rowers, rounded the party up.

At about eight o'clock, when the mood was growing mellow — the gallant Captain having brought some bottles of wine with him — one of Clanranald's men came and gave them the information that two Redcoat generals and fifteen hundred troops had landed just down the coast.

"I think the time has come for us to leave," said Charles, leaping to his feet.

"But this has been such fun, my dear prince. Why don't we take the boats and row across the loch. I know there's a bothy on the other side. We could just pack up the things and continue the party, as it were."

Lady Clanranald giggled. She was slightly drunk, as was Charles.

"A good idea, Ma'am. Who'll join us?"

"We will," chorused the two Macdonald rowers.

"If you will go, fair lady, then so shall I," said Felix, extending a hand to Flora who stared at it as if it had a strange odour — which it probably had.

They decamped, bearing the remains of the feast and liquid refreshment with them, rowed across Loch Uskavagh and carried on the festivity, just as easily as that. Lady Cranranald and Peggy left at five in the morning. Though they did not know it at the time, they were shortly to be arrested.

As the rest of the gathering packed up their things, Flora turned to Felix O'Neill.

"I am sorry, sir, but this will have to be the parting of the ways. I have been issued with a passport to travel to Skye accompanied by two servants, one male and one female. As Neil MacEachainn speaks Gaelic I have obviously chosen him. I'm most distressed about this but one has to be practical."

"But Felix has been with me throughout," protested Charles, realising even as he spoke that the words would fall on deaf ears, that to get away with the escape would take every ounce of nerve from all the parties concerned and a Gaelic speaker could only help not hinder.

The Captain gulped noisily but said, "It will be far more sensible if I leave you, sir. Miss Flora is right. But I'll catch up with you on Skye. Somehow or other I shall return to your side."

They were never to see one another again. Felix O'Neill was caught, threatened with a flogging which he barely escaped and finally taken as a prisoner to Edinburgh Castle.

At eight o'clock that evening they set out, the prince meanwhile having stripped down to a pair of breeches over which he assumed the disguise of a female named Betty Burke. Vital was the headdress, which consisted of a cap covering his whole head and most of his newly-shaven face. As he heaved on the calico dress, arms threshing like windmill sails, he turned to Flora.

"I want to carry a pistol under this lot."

"No, sir, that you cannot do. If we are searched that would give you away instantly."

Charles grinned, his face taking on some of its old charm.

"If they search me that closely they are going to find something that will definitely give the game away."

Flora averted her eyes, Neil MacEachainn bellowed like a bull.

Eventually nine people set forth for Skye, the two Macdonald rowers and a crew of other oarsmen including Neil. Lieutenant John Macdonald took the tiller, Flora lay down in the bottom of the boat and Charles turned his face towards the sea so that the others could not see the tears of gratitude that were starting in his eyes. Yet what lay ahead? Would he be paraded before Wee Georgy and the Butcher as a prize prisoner of war? Or could he, aided and abetted by a chain of silent supporters who would rather risk their lives than accept that blood-stained £30,000, leave the land of Scotland for ever?

Only time would reveal the answer.

CHAPTER NINE

The Prince in the Heather

He should never have doubted, never have thought for a moment, that he would be betrayed. Yet his very existence trembled on a knife's edge. A ransom was on his head that would keep a family in riches for the rest of their lives. Yet no-one — no-one! — who had helped him to live, to survive, to escape, had so much as whispered his whereabouts.

Butcher Cumberland had stayed on in Scotland until the middle of July, hoping to add to his glorious array of military honours the final glory of the capture of the Pretender's son. The Hanoverians had gone after him with fire and sword, they had put a chain of sentries stretching from Inverness to Inverary at all the major passes, Lord Albermarle had vowed that he would never leave Scotland — where he had taken command once the Butcher had left — until the Young Pretender was caught. And still Charles Edward Stuart slipped through their fingers.

All who were known to have supported him were taken prisoner and examined. All, without exception, disdainfully turned down the offer of £30,000 and said their actions had been born of common humanity, Flora going so far as to say that she would have done it for a beggar-man, let alone a prince. And all, without exception, were imprisoned. Yet the one that the Hanoverians wanted most of all eluded them like a shadow. For the Young Pretender was in the hands of a secret network — a network that conveyed messages by hidden codes and signals, which would pass him from person to person until he finally reached safe waters.

From Skye — having bade Flora MacDonald a courtly farewell and after burning the clothes of Betty Burke — who was described by one person who saw her as 'a lang odd muckle trallop of a carlin', the prince sailed for Scotland's extraordinary West coast and into the hands of the chain of clandestine companions who would safely guide him to freedom. He was to endure hardship, sleeping outdoors, in caves, travelling in the darkness. He also grew a beard and had red hair to his shoulders.

He was at the height of physical fitness, despite being plagued by midges. He climbed mountains, swam lochs, fished for food, the only thing missing in his life was female company. But, like everything else, Charles temporarily put it from his mind. His one aim and objective being to escape from this beautiful, awe-inspiring, wretchedly magnificent, land of Scotland.

In Moidart he came within a hair's breadth of capture. Having been informed that the prince was thereabouts, the Hanoverians ranged their militia in three parallel lines; from Fort William to Inverness, from Mull to Loch Arkaig, from Lochleven to Fort Augustus. The tightest spot of all was exactly at Charles' current location. Camps had been raised at half-mile intervals and look-outs were in earshot of one another. That night the prince and the two supporters who were with him, crept so near the enemy's sentry posts they were able to hear every word spoken. Having climbed yet another hill, the same thing repeated itself at the next. They had succeeded in breaking through the cordon, but the grim reaper was stalking Prince Charlie and hadn't finished his search.

Walking along a narrow slanting path, Charles slipped and plunged down to the edge of a cliff with a hundred-foot drop below him. He fell head first but somehow managed to grip a bush with both legs and hung staring death in the face until his two Highland companions hauled him up by the ankles. He was as pale as a ghost and trembling from head to foot.

"By God, sir, that was a close call."

"I thought I was done for. Thank you both, for saving my life."

"'T'was only a bit of a pull at your limbs, my prince."

Charles grinned wryly. "When one is gazing down into a sheer drop, one no longer cares what part of one's anatomy is put to use."

They all laughed with sheer relief and the trio continued on their way. Finally, on the twenty-fourth of July, the Highlanders delivered the prince into the hands of the Seven Men of Glenmoriston for safe keeping.

This particular wild bunch comprised the strangest people to be part of the hidden secret ribbon of Jacobites, who had been helping him since he met Flora Macdonald in South Uist. These Seven Men were brigands, fearless bandits, who had declared after the defeat at Culloden to fight a guerrilla war in the heather. They lived off the land, sheltering in caverns and grottoes or wherever they could. They spoke Gaelic and were as tough as rawhide.

The prince was allotted a particularly beautiful cave in which to sleep. A gentle stream of clear water ran through it and it was beside this that he lay down to rest. During the day he lived off the excellent food that the Seven Men foraged. But as Charles could not speak Gaelic with all its nuances, he could not understand a great deal of what they said — and when he gave orders they totally ignored him.

By this time he was barely recognisable. As well as his beard and hair, Charles' choice of dress was hardly princely. He wore a short philibeg

— or kilt — over which he had a shirt, splashed with mud and changed only when he could beg another one. He walked barefoot.

According to the spying activities that the Seven Men undertook, the hunt for him — which recently had been so devastatingly close — had slackened off. This — though the prince could not fathom the reason why at the time — was due to disinformation, spread by the spider's web of sympathisers, concerning his whereabouts. The captured Flora and Felix swore that he had departed for the mainland from somewhere entirely different. They, and others, gave the correct time but an entirely unrelated place. It was clever, cunning and effective.

Throughout this sojourn, the lean, hard men of the Seven protecting him, Charles felt safe. He knew that they would strangle with their bare hands anyone who came upon them in search of him. But eventually they passed the prince into the care of the MacPhersons. Six of the Seven raised their swords to their lips and bade him farewell in Gaelic, only Patrick Grant remaining with him. At nightfall, Grant and Glenaladale — another faithful follower — were dismissed, Charles giving the last of the splendid bandits a purse containing twenty-four guineas to share amongst them.

Lochiel — he who had been shot in both legs at Culloden — now took over the magical skein of supporters. Still limping and unable to run, he tried in vain to kneel to the prince. Charles would have none of it, clasping the man in his arms and kissing him fondly on the cheek. And the same occurred when Cluny MacPherson, another old friend, caught up with them. He too was greeted with a royal kiss of welcome.

Autumn came, arrayed in the colours of a woman of easy virtue — bright red, sharp yellow, voluptuous brown. Charles, hiding with his supporters in Cluny's Cage — cut into the rocks of Ben Alder, an impenetrable hideaway indeed — rather enjoyed himself, drinking whisky and eating well, for the surrounding country was rich in game. Then at last came the news which made his heart soar, brought by the chain of lookouts stretching to the west coast, their job to spy for French ships.

There were two vessels in Loch-nan-Uamh, which led out to the open sea. They were flying the flags of France.

So, the moment had finally come. Charles and his faithful cohorts set out in the darkness, hiding away during the glare of daylight. Yet impatience made him risk a final appearance during the hours of light, once more dressed as a woman, kicking at the long skirts as he hurried along. But *L'Heureux* and *Le Conti* were still riding at anchor. He had arrived in time to catch them. The prince wept with joy.

Dressed conventionally, though not yet devoid of his long hair and beard, he bade a fond farewell to Cluny MacPherson, who chose to remain in Scotland and await Charles' second attempt at overthrowing the House of Hanover. The rest of the stalwarts boarded the aptly-named *L'Heureux*, which meant someone with red locks abounding about their head. Then it was the prince's turn.

He paused at the top of the gangplank and turned to face Scotland. He had spent fourteen months in its wild and unyielding countryside, five of which had been as a hunted man with an enormous price on his head. Yet he had never been betrayed by any of that loyal band of men and women who had spirited him away and so cleverly laid a trail of false information that had utterly bewildered his pursuers.

But what had he brought to Scotland, other than suffering and despair? Nothing at all. Yet he would come back, next time with an army of French troops behind him, and he would free that loyal people from the Hanoverians for once and for all. Charles was determined, and equally his mind dwelled upon the fact that it might be from his hand, and his hand alone, that the death blow could be struck on that monster of cruelty — Butcher Cumberland.

Standing on the deck he glanced once more at that desolated and glorious land whose ruin he had brought about. Then he turned to face the open sea, watching as the light fell and the waves turned black. What lay in the immediate future? he wondered. Where would fate take him next? With a shake of his head Prince Charles Edward Stuart descended the wooden steps and went below deck.

CHAPTER TEN

Louise

There was a roar like that of a canon and Charles, entering his box at the opera in Paris, thought immediately that someone of great importance had come into the building and was under attack, or else that a riot had broken out. Dressed though he was to the inch, looking as divine as five weeks of life in France could possibly make him, he still carried a sword, and now his hand shot to it. The uproar continued. Creeping forward, the prince peered over the edge of the box.

The audience members were on their feet, facing his loge, clapping, shouting and whistling. He glanced over his shoulder — there must be somebody famous behind him. There was no-one. And then he heard it. Female voices were calling his name, male voices were shouting, *Bravo, monsieur*, the Parisians had risen to their feet and were going wild at the sight of him.

His heart thumping with unexpected and enormous pleasure, Charles bowed. The audience stamped in approval. He bowed again. The cheer rose in a crescendo. The prince was forced to make a swift decision whether to continue or to let the performance start; he gave another deep bow and sat down. After a moment or two, the theatre-goers did likewise.

His cheeks scarlet, his wig very slightly askew, Charles knew that from the awful apparition that had recently left Scotland, prince charming had returned. It was a social triumph.

As the performance started he swiftly ran through events since his arrival. A storm of adulation had swept over him as soon as he set foot in France. His five months in the heather had captured the imagination of not only the general public, but of kings and princes too. Charles had received an admiring letter from Frederick the Great, Marshal Saxe called him *the hero of the century*, Madame Pompadour invited him to supper at Fontainebleau. Charles' star was in the ascendant, he had even played the cello, accompanied by his brother Henry on the harpsichord, to charm the Duc de Luynes. He was the darling of Parisian society.

Women, of course, flocked to meet him. He dillied a little, and dallied a little more. It was sublime. And then came an evening when — having moved out of Paris to St Ouen, a charming town in the countryside — the prince was invited to take supper with his cousins, the Rohans, the Polish royal family.

He entered their salon to see a small gathering already assembled; its members turned as he entered. Charles lingered in the doorway a second longer than was necessary, a new trick of his. There was a smattering of subdued applause. Then, a figure detached itself from the mass and rushed towards him. An arm slipped through his and a sweet little voice said, "My dear cousin, how delighted I am to meet you."

The prince looked down into a pansy-flower of a face and it seemed to him that at that moment, just for a second or two, his heart stopped beating. He was totally captured by the childlike creature that clung to his arm.

"Not as delighted as myself," he said, and inclined his head.

The little person, beautiful in silver tissue, giggled. "You don't remember me, do you? Well I am Marie Louise Henriette Jeanne de la Tour d'Auvergne, Duchesse de Montbazon and Princesse de Rohan. We are first cousins, sir, because my mother and your mother were sisters."

Charles felt a smile cross his features as he attempted a serious expression; an attempt that completely failed.

"I take it you know who I am?"

"You are the talk of Paris, sir. You are Charles Edward Stuart and you are the son of King James III."

"And what am I to call *you*, from amongst your many names and titles?"

"Louise, sir. That is how I am generally known."

"Then, my dear, let us proceed into the salon and make merry with our fellow guests."

The prince, as always, was lionised by the assembled visitors, the women casting him glances, often with a great deal of meaning in the look. The men were slightly in awe of one who had so bravely gone to Scotland and been on the run from Butcher Cumberland for five whole months.

But it was to his cousin that Charles felt his eyes turning, again and again. She was as fresh as a flower and saucy with it, because whenever he glanced at her she would lower her lids and continue to stare at him for a moment before she looked at the person with whom she was conversing. By good fortune she was seated next to him at supper, so Charles was able to observe her properly.

The face was shaped like a heart, though the general impression it gave was that of a butterfly in flight, because it danced and sparkled and changed expression even when she was sitting still and listening avidly to what the prince was saying. Her hair was a rich glowing mahogany, while her eyes, dark though they appeared, had amber lights running through them. To say that Charles was fascinated would have been utterly to understate the case. He was enraptured, captured, totally and immediately under Louise's spell.

He was stricken to hear that she was married and the mother of a son, even though still just twenty-one years of age. If she had been single he knew that he would have gone down on one knee and proposed to her forthwith. And even his father would have considered it a good match.

Under the pretence of dropping his napkin, Charles reached down for it and gave her hand a meaningful squeeze. When he straightened up she was staring at him alertly.

"What was that for?" she asked, giving him the most mischievous of glances.

"Can't you guess?"

"To say that you enjoy my company, perhaps?"

"More than that."

"You thought me a child when we first met."

"Did I? Then I obviously wasn't looking at you. But now that I am I know that it will take a great deal to make me look away."

She dropped her eyes and the dark lashes drooped on her luscious cheek.

"I don't know how to understand you."

"There is nothing to understand, princesse. I find you immensely attractive and I want to see you again."

"No doubt you will at some—"

Charles' voice cut across hers, not loud but extremely incisive. "Listen to me, Louise. I am not good at fancy speaking, having just spent five months in the deep heart of Scotland running for my life. But I know that I find you quite irresistible. I would like to meet with you again — and again. That's all."

She stared into his face, thinking that he was quite gorgeous in a rugged sort of way.

"Well, that should be easy to arrange, your Highness. My uncle lives next door to you."

The prince's eyebrows shot up. "You mean the Comte d'Evreux, that nice old boy who falls asleep in the sun?"

"One and the same. So when I call on him tomorrow I can drop in on you perhaps."

"There is to be no *perhaps* about it. Please do so."

"Is that a royal command, sir?"

"Indeed, my dear, it is."

Subtlety was not an art with which the prince had been greatly endowed, and by the time the supper party finally came to an end he was finding it difficult to keep his hands off his fascinating cousin. In fact he was quite glad to get away and be in the carriage picking its short way home. Once in bed he was consumed by devouring passion and knew that, come what may, he was going to pursue Louise — cousin or no cousin, married or otherwise.

But she, little minx, called so late at his house next day that Charles was on his way upstairs to retire. He turned as he heard the sound of the front door bell.

"I have come to visit His Highness the prince, if you please."

"If madam would like to step into the parlour I will discover if he is available."

"I am available and very anxious indeed to see the princesse," he called from the stairs and flew down them on the quadruple. The little package of naughtiness was just settling herself in a chair when, brushing his servant aside, Charles stood in the doorway. Then, with a very besotted smile on his face he made his way towards her, arms outstretched.

"Ooh," said Louise, and allowed herself to be pulled into his chest.

"You're actually here," he answered and bent his lips to kiss hers.

The response he got startled even him. Most girls returned their first kiss with a new sweetheart with a certain measure of restraint, but not this little minx. She opened her mouth and out came her twitching, teasing tongue. The prince felt an overpowering pull in his breeches and could hardly credit what was happening. And the next sensation was Louise's hand sliding down his chest and stopping just short of his penis, caressing his thigh.

"My God," Charles breathed against her mouth, "you want it as much as I do."

"I have only had one man, sir, my husband, and he is not to my liking. But *you*, my prince… I want to lie in your arms and be truly aroused."

"Then so you shall be," he answered, and without further ado they made their way upstairs.

The sexual act was pure delight for them both. The ease with which he entered her, her shouts of sensual pleasure, the very fact that they climaxed together like lovers of many years, said it all.

This couple was destined to be together.

*

At first it was relatively easy. Louise's husband — father of her young son — was away in Flanders, fighting for the flag. When she was in Paris the prince made his way there and entered her grand house by a back door which was opened for him by a faithful servant. Then he crept to her bedroom, right under the nose of her formidable mother-in-law the Princesse de Guéméné, spending whole nights in the arms of his little rebel lover Louise.

They had intercourse in every way possible, gluttons for gorgeous sensation. And Charles, for the first time in his life, was genuinely in love. He knew it when he caressed a tendril of her bright hair round his finger, when he saw her sitting on the bed, stark naked and round-breasted, when his fluid cascaded into her and she cried and laughed in triumph.

He offered her everything that he owned but for that one unchangeable thing — he could not offer to make her his wife. She already had a husband.

Yet she seemed happy enough with the situation, whereby the prince — who by now was planning to move to Paris to be nearer to her — made love to her several times a week. Charles was using his full cloak-and-dagger techniques to get past Louise's redoubtable mother-in-law but even he was not quite clever enough.

On the twenty-ninth of October 1747, a report, of something odd happening at night, landed on the desk of the Comte de Maurepas, secretary of state to the King of France, Louis XV. It came from the chief of police in the St Denis area of Paris, some five odd miles from the centre of the city, and stated that for some while his men had observed a hired carriage which, several times a week, at various times between ten in the evening and five in the morning, lingered near the prince's house in St Ouen. A tall figure, sometimes wearing a white frock coat, would emerge and disappear down a lane leading to the house.

The comte had raised his eyebrows in surprise and then read on. It appeared that a local neighbour had lodged a complaint. He — the busybody — had approached the coach to ask its business and had been told in no uncertain terms to back off, a pistol being flashed in the interior. He had, of course, made a formal protest to the authorities. The comte smiled cynically, imagining the scene — but still there was much to be considered. Once King James was dead, the next heir was Prince Charles Edward. Could this be a Hanoverian plot to rid themselves of the Stuart's claim to the throne? Could the mysterious carriage contain a would-be assassin?

He felt sufficiently alarmed to issue an order immediately for a second team of police and informers to begin enquiries in Paris.

At first they made no progress. The curious coach and its occupants had apparently disappeared; the Bonnie Prince was alive and well and could be spotted walking in his gardens in company with his cousin, the pretty little Princesse Louise, and several gentlemen; but where had the carriage gone? The chief of the St Denis police was convinced that it was still there somewhere and ordered a search to be made along the river road. His suspicions were fully justified. Since the nosy neighbour incident, the vehicle was now approaching by another route.

What followed were a series of sightings and manoeuvres that would not have disgraced a French farce. The report that finally arrived on the Comte de Maurepas' desk stated that a gentleman of the prince's household left the coach and proceeded to enter, through the porter's lodge, a house near the Rue de Minimes. This same coach, bearing Charles' valet, then went on to another destination. It added that without doubt the prince would be grateful that the French police were so active in their quest for protecting him against any malefactors. The comte smiled another cynical smile. He, who lived at the court of Versailles, very much doubted that it was as innocent as all that.

The next thing that happened was the arrival ofa letter from the prince's household at the office of the lieutenant general of police, Nicolas-René Berryer. It instructed him to call personally on the Young Pretender. Accordingly, feeling nervous and wearing a somewhat ill-fitting new suit of clothes, Berryer obliged.

He was shown into a receiving room which overlooked the beautiful gardens, and no sooner had he nervously taken a seat on a very fine scarlet sofa than a man appeared at the French windows. Smiling, the stranger came in and the police chief realised that it was the prince himself. He stood up and bowed deeply, then rapidly scrutinised the heir to the Stuart throne.

Charles was twenty-seven years old and dressed sublimely. He wore a fashionable wig falling back to curls over his shoulders, secured with a satin ribbon in the style known as queue de renard. His suit was impeccable, blue shot silk, his breeches breathtakingly tight, his white silk stockings fastened with a buckle at the knee. But it was to the twinkling tawny eyes that Berryer's gaze was drawn. There could be no question about the message that they were barely concealing. The prince had been up to naughty tricks, it would seem. The look was so infectious that, try as he might to supress it, the head of police found himself starting to grin.

"Ah, monsieur," said Charles Edward, smiling broadly in return, "you are here for an explanation, I believe."

"Well not exactly, your Highness. If you remember you wrote to me and said you would explain all."

"To be sure. But take a seat, monsieur. Would you like some refreshment?"

Bowing and nodding simultaneously, Berryer perched on the edge of the exquisite sofa. Charles said nothing further until they both had a glass of wine and the servants had been dismissed from the room, then he raised his.

"To pretty women everywhere."

"Agreed, my prince."

"I'm sorry I lead you such a dance."

Berryer stared at him, nonplussed.

"You got everything right, didn't you, my clever friend? Except that I was the man in the coach all along."

"You mean…?"

"Yes, I was the one who alighted and vanished through a porter's lodge. The man who continued on his way was my servant, Daniel O'Brien."

Charles burst out laughing at the look of incredulity on the face of the chief of police, then his expression grew sharper.

"You do not know the identity of the lady in question, do you?"

"No, sir. We thought you were visiting the house of the de Dampierre's in the Rue de Minimes."

Charles chortled. "How quaint. I don't even know them. But, monsieur, I must ask you to keep this conversation totally confidential. Nor do I wish any further investigation into my life."

"It will be utterly as you wish, my prince. Nothing further will be examined. And may I just say, sir, that your escape from Scotland was one of the most daring exploits I have ever heard. You are the hero of Paris — and rightly so."

"Thank you, Monsieur Berryer. And now, let us finish our wine as two friends should, in an enjoyable harmony."

"The pleasure will be entirely mine, sir."

A week later, Charles — this time with no peering eyes following his every move — undertook the journey to Paris again. Louise was waiting for him and opened the door as soon as he gave a quiet knock. Charles slipped through the shadows to find her hands tearing at his breeches.

"Having a lover makes me feel like a woman of the world," she stated as Charles stepped out of them, excitingly and immediately erect. Louise sank to her knees before him, embracing him like a glutton. He stood in ecstasy, leaning against the wall, eyes closed, as she set up an exquisite rhythm. Finally, though, he pulled away.

"Enough. I'll be no use for the rest of the night."

"Oh don't say that. I was enjoying it."

"You're a wanton hussy. You've all the manners of a street urchin."

"Look who's talking! You're one of the sexiest men alive."

"And you would know, of course. Having slept only with your husband before I showed you a thing or two."

"More than *showed*," answered Louise, sighing as she stood up. "You have actually put your permanency within me."

"What do you mean?" the prince asked, lying back on the vastly comfortable bed, not a stitch of clothing on him.

"He," Louise answered, flicking him with her finger, "has been a very naughty boy."

"In what particular way?"

"He has made me *enceinte*." And Louise's eyes, so happy and glistening usually, filled with sudden tears.

Charles sat bolt upright. "You mean that you are *pregnant*?"

She nodded her head and indulged in a sudden spasm of weeping.

"Are you sure?"

She looked up, doleful as a miserable child. "I have had no monthly show for ten weeks. I am certain that I carry your baby, sir."

Charles was on his feet and pulling on his drawers and breeches in one movement. Then he put his arms round the weeping girl.

"Hush, my darling. Don't upset yourself. It is such wonderful news. I am to be a father! I couldn't be more pleased."

She nestled in his arms and he had never felt more loving. It did not occur to him that to adore anyone so deeply was highly dangerous; all the prince could think of was that this little bundle of womanhood was going to give him a child. He kissed her naked stomach.

"Hello, sweet baby. I'm your papa. We shall play some jolly games when you arrive. I shall teach you how to ride and shoot and all sorts of wonderful things."

"Supposing it's a girl?"

"Then she will be the most beautiful woman in the entire world and her hand will be sought by the most powerful men imaginable."

Louise stood up and slipped on a lace-trimmed nightgown.

"As a mother, I must dress respectably."

"You, my little vagabond princess, could never be respectable, even if I give you eleven children."

"Oh, pouf. You seem to forget that I am an honourable married woman. Which reminds me that Jules will be back soon and I shall have to go to bed with him to give this child a nominal father."

"What?" The prince was astounded. Louise had spoken so matter-of-factly, just as if it were a matter of routine. "But *I* am the father. I won't have my baby foisted on another man. I simply *won't*."

Louise looked at him, her beautiful face suddenly grown sharp as an arrow.

"Well, what other choice is there?"

"We could run away together. Set up home. I fear nothing, least of all scandal. We can live as husband and wife and raise children."

"But you are a prince of the blood."

"Who cares?" said Charles, shrugging eloquently.

"I do, for a start."

"Why?"

"Because I would become an outcast, shunned by society. I would lose everything. Besides there is my little boy to consider."

"And there's *my* son to consider as well."

"Oh Charles, don't be so hot-headed. I have a fine position here in this grand house. I can't throw it all to the winds."

"Why not? We can set up home as a married couple would. People would not be shocked. Remember that I am heir to the throne of England and you most definitely would not be an outcast. In fact you would be the most envied woman in all society."

"Oh Charles…"

"*Oh Charles* nothing. I truly love you, Louise. For you I have given up my claim to the family jewels, which *your* family are after. I offer myself to you and our unborn child completely. Do not, I beg you, return to your husband."

"But I owe Jules a certain loyalty."

"Then, if I may say so madame, you have not served that loyalty well of late."

She turned away with a pretty little pout, but something died in Charles' heart at the sight of it. The thought of her offering herself to her lawful spouse, of lying naked in Jules' arms, revolted him. Of allowing her husband to place his most private part in her body where Charles' child was growing, filled the prince with a furious jealousy.

And once Jules, Duke de Montbazon, was safely back from the front, Louise insisted on a period when she had intercourse only with him. Charles, arriving late one night to be with her, paced the streets in a fury, there being no sign of Louise's valet, who usually saw him safely into the house. And when this time of abstinence was over, Charles' mistress further pointed out that they could not meet until the duke had retired to his own bedroom for the night. This was frequently well after midnight — and winter was approaching.

The journey from St Ouen to central Paris was becoming decidedly chilly and the Bonnie Prince was suffering from severe lack of sleep. In order to ease his predicament, Charles moved to a goodly-sized house in central Paris where he could entertain his new friends who frequented the salon society of which he had recently become a member.

But he could no longer put up with the situation. Louise pleaded with him not to ruin her life by insisting that he have full access to her bedroom whenever he liked, despite the fact that Jules was once more living with her. The young duke had not, as yet, heard the slightest whisper that his wife was involved in a passionate affair, despite the gossip and rumours that were already circulating in Paris. In those haughty salons it was generally agreed that Louise was a complete adolescent and could not handle a lover, however royal he was, that she was childish beyond measure. The couple staggered on through Christmas and then on the twenty-third of January, with Jules away attending the court in Marly, the axe finally fell on their relationship.

Louise's mother-in-law, the sharp-eyed Princesse de Guéméné, together with Louise's father, to whom she had confessed the secret of her torrid affair and who was, as a consequence, deeply upset, faced the wretched girl with the truth. Despite the infantile screaming in which she indulged, Louise was forced to sit down and write a letter to Charles, putting an end to the affair.

A few days later she wrote another, entirely secret, letter. In this, blotchy with the tears that fell all over it, she wrote the piteous truth; that she would always love him and would do so for the rest of her life. And to remind him that she was carrying his child.

Charles read the letter in the privacy of his study. A war of emotions swept over him, but overriding all was the feeling that he was being hunted. A nasty reaction this, and one which made him stir with unease. Back came all the fears and frights of his journey through Scotland. Then he had been entirely in the hands of those loyal to the Jacobite cause, but during those months of pure hell he had been forced to grow up. Now the tear-stained letter he had just received seemed like the rantings of a small girl.

With a great sigh Charles tore the letter up and went out to get a little grown-up company and enjoy the witty, stylish and definitely adult conversation of the Parisienne smart set.

CHAPTER ELEVEN

The End of the Affair

It was the letter from Anne-Françoise de Carteret that drove home the stupidity of continuing the relationship with Louise. De Carteret was a woman of good Jacobite stock — her brother had fought in Scotland — but alas, the family had fallen on hard times and she had written to Charles asking for a pension. Realising that Anne-Françoise was a friend of Louise, Charles had been only too happy to oblige. In return, he had asked for a favour. A little gentle spying on his behalf. And now a long letter in reply to his, which had required her to tell him exactly what had happened on the night when Louise had been reduced to hysterics, had finally arrived.

Reading it, Charles Edward sighed.

What Louise's father had reportedly said infuriated him. He could almost hear the man exploding as he spoke:

"Merciful heavens, what a wretch the beastly boy is! To think after all I have done for him and his family that I should be rewarded with this! He has dishonoured my daughter in her own house. The man is a snake-in-the-grass, d'ye hear me?" This statement no doubt followed by a string of expletives.

The man who had risked his life so often in the towering crags of Scotland stood back from the exuberant young lover and thought seriously. First and foremost there was the feeling of a trap closing around him, its steely jaws trying to make him into something that he was not, nor ever would be. Secondly, the way that the Duc de Bouillon — Louise's father — had insulted him hurt his royal dignity. One did not call the King of France a snake whenever he took a new mistress, so why blame the heir to the English throne for doing the same?. Charles physically shook himself. It was as if he had spent the last six months under some kind of love spell. At that moment he decided not to reply to the soggy, tear-stained compositions that Louise insisted on sending him. She must be cut out of his life.

But it was not so easy. The sobbing wreck started to write to his servants, begging O'Brien — who had great difficulty in reading anything — to tell her what had happened to the man she loved. If he no longer loved her, did he not have mercy for her? And so on and so forth. Other members of staff received piteous notes as well. Charles remained aloof meanwhile, punishing her for being so craven, so subservient. If she had had one ounce of fire in her, she would have stood up to her mother-in-law and her father. She would have accepted his offer — made in good faith at the time — to run away and live with him.

As if he wanted to taunt Louise — which by this time he did — Charles sauntered around Paris, dressed in striking clothes and a selection of breath-taking headgear. He acknowledged everyone who turned to stare at him with an inclination of the head. He also started to visit the opera on a regular basis. He attended balls and parties. But there was one invitation that he would not accept. And that was to socialise with the Rohans or Bouillons.

Did they really think that he would sit down and make polite conversation with someone who thought of him as a *beastly boy*?

It was at a salon given by the Duchesse d'Aiguillon — an eccentric woman much admired by the cream of Paris society — that Charles first laid eyes on the Princesse de Talmont.

Louise had a pert face — or rather she did when it wasn't screwed up and howling like a miserable monkey. In contrast, de Talmont had that sweep from eye to chin of glorious cheekbones which became shadowed in the candlelight, whilst above them a pair of deep blue eyes would turn indigo in the flickering light. She held herself well, her skirts whispering along the floor so that they gave a sensuous rustle as she approached. And — greatest attribute of all — she had about her a worldly air, an air that suggested sophistication, a look of human knowledge that would most certainly *not* allow hysterical or childish behaviour.

Charles turned to his hostess. "Introduce me to that fascinating newcomer, if you would be so kind, madame."

The duchesse gave him a sideways look full of good-humoured mockery.

"I knew that she would catch your eye immediately. A wondrous creature, is she not?"

"Glorious. Tell me her name."

"Marie Louise Anne, Princesse de Talmont. So you'll have no problem if you talk in your sleep."

Charles looked down the length of his nose at her, smiling faintly. "She is married, I take it."

"Correct. Her husband is the Prince de Talmont. He is ten years younger than she is and — if what I hear is correct — has a great liking for beautiful young men."

Charles chuckled. "So she may be open to a little flattering speech or two?"

"My dear prince, if she so chooses, she could have a dozen of them before noon each day."

"She is popular with the gallants then?"

"That would be the understatement of the century."

Charles raised an elegant eyebrow and the next instant was bowing low before the sumptuous woman, who stood regarding him with a slightly amused expression on her face.

"Madame la princesse," said the duchesse, "may I present to you Prince Charles Edward Stuart."

There was the swish of taffeta as the princesse curtsied deeply.

"I am greatly honoured, sir. Your exploits in Scotland are much discussed in Paris. You are regarded as a hero. Are you such?"

Charles looked up, surprised, and saw that the splendid eyes — full of rather secretive thoughts — held a provocative gleam.

"Some think so," he answered. "There are others who would refute the claim."

Straightening up, he kissed her cool hand and held it just for a second longer than etiquette dictated.

"It is so with everyone, I believe. There are those who would despise us because they are more than likely jealous of our achievements," answered the princesse.

"I see that you are interesting as well as beautiful, madame. Would you do me the honour of dancing with me?"

"How could I refuse the hero of Scotland?"

To say that the ballroom stood in awe when the prince went on to the floor would have been an overstatement. Nevertheless, a space cleared around him when his tall, elegant figure appeared in the entrance and there was a hushed whisper that the darling of Paris was about to dance with that most celebrated of courtesans, Madame de Talmont. And after the dance there was a great deal of whispering behind fans that the two of them were deep in conversation and were sitting closely beside one another. It was obvious that the prince was utterly enthralled, while the princesse had a certain glow in her magnificent eyes.

"I don't know what I am to do," Charles was confiding to her. "She is driving me and my staff out of our minds. Every day she writes to one or other of us, while I am hourly inundated with soggy letters."

"Why so?" exclaimed the princesse in mock horror. "Surely the wretched girl has not lost control of herself?"

Charles, who had drunk more glasses of wine than he cared to remember, grinned.

"Not yet. Though I expect that will be next."

"I see. Let me think about your problem for a moment or two. Perhaps I might come up with a solution."

"If you do, I will lay my heart at your feet. And if you don't, I will do exactly the same."

De Talmont laughed. "Be careful what you say to me, Charles Edward Stuart. I might not treat it as a joke."

"Nor is it meant as such, my beautiful new friend."

"I would advise you to get rid of one amour before you begin another, sir."

"Why, madam," Charles answered, sitting up straight, "that is precisely what I intend to do, with the help of a woman whom I hope will become the most personal of friends."

De Talmont's fan gave him a wrap on the knuckles.

"You're very forward, young man."

"I cannot help it, princesse, your perfume fills my senses."

And he was not playing with her. For with every movement she made, a dusky aroma, which spoke of spices, of deep red roses, of the warming fulfilment of rich, dark wine, stole into Charles' nostrils.

"Tell me," she said, her face pensive, "has the lady written about going to the opera in order to look at you?"

The prince stared. "Are you a mistress of the dark arts? I'll swear that you might be. A letter arrived this very morning saying that she would go to the opera two nights hence just to get sight of me."

De Talmont chuckled, a deep and lovely sound. "Then you must go, monsieur."

"But I don't want to see her again!"

"Not even if I am sitting next to you and we do not so much as glance in her direction? For I can think of no better way of seeing off an unwanted lover."

Charles gazed at her in incredulity. "Madam, you are indeed a creature of many facets. I would never have thought of such a scheme."

De Talmont turned on him a very knowing expression. "And remember, my prince, that any future dealings you have with her will merely be because your body is speaking to you — not your heart."

"If it speaks then I will ignore it, for you have bewitched me, Madame, and I fall most graciously beneath your spell," Charles answered, and once more kissed her hand.

*

As was customary when the prince entered his box in the theatre, the entire audience erupted. He walked in — a step or two in front of his companion — and, as one, everybody rose from wherever they were seated and made a deep reverence before bursting into wild applause and cheering. The shouts grew even louder when they saw that his companion was the beautiful Princesse de Talmont. As he swept into his loge, Charles glimpsed from the corner of his eye a figure sitting in the box directly opposite. It was staring at him like a creature possessed. Keeping up his Prince Charming image, Charles turned to his lovely companion and handed her into her seat. The crowd went mad. Eventually, after bowing several times, the prince sat down and the performance began.

Louise, alone in her loge, watched them like a forsaken child. She could see at a glance that they were a couple in every sense. Her suspicions had been right. Her beloved had found somebody else to love, while she went to bed every night clutching a lock of his hair and gazing at his portrait. At that moment the child within gave her a hearty kick and Louise let out a tiny cry.

Nobody even looked in her direction.

*

The next day dawned with all the crispness of a spring morning, the buds on the trees exulting in the early sun that would see them open beneath its warmth. The sky was the blue of an artist's palette and this was reflected in the river Seine, which flowed beneath the dank, ancient bridges with a slapping wave caused by the craft which plied up and down its shimmering surface.

The prince, however, saw none of it. He was in a state bordering on exultation as he kissed every inch of de Talmont's body, rubbed in scented oils — some with a definite opium base. Sex with Louise had been good, but this was something else, something infinitely more rare. De Talmont — Charles could not bear to use the name Louise — was older than he was, sophisticated, witty, had an engaging mind and could converse on any subject. In her, he had met his match. He engaged with her body deeply, feeling that he was at last making love to an equal, not some awful little snotty schoolgirl, which was how de Talmont referred to the *other* Louise.

But the schoolgirl was not quite finished yet, for all that she was snubbed. Since Charles no longer answered her letters, she had kept up a correspondence with members of his staff, particularly Daniel, his valet. The morning after the visit to the opera, the morning when spring was awakening, when Charles and de Talmont made love turn to passion, came the most tragic missive of all. In it, Louise — after wailing interminably about her miserable lot — hinted that soon she would be able to visit the prince at his house in perfect safety. *Won't he be pleased?* she said to Daniel.

A few days later, when de Talmont was visiting other friends, Daniel finally showed the letter to Charles, who reluctantly read it. It was her writing about death that stirred him to act on the tear-damped scrawl, finally putting the missive down on his desk and looking up at his valet.

"This is most distressing, I must confess. She talks of dying, which makes me fear for the child. And what's all this about my having to leave France?"

"Well, as you know, sir, Louis XV's ministers are — even as we speak — negotiating with the Hanoverian envoys, their aim being to drive you out of the country."

Charles sat back in his chair, casting his eyes on the beautiful garden that lay behind the French windows. Outside, two birds were circling in flight then landed on the bird bath and preened in its waters. Drops of liquid appeared on their wings and they raised their voices in a sweet-noted anthem. Daniel stared at the prince, who seemed utterly absorbed in the scene.

"Your comments, sir?"

"I was thinking how beautiful and how ugly nature can be."

"Your meaning?"

"That if Louise were to take steps to end her life, my child would die as well. It is not a pretty thought, my friend. Do you think I ought to talk to her?"

"But if you do, my prince, she will want to resume your tired affair. You will forgive me if I speak frankly?" Charles nodded. "She has been a rope around your neck these last few months. You have subsequently met a beautiful and charming woman. What is it you really want, sir?"

"To ensure that my son or daughter comes safely into the world."

"Think, sir. Louise will bombard you with questions. Do you still love me? Can we be together always? Will you write to me every day? Et cetera, et cetera ad nauseum."

Charles laughed aloud, he couldn't help it.

"I know all that. But she did sound quite serious about suicide."

"So, are you going to see her?"

"Yes. Write that if she makes all the arrangements I will agree."

Daniel shook his head. "You don't know what you'll be getting yourself into, sir."

"I'll worry about that when the time comes."

"And don't forget to bundle yourself up well in your redingote, just as you used to, and to have an early night as Madame Louise suggests," Daniel called cheekily, heading for the door and dodging the book that came flying at his ear.

*

For reasons best known to himself, Charles said nothing of the arranged meeting to his new mistress and was all set to go to the assignation when a last-minute note arrived from Louise. Her mother-in-law, the Princesse Guéméné, was on the war path and had posted her spies all around the prince's house. Instead, Louise would go to the Pont Tournant at midnight and await him in a hackney coach.

It was the most awkward meeting of the prince's life. The coach was small and confined, Louise was pregnant and bulky, he was wrapped up in a thick coat. It was the first time they had seen each other in four months and the girl wept with joy and continued to do so throughout their time together. Intercourse, which she begged and pleaded for, was virtually impossible, but by reason of her sitting on his lap with her back turned, just about manageable. Moreover she fired questions at him for the whole time they were together.

By the time the session came to its horrendous end the Bonnie Prince was green about the gills and Louisa was smiling and crying simultaneously.

He confessed all to de Talmont the very next time they met.

"Serve you right," she answered, grinning like one of her pet pug dogs. "Did she ask if you still love her and, if so, I will wager you replied yes."

"I told her I did, but not so much."

"Tiens, tiens! You are like a comfit, monsieur. Everyone likes to lick you and you are sweet to all comers. Shame on you."

"I couldn't help it. She had me cornered. What was I to do?"

"You should have told the truth and then have left the carriage on the instant."

"She is expecting my child and has threatened suicide."

"Really, my prince, you know nothing of the world. Those who talk about killing themselves rarely do it. Now, I'll hear no more of the silly little strumpet. She should have taken care of herself like an adult woman would."

"You have never been caught?"

"I have a son, as you know. He is the child of my husband, so no, I have never been caught out. And now, sweet Charles, if you will listen to my advice you will get rid of that snivelling little ninny for once and for all."

The prince listened, liked what he heard, and acted accordingly. Truth to tell he had lied through his teeth when he had seen Louise in the hackney coach; the closeted atmosphere, the whimpering voice begging for love, the close confinement, had driven him to it. For the sake of his unborn child he had told the pitiful girl exactly what she wanted to hear. But now, listening to the words of his worldly-wise mistress, he realised just how wrong he had been. Louise was seven months pregnant and the likelihood of her damaging the child was by now minimal. He was only prolonging the agony by telling her a pack of untruths. He must not write to her again.

He did, of course. But this time the letters took a different tone. He once again criticised her lack of courage in not standing up to her dragon of a mother-in-law, the Princesse Guéméné, instead being led by the nose like a small child. He refused, via Daniel, to meet her again in a small carriage — or even a large one, come to that.

Louise wrote back that she was prepared to give up everything just for a glimpse of his dear face, because life without him was not worth living. And then things came to a violent and noisy head — and all this in the public streets.

Rounding the corner one day and in a buoyant mood, Charles ran straight into his bête noir, the Princesse de Guéméné herself.

"Vile seducer," she screamed at full pitch.

"How dare you?" he answered angrily. "How dare you, when your daughter-in-law *begged* me for my attentions? It would suit you in future, madam, to keep your mouth closed."

"You evil monster, you bare-faced liar! You're not fit to be a prince of anything unless it is disgrace. You're nothing but a cheap-jack son of a whore."

Charles shook off Daniel, who was holding him back by the elbow, and raised his stick.

"You will *never* insult my mother while I live. My God, madam, if you were a man I would thrash you where you stood."

"Come on then, I dare you. If you hit me in the public streets you will be finished for what remains of your miserable existence."

"You wretched old hag. Go back to the hell from whence you came."

"You have ruined my daughter-in-law's life."

"Ruined, you say? Why, the little slut was rampant for it."

"May the filth that comes out of your mouth choke you!"

"I hate you with a passion, you particularly unpleasant old woman."

"Come here and let me thrash the life out of you, you yellow-faced dog!"

They were screaming at one another at the tops of their voices and a small crowd had gathered round. The princesse had gone purple with rage and the prince's beautiful wig had slipped to one side. Both carried a walking cane and these had been raised in angry fists.

"Walk away, sir, please do," said Daniel. "The police will be called at any moment."

But Charles was beyond listening; beyond anything except the pressing desire to kill the woman shouting at him.

"Your spittle is running from your blackened teeth, madam. You are a travesty of your sex."

"When you are dead, sir — which pray God will be soon — I shall dance on your grave."

"And I will piss on yours," the prince retorted.

There was a loud cheer from the crowd, none of whom liked seeing the darling of Paris insulted by a stuck-up old dame. And it was on that note that Daniel finally managed to drag the prince down a side-street and away from the menacing besom who was still screaming and waving her stick.

"We are going to a tavern, *now*," said the valet firmly, taking Charles by the arm.

He nodded his response, too breathless to speak.

When finally they were seated in rather a dingy place, the first the valet had been able to find, Charles spoke.

"Well, did I win, do you think?"

"Do you want me to be honest, my prince?"

"Yes."

"Then in that case, I think it was a draw."

"She's certainly got a mouth on her. If she had been a man I would have challenged her to a duel and she would by now be lying a crumpled heap on the cobbles."

Daniel smiled a knowing smile. "Then she must thank God she was born female."

Charles raised his glass. "Well, it has at least cleared the air. She and her little strumpet daughter-in-law have finally gone."

The valet nodded. "Yes, my prince. I think we can truly say that the affair is at an end."

They clinked glasses and drank. It was time for Charles Edward Stuart to move on.

CHAPTER TWELVE

De Talmont

He could never marry her, although she delighted him in every way. He had never met anyone so utterly absorbing before, yet she had a husband, a child and others who were interested in her as a mistress, no doubt about that. And yet, when the prince was away from her, alone in his beautiful garden, the many problems surrounding him bore home quite cruelly.

He was a complicated young man. Underneath all the layers that had added to his personality as he grew, was a brave and courageous person. His time on the run in Scotland proved that beyond any doubt. Unfortunately his sexual drive sometimes overcame his basic good sense and he had been thrown completely off course by the blandishments of his nymphomaniac cousin, Louise. By the end of their affair he had felt himself in the stranglehold of an octopus and had ended up hating her, running instead to his new sophisticated mistress, de Talmont. But as he strode through his grounds in that budding June sunshine he knew that, despite her charms, his entire future lay in jeopardy.

All about him were sweeping and gracious lawns, fresh with new green grass. Birds flew through the azure sky, cutting through the warm air in swift incisive movements. Flowers, glowing in shades from childish pink to fully thrusting crimson, loosed their vapours onto the joyful breeze. Everywhere the prince looked was loveliness and he imagined for one brief untroubled moment that his future was mapped out peacefully before him.

He would marry a Protestant princess — Charles could almost visualise her: plump, pretty and acquiescent — then settle in her country. He would then march — reinforced by an enormous French army — back to the land of rearing, roaring mountains and mighty glittering lochs, and see off the wretched Hanoverians once and for all. He would eventually claim the throne as King Charles III — when his father decided to die, of course — and rule in harmonious majesty surrounded by his many loving children. Amen.

But it was ludicrous even to imagine. First of all his envoy, Sir John Graeme, had so far had no luck despite scouring the various European courts for a bride. Secondly, unless Louis XV had a brainstorm, there was no hope of raising a French army. Thirdly — and sickeningly — the Hanoverians seem to have dug themselves into British affections. It was all a pathetic pipe dream.

And yet, Charles had to keep hoping against hope. He had promised the Scottish people he would come back to save them and somehow he must fulfil his destiny, both for their sakes and also for his own. For a minute he stood near to tears on the glorious golden June day. Then he thought better of weeping and turned his feet towards the house.

*

The summer was slowly passing; wine and kisses, flirting and funning, empty laughter and progress none. The Young Pretender was hoping for a positive reply from Princess Caroline-Louise of Hesse-Darmstadt. Meanwhile, he was making jokes about Butcher Cumberland.

Fick, as Charles rudely called him, had gone to London to be cured of the pox in anticipation, no doubt, of his hoped-for marriage to Hack — short for the nickname Hackney — the Princess of Prussia. But it wasn't all nudging and winking, for on the twenty-ninth of July the wretched Louise went into labour and gave birth to a son.

Charles was unusually quiet that night, staring into the shadows as he sipped his wine. De Talmont, in that uncanny way she had of knowing what he was thinking, asked a question.

"Has the silly girl given birth yet?"

"Yes, today actually. Daniel heard from one of the servants. She had a boy."

"So the hero of Scotland is father to a son. Are you going to acknowledge him?"

"Of course not. Louise successfully passed him off as Jules' child. She slept with him as soon as he returned from the war."

"So the chit has some brains in her head."

Charles smiled without humour. "It will be awkward though, if he grows up and resembles me."

" Jules might have to think twice in those circumstances."

"Oh, damn the whole wretched family. Particularly that old hag Guéméné. I hope my son grows up loathing her."

Had there been the faintest catch in his voice when he said the words 'my son'? His mistress noticed, but decided not to comment on it. Instead she raised her glass.

"Let us drink the boy's health and then say nothing further of him."

Charles lifted his in response. "To my son. Long life and strength to him always."

Then he drained his wine and brushed away a solitary tear.

*

Louis XV was growing extremely impatient. He had three times formally requested that Charles Stuart leave France. He had signed a peace treaty with the English and it was now imperative that the son of the claimant to the English throne should leave French soil. But the Young Pretender remained where he was.

The lease on the prince's house had run out, but having failed to find another property — discreet ministerial pressure? — he had remained where he was, to the extreme annoyance of the prospective tenant. Each time the king had intervened, using the Duc de Gesvres, a kind and gentle man who was fond of the prince, to deliver the letter asking Charles to quit the house. Each time the prince had listened, affably enough, but had refused to budge. He had said that he would fight to the death to remain in France. The only way ahead, Louis reckoned, was to enlist the help of Charles' father, King James III, who still resided in Rome. Ask him to write a letter to his son and explain the delicacy of the situation.

At first, de Talmont had encouraged Charles to resist all efforts to make him leave, to remain haughty and ignore the summons, as did she. But lately a nasty rumour was circulating and had reached her ears, namely that Louis intended to send *her* into exile, if she continued to influence Charles further. Great forces were at work, powers that even she could not resist. So it was that one evening she sought out her husband, ten years younger than herself and still maintaining his boyish looks — much to her annoyance.

"My dear, how are you? I have not seen you in a while," was her opening gambit.

"Have you not? I really can't remember. Surely we met at breakfast a few days ago?"

"Oh yes, you're right, I think we did. How are you these days?"

"So-so. My devotional duties take up a lot of my time…"

De Talmont adjusted her lips into a sympathetic smile.

"… and I have taken an interest in a young courtier, a nephew of the Duc de Vallier. Very sweet fellow."

His wife nodded, charm dripping from every pore.

"I'm so delighted for you, my dear. You mustn't allow yourself to become bored." She paused, then continued. "You are spending a deal of time at Versailles, I'm told. How lovely for you. How is the king these days?"

"Getting rather fed up with that Pretender fellow. One of your lovers, isn't he?"

De Talmont heaved a deep sigh. "Oh yes, I have toyed with the boy from time to time. But, my dear, he has frankly turned into a nuisance of late."

"Really? In what way?"

"He strolls round this house morning, noon and night. Why, one would think he owns the place, the way he uses it."

"Now you come to mention the fact, I have spotted him lurking round the corridors occasionally. And once in the garden. Is the chap bothering you?"

"That would be to overstate the case. Let us just say that he has become passé."

"I see. Can I do anything to help?"

"I suppose you could mention it at court — but only if you have the time, of course."

"Yes, yes I will. It's not often I speak out but I can't have some lout wandering around my house and grounds as if he owns them. Don't worry, my dear. I'll see him off."

De Talmont smiled the smile of a smouldering tiger. "Mon cher, I don't know what I would do without you." She rang a bell and said to the servant who answered, "A decanter of port and some sweet biscuits, if you please. And be quick about it. Monsieur is somewhat thirsty."

She settled herself on a comfortable sofa and patted the space beside her.

"Come and sit with me, my dear. Let us converse of life and laughter."

Inwardly, she breathed a sigh of relief. The nasty rumour that Louis XV was about to exile her had been growing in intensity. She had made the only move possible. When push came to jostle, lovers were best dispensed with, however heroic their pasts, even be it only for a short time.

*

Charles simply could not understand it. He had turned up at his mistress' house for his usual afternoon of unbridled love making and been told that there was no-one at home. He had argued but the servant — an enormous hulk of a creature with a nasty cast of features — had remained utterly adamant.

"I said they was out and out they are, even to the Pope himself," the fellow had said, and fingered a mighty cudgel which he kept in his box in case visitors should turn ugly. The prince had had no option but to leave, cursing.

Meanwhile, de Talmont had set forth that very night for Versailles, making a point of having supper with the queen, informing Her Majesty of the incident, saying, with a pious look on her carefully arranged features, that a husband should always be master in his own house. The queen, giving a sympathetic sigh, entirely agreed.

Charles, who by now was in a fury, called at the house at eleven o'clock the next morning and had been on the point of attacking the lodgekeeper when a senior Jacobite had arrived — by coincidence? — and calmed him down. That night, determined to put on a show, the Young Pretender attended the opera, looking so handsome that several young ladies became quite hysterical at his entrance. The Parisian audience rose as one and cheered and shouted as he entered his box. Bowing effusively before he sat down, Charles mentally raised a finger to the French King as he blew several kisses to the plump soprano who was singing the leading role.

Despite his immense popularity with the people of the capital, his mistress publicly announced that if he dared darken her doors once more she would have no choice but to shoot him dead. Remembering his escape from Scotland, and how the ordinary people, in the face of being offered a fortune for information, had banded together to aid him, Charles felt confident that the citizens of Paris would put up a fight rather than see their hero publicly shamed. Announcing that he would commit suicide rather than leave the city, the prince continued to make his flamboyant appearances in the streets, bowing graciously to the many people who called him by name. The opera house and the theatres he attended nightly. The final deadline given by Louis XV came and went and the prince was still in town.

He was sauntering to the opera house one evening, a step or two ahead of his three companions, when suddenly five shadowy figures appeared in front of him. Charles paused, not sure whether to run or push past. He had been receiving warm-hearted warnings from well-wishers; notes had been delivered to his house, people had called out as he walked in the Tuileries that he was in danger, somebody had even shouted to the coach that carried him on the early part of this journey, begging him to turn back. Now he stopped dead.

"Excuse me," he said icily.

"No, sir, please excuse *us*," one of them answered, and the next minute he had been grabbed by three of them and hurried off down an extremely narrow passageway. Behind him he could hear grunts and groans as his companions were set upon.

At the end of the cul-de-sac was a gateway which led — much to Charles' surprise — into a courtyard of the Palais Royale. So far, his feet had not touched the ground but now he was set down with a thump that shook every tooth in his head. Facing him, dressed in full regimentals, was de Vaudreuil, major of the guards.

"Charles Edward Stuart," he said in a small menacing voice, sending out specks of saliva as he did so. "I am arresting you in the name of the King of France."

"I don't believe you!"

De Vaudreuil gave a sinister smile.

"Will you be so good as to hand over your weapons?"

The prince stood helplessly while a pair of hard hands held him rigid as another soldier disarmed him, even going so far as to peer into his breeches in the search for pistols.

"Nothing there," Charles gasped.

For answer the soldier rolled his eyes and said, "Not much."

Normally he would have yelped with laughter but on this particular occasion he felt genuinely nervous and stared at his feet.

"Bind him," ordered the major.

From nowhere ells of crimson silk cord appeared and the prince, still in the grip of two soldiers, was wound round and round from his heels upwards.

"My God, this is not necessary."

"Sorry to inconvenience you, sir. Let me assure you that it is entirely for your own good."

"I don't—"

But his voice was cut off as a soldier with a twisted sense of fun slipped the cord between his teeth. The final indignity came when he was lifted and carried like a corpse into a waiting carriage where he was laid out lengthwise on one of the seats. Then the conveyance clattered off, leading a convoy bristling with mounted militia.

Insult was heaped on indignity. On reaching Vincennes, on the outskirts of Paris, Charles was not invited to stay in the comfortable chateau but instead shown into a gloomy cell in the donjon. His host, the Marquis du Châtelet, an old friend of the Stuarts, nearly died with embarrassment when he saw who the prisoner was. The major, full of spite, informed the marquis that Charles had not been thoroughly searched and proceeded to peer into every article of the prince's clothing including his drawers, groping round his genitals with a nasty look in his eye. All they could find — not in his underwear — were a compass and a wallet which were duly seized. Charles said nothing, fixing his eyes on the ceiling while the marquis looked sick. Eventually, after dragging out the proceedings to an agonising point, the major left for Paris, handing the royal prisoner into the charge of du Châtelet, who promptly fell on his knees before the prince, begging his forgiveness.

"Please, old friend, do not distress yourself. I suppose in a way I asked for trouble."

"Whatever you did, Highness, nothing could justify this."

"Well what's done is done. There's no point in dwelling on it. I trust you are going to make my stay as comfortable as possible."

"Of course, my prince. You shall have full use of the spacious room adjoining your chamber where you may dine in comfort."

"I knew I would be treated well. And now, my friend, I think I shall retire for the night. That is, if you have no objection."

Charles nodded his head in the direction of the two guards who were under orders to remain in his cell.

"Are they to stay with me all the time?"

"I'm afraid so."

"Oh, well. Could be worse I suppose."

Half an hour later things had grown very quiet. The two soldiers played cards by the light of a solitary candle. The only other candle had been blown out. It stood beside the bed where the prince slumbered fitfully, dreaming that he was back in the cave of the Seven Men of Glenmoriston, where he had slept in perfect peace. But when he awoke all was darkness and he could dimly see the outlines of his cell.

He did what he had always done in moments of extreme difficulty. Charles Edward Stuart prepared himself for whatever fate was going to throw at him next, then went back to sleep.

CHAPTER THIRTEEN

De Talmont Continued

There was a rustling of silken sheets as the Princesse de Talmont stretched out her arm to the bedside cabinet and removed from it, first, a document written in code and, secondly, a fine gold-stemmed wine glass containing a swirling concoction drunk by the ladies of high fashion to enhance their sexual appetites. Not that de Talmont needed any assistance in that direction — but the Comtesse de Vasse had spoken of it highly and de Talmont had promised to try it.

But the coded letter was of far more interest. Because it was from the young man presently incarcerated in the donjon at Vincennes. The young man with whom she had so publicly fallen out, whom she had threatened to shoot at point blank range, who had been barred for ever from her magnificent home. Leaning back on her pillows, de Talmont laughed aloud. How well her little trick had played out; even Charles Edward himself had been deceived. That was until she had smuggled a tiny love token into his prison, via the good offices of one of the prince's gentlemen. Now they were exchanging coded messages to one another — and arranging to meet again, one day.

She sat up straight and finished the rest of the glass, and had to admit that it sent a feeling of abandonment to her limbs. Smiling, de Talmont filled the champagne flute with some more gorgeously exuberant wine.

There was a gentle knock on her door and a quiet voice called out, "Are you awake, my love?"

It was that amiable, dim, bisexual husband of hers. Inwardly, de Talmont sighed, but aloud she called in a soft, sweet reply, "Come in, mon cher."

The door opened quietly and there he stood, his night-rail hanging loosely, a cap on his head, a silver candlestick in one hand.

"May I enter?" he asked, tentatively.

"Of course you can, my dear. I am not entertaining tonight."

"I have not seen you in a while and I wanted to have a little chat."

Thoughts went through de Talmont's mind. Ought she to have intercourse with him? She supposed it was high time — but did he regard it as much of a duty as she did?

"Come and sit here, my sweet. Let me pour you some champagne."

She quickly produced another glass and filled it with sparkling liquid, topping it up with some aphrodisiac for good measure.

"Here," she handed it to him and he swallowed it down in one.

"That was nice," he said, smacking his lips.

This time she put a larger amount of love potion into his brew, thinking to herself that she may as well enjoy what was coming. She smiled at him.

"What do you want to chat about, Porcin?"

This was French for 'piggy' and a nickname that de Talmont had given him on their wedding day.

"About that lover of yours, the prince fellow. Do you know there has been the most awful stink about him being imprisoned? The dauphin burst into tears, the king was told off by most of his family and the people of Paris practically rioted."

"I know. I wrote to His Majesty that I thought it was in very poor taste."

"And he's *still* muttering about exiling you, my dear. It is not wise to write and tell him what you think, you know. He is a shrewd old fellow and he's not sure that he believes you have finished with the pretender chappie."

A delicate hand flashed with rings as de Talmont clutched at her throat. "How could he *think* such a thing?" She swallowed down another glass of potion.

Her husband laughed. "Probably because it's true, old girl. I wouldn't put anything past you."

"Porcin! Have you no trust in me?"

"None, actually. Not for a long time. But that doesn't mean we can't rub along together, does it?"

De Talmont laughed. Her husband could be quite sweet, in an innocent sort of way.

"Get into bed, Porcin."

"What — now?"

"Yes, now. I want to feel your plump little body next to mine."

"Is it time for me to use my cockalorum?"

"If you haven't forgotten how, the answer is yes."

"This is going to be great fun. Hang on a minute."

With amazing agility, de Talmont's husband divested himself of his nightclothes and leapt on top of her. Plump he may have been, but he was not badly formed, and a moment later he set up a rhythm that had the courtesan giving a loud shriek of enjoyment.

"We should do this more often," she gasped, thinking that the concoction really was working well.

"Tremendous," panted Porcin, going at it like a true hero.

"I'm coming," yelled de Talmont in sudden great surprise.

"By golly, so am I," he answered, and they collapsed in each other's arms, laughing hysterically.

*

What her husband had said about the reaction to Charles' capture was perfectly true. He had emerged as the hero and the French police as the villains of the piece. But public opinion was not enough. The Young Pretender was offered a simple choice as a means of leaving gaol. He could be released and head for the French border and onwards with a few guards and several of his gentlemen. Or, he could travel alone, but with an escort of a whole detachment of musketeers, for a destination beyond the Alps. He chose to go to the border.

At this news the Princesse de Talmont — nicknamed by the dauphin and his sisters *Maman Putain* or *Mother Fuck* — wrote to the king again, asking permission to see the prince before he left.

"I am sick of this old woman and her little-boy lover. God's life, but I've a mind to exile her and her small pansy husband to their country estates in Lorraine."

"But, sir, she is cousin to the queen and you can't punish her for having an affair."

The king raised an eyebrow. "No. But we can bring strong pressure to bear on the husband to get her out of Paris and into the depths of the countryside fast. She is no longer a fresh-faced girl but an over-rouged hack. Everybody knows it, even my children have the rudest nickname for her."

The courtier chuckled and left the room.

But the over-rouged hack — or Maman Putain as the dauphin continued to call her — was too old and wise a warrior to give up on her handsome young prince. Instead she set up a network of contacts so that she could remain in constant coded touch with him. As for Charles himself, he rode out from Vincennes early one morning towards the border and an uncertain future, knowing that the people of Paris loved him dearly but that he would legally never be able to set foot in France again.

His thoughts went briefly to his son, to the cloying, killing love of Louise and how brutal it had been to shake her off. He wished — just for a second — that he had seen the child; but that would have meant meeting *her*, and braving her horrendous passion once more. It was for the best that he had never known the boy.

With that belief in mind the Bonnie Prince cantered off into a cold December day, wishing that the country which had shown him so much friendship had not turned its back on him and forced him to become a man on the run once more.

CHAPTER FOURTEEN

Exit de Talmont

He had hidden in God only knew what hell-holes during his escape from Scotland. He had put up with dastardly situations and not uttered a word of complaint. He had faced, with bravery, appalling destruction. But this — this *indignity* — was something entirely new to him. Ruled by his mad desire to see his wonderful mistress, admittedly much older than he was but oh so witty and so wise in every way, the prince was back in Paris once more.

Charles had entered the age of disguises. False noses, wigs, beetling eyebrows, cloaks; all had become part of his daily life. Beards, long and woolly, like that of an ancient hermit, or sharp and pointed, aping a Spanish grandee, became his speciality. Moustaches too, either his own or fake, twirly-ended or long and drooping, were very much part of his new scene. And so it was in the dress of an Italian officer that he now awaited — in great discomfort — a tryst with the immortal de Talmont.

He had ended up in the papal state of Avignon after his flight from France, and there had been treated like a conquering hero. It had come as something of a shock to be as adored as he had been in Edinburgh, but Charles lapped it up. There were sumptuous dinners, balls at which he had danced with his usual stylish élan, colourful carnivals in the streets. There had been music and laughter and wonderful wine — and there had been vigorous protests from both England and France that the Pope should be seen as harbouring the outlaw. This had followed with Charles, having had a wonderful time and realising that it was coming to an end, leaving in the dead of night and not returning.

The city was relieved, France was irritated, England was delighted, the Pope was pleased, the prince was triumphant. He had had the time of his life and in so doing raised two fingers at Louis XV and Charles' own brother Henry — the one adored by their father and always in the right — who had entered the church of Rome and now become a cardinal. And now here he was, disguised and back in Paris, and hiding in a horrible little niche not big enough for him to stand up in with only a small chamber pot for his convenience.

The plot had been conceived by the Princesse de Talmont herself. She and Charles had never ceased to communicate regularly and now were finally together again. Quite typically of her, she and two other ladies of the court — Mademoiselle Ferrand, a charming and delightful girl, and her friend the Comtesse de Vasse — had taken rooms in the convent of St Joseph. Not because they had become ultra-religious, but because the convent offered dwelling space for great ladies looking for a quiet retreat.

These lodgings suited the Young Pretender down to the ground, except that he had to spend hours behind the walls of the various rooms in what had once been hidey-holes for, presumably, lovers. During the morning he crouched behind Mademoiselle Ferrand's quarters, in the afternoon moved down to the Comtesse's, then by night crept down a hidden staircase to de Talmont's bedchamber. This had been all very fine to begin with, but Charles had rapidly grown bored with hunching in half for hours on end and had said as much.

"My darling girl, I can barely stand upright. It is so cramped in those wretched little niches."

"I'm sure it is, my dear. But what is the alternative? You can hardly stroll up and down the public streets as you used to. If you want me I'm afraid you will have to put up with it."

"I don't altogether like your tone of voice, madam."

De Talmont gleamed dangerously and Charles was suddenly reminded of a serpent disturbed in its slumber.

"Oh, what a pity! To think you have come all this way and in such elaborate disguise just to find it wasn't worth it after all."

"I did not say that."

"No, but you were about to, weren't you?"

"Oh, be quiet woman. I think you are going off your head."

She flew at him, fists pummelling his chest and hurting him. Charles pushed her away, hard.

"Don't you dare address me as *woman*. I am a princess of noble birth, I'll have you know."

"And I am a prince of the blood royal and I'll not have some over-blown strumpet telling me how to behave."

She slapped him in the face, so hard that it sent him reeling backwards, a hand clutching his jaw. He knew he shouldn't have done it — but almost as a reflex he struck her back. De Talmont collapsed onto the bed, wildly weeping, moaning loudly, and generally making a scene. Instantly, Charles was at her side, picking her up and holding her tenderly, saying that he loved her more than any other mortal thing.

"How can you utter that?" Loud sob. "You have just slapped me!" Even louder sob.

"I am so sorry, darling heart. But you were nagging me and I struck out in a rage. I am truly, truly sorry." A wicked thought occurred to him. "Do you think the two ladies are listening in?"

De Talmont's beautiful tear-filled eyes grew large at the idea of intrigue. "I'm sure of it. Shall we make love noisily?"

"Oh yes. That would give them something to think about. I could do it right now actually."

"Then please, begin," she whispered, and raised her skirts.

It was not difficult to cause a scandal. The prince — with much loud shouting — glided into her and yelled loudly with every stroke. And, as usual, de Talmont screeched in ecstasy, letting the whole world hear her pleasure. Afterwards they got into bed, where they slept peacefully, all forgotten and forgiven. Until the next time.

Master of disguise as he was, the prince kept a promise that he had made to himself and went to the opera. He dyed his hair black, grew a beard and dyed that as well, and put the finishing touch to his eyebrows. He then asked Elisabeth Ferrand to buy him a long robe of the type worn by Jewish nobility, and Charles put this on together with a skull cap. A woman sitting next to him glanced at him throughout the performance, but the prince — speaking French with a Yiddish accent — gave her the glad eye and she became slightly nervous.

"Good night, my lady. Mazel Tov," he said on departing. "Let it be hoped that we meet again."

She dropped a faint curtsey and hurried away, but whether she was suspicious or not the prince never afterwards knew. What he *did* know, however, was that the authorities had got wind of the fact that he was in Paris and had started a man hunt. In the guise of a priest, Charles immediately left for Venice, then, masked as an ascetic man of learning, went on to Luneville in the Duchy of Lorraine.

Eventually, after much skulking about trying to find a permanent home, many countries having decided not to shelter him because of the threats of mighty England, the prince decided to stay in Luneville. Sex-starved and lonely, he sent for de Talmont, who arrived in a flurry of fun and flowers.

"Dearest prince. My adored king. I love you a million times, truly I do."

She swept a court curtsey, down to the floor, skirt spreading out, one arm elegantly folded across her breast. Charles bent to raise her up, noticing that she wobbled quite considerably as she rose.

"Queen of my heart. Are you quite well? Was the journey very tiring?"

"I had a slight headache, beloved. I have taken a little opium to cure it."

He made a great fuss of her, kissing her better, and afterwards walked with her arm-in-arm to the house he had rented for her. She exclaimed with delight at the beauty of the building and rushed excitedly into the garden. It blazed with summer colour. Red roses were everywhere, wisteria wove excitingly through the hedges and then splayed across the walls of the house in a vivid and divinely beautiful pall of purple. A solitary peacock — brought in specially by the prince — looked up in alarm at the intrusion and displayed its gloriously vivid jewels at a swish.

Charles, looking at his beloved closely in the unrelenting daylight, thought that she looked slightly ravaged.

"You're staring at me, beloved. Is anything wrong?"

"No, darling. You are as beautiful as ever."

But he was lying through his teeth and was horribly aware of it. She, however, felt rejuvenated by his compliments. She giggled and teased and fondled him all the way through their supper, getting up from her place at the table to feed him a morsel of food, then taking her place again with a girlish laugh and much swishing of her skirt. A bell was ringing in the back of the prince's mind, a vivid and unpleasant bell that had the name *Louise* in its sound. Surely the vivid, witty, worldly-wise woman with whom he had fallen in love could not be turning herself into an older version of that tormented and torrid young creature? Out of the relationship with Louise a son had been born, a son he had never seen. Charles shrivelled at the very thought.

After supper the Young Pretender escorted de Talmont to the wisteria-clad house and then, though invited to spend the night, he found it hard to make love to her, which was very out of character. Slowly but surely, the rot had started to set in.

"Good morning, my prince, king of my heart," she said next day.

"Good morning, my queen. Thank for you all you have done for me over the years."

She looked at him suspiciously. "Why do you say it like that?"

"Like what?"

"As if we are on the brink of parting."

Charles made an uneasy sound. "Why do you have to nag me every time I pay you a compliment?"

"I? Nag? I think you are confusing me with somebody else, sir."

He hesitated, not feeling that he had the energy for even a minor row. Instead he said, "I must apologise for my poor performance last night. Do you forgive me?"

She was in a testy mood and not willing to overlook a single word he uttered. Where Louise would have answered, 'Just to be near you is enough for me,' de Talmont said, "It is quite a common occurrence in men of a certain age."

The prince was incensed. He was twenty-nine years old, the hero of Scotland, generally hailed as a man of wit and courage. To be accused of failure by a woman older — much older — than himself, hit him on the raw.

"If that is your opinion of me then I shall immediately take my leave of you. I bid you good day, madam."

Leaping out of bed and sweeping her a deep bow, despite the fact that his bottom was dramatically exposed to anyone who happened to come in at that moment, Charles seized his clothes and made his way out.

As soon as he returned to his own house he dressed carefully and, mounting his second-best horse, rode out to a high-class house of ill repute and spent the afternoon in the arms of a top-notch madame. Then, thoroughly exhausted, he returned home for an early night. But it was not meant to be peaceful because the prince was beset by a most vivid dream which greatly disturbed him.

He was back in Scotland, this time alone, staring at the great vista of lochs and towering mountains that stretched before him. He was dressed meanly in a grey philibeg and tattered shirt, his bare legs muscular with walking, his red hair long, his jaw roughly shaved. There was not another living soul in sight and suddenly the prince felt frightened at the enormity of the world before him. Then, faintly but distinctly, came the sound of someone playing a solitary set of bagpipes and he hurried towards it, glad of the company, pleased that there was a being left alive.

Descending the steep mountainside was not easy but by slithering and sliding Charles arrived at a small cottage on the bottom slopes, outside which sat a young woman. She had the blowpipe in her mouth and continued to play but she winked at him, and with a nod of her head invited him to sit beside her on the ancient wooden bench.

She had curly auburn hair, a mass of tight bright locks that formed a halo round her head and a pair of vivid green eyes. Charles knew the moment he looked at her that she was his ideal woman. That all his life he had been searching for her and was never able to find her. That mistresses of all ages, colour, size and shape, would never be able to match up to her delicious freshness and vivacity. She was his dream woman. The woman he had never met.

Taking the pipe out of her mouth, she smiled at him and said, "Hello, my dear. So you've found me at long last. Not before time."

Charles answered, "I've been searching for you, always. And now that I have found you I promise that I shall never let you go."

She laid one of her beautiful little hands in his own, unkempt and travel stained as it was.

"Wherever you travel, my dear, whatever fate has in store, I will always be at your side. But only if you seek me."

"I have constantly been looking for you, you know that."

"I do, but nevertheless you must fulfil your destiny. Yet I will be waiting for you in the shadows. I promise you that. Now, I would like to kiss you farewell."

It was the most rapturous kiss, his mouth on her beautiful lips. Charles knew at that moment that he was hers for ever more, that when he met her in the living world he would never leave her.

And then he woke up, thoroughly disgusted with this life and all that went with it. When he raised his hand to his cheeks it was to find them wet with tears. He buried his face in the pillows and sobbed like a child, all thoughts of his association with de Talmont ashes in his mouth.

*

Though he had said nothing in actual words about their relationship dying, she, of course, sensed it.

"Listen to me, Charles, and listen well. Unless you improve in your manner towards me I am leaving forthwith. In fact I shall be glad to quit this beastly place and to return to dear old Porcin."

"Yes, the poor chap must be wondering what you look like."

She shot him a glare of pure poison. "Is that meant to be funny?"

"No, my dear, it isn't. Funny, I mean. You must forgive me for my lack of manners. I have a great deal on my mind."

De Talmont decided to be caring. "I know, my prince. I do realise what a great burden it is you carry. Over the years I have done my best to help you."

A rush of conscience filled Charles and he turned to her with a sad face.

"I'm sorry, my dear. Have pity on your faithful subject. I don't want to die of chagrin and despair."

"And you certainly won't, if I have anything to do with it."

"Thank you. It is kind of you."

"I'm afraid, though, that I must leave you and go to Paris soon, dear one. I need to see the poor old fellow again," de Talmont continued.

"Are you referring to my cock or your husband?"

"For a prince of the blood you are the rudest person I know."

"And don't you love it?"

All was well while they were playing delightful games but that was merely a temporary shelter. In his heart Charles was bored with her but really could not see a clear way out.

"I'm afraid I must go, Charles. Poor old Piggywill be going frantic."

"On consideration, can you delay your departure for an hour or two?"

For answer, de Talmont frothed her skirts excitingly.

*

And so the situation went on, until something happened to change the circumstances. The princesse's sister fell dangerously ill. It was critical that de Talmont make her way to France — and quickly. Charles, on a whim, decided to go with her and despite the risk — which secretly he enjoyed — they journeyed to the capital. On arrival, however, they parted company.

Glad to see his mistress' departing form, the prince rapidly moved from place to place, sheltering with various people and thoroughly relishing all the intrigue. An idea had been born in his mind, namely a dangerous visit to London. Rumour was flying that George II was rapidly getting old and past it. Charles determined that if he could be in England when the king died, he might organise a rapid coup d'état before the Butcher seized the throne, proclaiming his brother Frederick too weak to rule, and naming himself as regent.

On this visit he stayed with Elisabeth Ferrand — a gift of a girl whom he had rather overlooked when they originally met. He gave her a nickname Luci. Together they worked out a silly code that would mask their future correspondence. De Talmont was to be known as la vielle tante, the old aunt. Roaring with laughter, Charles moved on and put word out that he had left Paris. But his lusty nature — something he found, try as he might, impossible to overcome — possessed him once more and he called at midnight on de Talmont, who promptly had him turned away from her door, then apologised next day and asked him to try once more. He sent word to her that he would leave the capital and not bother her again. And this time, he really meant it.

He left Paris by the skin of his teeth. Someone who could identify him, possibly the porter at the Princesse de Talmont's house, had betrayed him. The yellow wig and pallid complexion he had adopted were rapidly disposed of at Luci's apartment, and a swarthy creature with pebble glasses and a nasty scar made his way through the check point and out of Paris.

Back in Luneville, the prince called his most trusted advisers to his side and discussed the London situation in full. It would appear that he had a virtual arsenal of weapons at his command and that these could be shipped over to England as soon as Charles sent word. He wrote secret messages to the doyenne of English Jacobites, Anne, Lady Primrose, at her house in Essex Street, off the Strand. The message came back that he would be gladly received. Writing a quick note to Luci, Charles prepared for his journey. It would be his first visit to England and would mark his fateful return after his departure from the shores of Scotland. Furthermore, Madame de Talmont would know nothing at all about it.

CHAPTER FIFTEEN

Lady Primrose

It was with great emotion that the prince glimpsed the white cliffs of Dover through a somewhat misty telescope. He had sailed from Ostend, preferring to journey the long way round rather than risk departing from a French port. But now he was here, looking at the country which one day he might, with any luck, rule. A stir of emotions filled his heart. Despite everything that had happened to him, despite his most unfortunate affairs with women, Charles Edward Stuart still had a boyish and rather childlike enthusiasm for living life to the full. Now, as the boat entered British territorial waters, he was overcome with emotion; he felt a pain in his chest and barely controlled his tears.

He was disguised, as usual, this time as a typical Frenchman, anxious to see something of London and its inhabitants. He wore a rather battered tricorne hat pulled down over his eyebrows, to which he had added minimal red ochre. His own hair was clipped short and he wore a simple, yet fashionable, tie wig. His clothes were in good taste but did not shout of high fashion.

He was accompanied in this instance by John Holker, whom he had met in Belgium, an ardent Jacobite prepared to protect the prince with his life. Strolling down the gangplank in a throng of passengers, Charles spied a dockside tavern. Three brandies later and feeling a great deal stronger, he and Holker started their 'great adventure' in the capital.

They spent the night at a coaching inn in Dover, but had to rise at four next morning to take the post-chaise to London. This duly arrived and deposited them in the Strand the same evening.

"I suggest we go immediately to Lady Primrose's. Essex Street can't be far away."

"Yes, Highness. I agree."

It was with a delicious thrill of making his way through the early shadows that Charles, sniffing the air and not finding it as noxious as that of Paris, strolled down the pleasant side street, having located it with surprising ease, and much amazed by the recent innovation of oil lamps in the public ways. The house was half-way down and he allowed Holker the task of rapping the dolphin-shaped knocker. A servant answered. The prince spoke out of the darkness.

"Dr Thompson to see Lady Primrose, if you please."

"If you would like to step inside, gentlemen, I will enquire whether her ladyship is at home."

The house was buzzing with conversation from a room upstairs, and after a few minutes Charles Stuart and John Holker were told that they could join the company. Climbing the curving staircase in silence, they went into the grand salon.

Not quite sure which one was Lady Primrose, Charles hovered in the doorway, looking around. The scene was one of quiet elegance. Beautifully dressed women sat with polished and aristocratic men, all holding cards and seated round small baize-covered tables in groups of four. He had interrupted a card party.

One of the women glanced up and made eye contact with the prince. The effect was amazing. She let out a small scream and clutched her cards to her breast, almost dropped them, then hastily recovered both the cards and herself. Rising from her place she headed for Charles and extended a hand. He could not resist it. As he straightened from putting a kiss on her extended fingers, he winked, long and slowly. Lady Primrose did not know where to look.

"Oh my dear sir, how nice to see you…" she said, adding the word 'again' loudly enough for the gathered company to hear.

"My pleasure, ma'am," he answered. "May I introduce my companion, Mr John Holker."

Holker bowed low and, with a smile, so once again did Charles.

"How do you do, sir. Please to come in, the pair of you. I have a few friends round for cards. Do join us please. Ladies, gentlemen, these are some old acquaintances who have come to call. Dr Thompson and Mr Holker."

The gentlemen rose slightly and bowed, the women inclined their heads graciously, one or two fanning themselves slightly as they took in the handsome features — disguise or no — of the younger newcomer. One extremely pretty female, with lips that were sweet and ripe, gave the prince a very merry glance. He grinned back, glad that he had disguised himself as a young man of learning, rather than an old money-lender or a beetle-browed book keeper.

They were put at a side table from which they could observe the other guests. Holker leaned forward and whispered.

"Your hostess nearly gave the game away."

"Almost. But she can say she was startled by our arrival if anyone asks. By the way, I think this room is most pleasant. I can honestly declare that so far, I like what little I have seen of London."

"I agree. Pity our mission is so perilous."

"Nothing — but *nothing* — is perilous after escaping from Scotland with £30,000 on your head."

Holker bayed a laugh and several of the card players turned to look in his direction before turning back to their game.

"You're attracting attention," Charles mouthed.

"Sorry, sir."

But there was no further conversation, as Anne Primrose was bearing down on them.

"Gentlemen, some wine or refreshment to keep you going until supper?"

Charles rose from his chair, the height of good manners and charm.

"You are very gracious, madam. I am a little peckish."

She smiled at him. "You've travelled quite a distance, sir."

"Yes, madam, I have indeed."

They laughed gently and Holker joined in, quietly this time.

"There are several people who would like to meet you. What shall I say your Christian name is?"

"Tobias," Charles answered, grinning. "Tobias Thompson. It has a certain ring to it, would you not agree?"

"It has indeed, sir."

So later, when the game of cards was finally at an end and several people approached politely, Lady Primrose did the honours.

"May I present a very old friend of mine, Dr Tobias Thompson, and his companion, Mr John Holker."

Charles made much of bowing and hand kissing, particularly to the young woman with the lovely lips.

"I noticed you when I first walked in," he murmured, drawing her slightly to one side.

"And I you, sir. Have you travelled far?"

"From Scotland," he answered with the hint of a smile.

"Gracious. What rough territory. Did you enjoy it, sir?"

"I liked Edinburgh," he answered, his eyes twinkling and all the old allure returning.

"Perhaps you will tell me something of it. Scotland is a place that I would rather like to visit."

"Madam, command me to talk to you about Morocco and I will be glad to do so."

"Morocco?" she asked, puzzled.

The prince laughed, knowing that he had captured her interest.

"I have never been there but I will gladly make anything up as long as I can remain in your company."

"I think you flatter me, sir."

"I could spend all night doing so."

She was captivated and so was he. Nothing would satisfy him now until he had a private meeting with her.

"Tell me your first name. You were introduced only as Miss Carthew."

"It's Helena. And yours is Tobias, I believe."

Charles smiled. "Yes. Do you like it?"

"Very much."

"Then, beautiful Miss Carthew, will you allow me to escort you somewhere that you would greatly like to visit?"

"Yes. Provided that Papa gives his permission, of course."

Charles winked a confident eye. "Leave that to me, Miss Carthew. And now, if you will forgive me, I see our hostess coming towards me. Au revoir."

The evening was drawing to a close and the guests were making their farewells. The prince, alias Dr Tobias Thompson, had scored a definite success with all and sundry. He had been on his very best behaviour and had slipped easily into the role of an intelligent and somewhat-learned young man. However, his request to accompany Miss Helena Carthew to a place of her choosing had been met with a certain amount of resistance.

"But my dear sir, can you not call on us at home? That is the usual form of address."

"Alas Sir Edmund, I'm afraid that will not be possible. I live in Paris, you see, and am in town for a brief visit only. Indeed, my poor father is ailing and I might be called back at any time."

"That is bad news indeed. So why are you interested in my daughter, may I ask?"

"Only as a companion to show me the sights of London. I say that with a heavy heart because if I could stay longer I would pay her respectable court."

"I see. Well, let me speak to her mother."

Lady Primrose bore down on them. "Can you stay a while, Dr Thompson? And your friend of course?"

"Certainly, milady."

In the end the departing Sir Edmund told Charles that he could escort Helena, provided that her brother went as well. Satisfied, the prince and John Holker settled down for the rest of the evening, both delighted when Anne Primrose invited them to stay with her for the duration of the visit.

She had drawn up an entire programme for them and within a few days Charles was invited to address a meeting of sympathisers at a house in Pall Mall. Amongst the great men present was the Duke of Beaufort. By the end of his talk the prince knew he was defeated. He was persuaded that the task could not be undertaken without the assistance of some foreign power. That his request for four thousand men could not be met by the English Jacobites. That perhaps he should try to organise an uprising somewhere other than the capital.

"It's no good, John. They're not going to help me."

"Still, sir, it would be worth a tour of the London strongholds."

The only answer had been a weary nod of the head. But Charles brightened when the next night he called in a hired carriage to take Helena Carthew and her brother Cuthbert out on the town, only for them to insist that they go by water to the Vaux Hall Pleasure Gardens. The coach dropped them back at Essex Street and they walked down to the Thames and picked up a wherry at Temple Stairs.

It was September and there was a chill in the evening air. Charles, determined to play the gallant, snatched off his redingote and put it around Helena's shoulders. She gave him a smile of thanks and the prince thought that if he played his cards correctly he could expect — at the very least — a kiss before the night was out.

Vaux Hall Gardens proved to be everything that he could have wished for. Crowded with women of all types, from the highest born to the dark-eyed whores strolling about the many walkways, it also had its cross section of men. Lords and louts rubbed shoulders, bully-boys shouted orders at harassed waiters, young rakes leapt over parapets and bothered the women sitting in the supper boxes, raddled old men leered at girls younger than their daughters. It was a great, rich, boisterous panoply of life itself, and Charles loved it.

"Well, do you like it, Dr Thompson?"

"Tobias, please. I adore it. If I lived in London I would visit regularly."

"And I could show you the sights of town," she whispered, so that her brother could not hear. Cuthbert, however, was far more interested in getting a supper box and securing the comforting contents of a bottle of champagne. Proving to the world in general that he was indeed a member of the beau monde, he promptly obtained one, close enough to be able to glimpse the singers and orchestra, and also acquired several bottles. He then proceeded to eye-up assorted women with the aid of his quizzing glass.

"How old is he?" Charles whispered.

"Twenty."

"Starting as he means to go on, I see."

"I'm afraid so."

"Why afraid? Life is for taking by the throat and making the best of."

"Sounds rather nasty to me," Helena answered, with spirit.

Charles could do nothing but smile at the absurdity of it all. Yet, as the evening wore on and Cuthbert saw a group of old school friends and went off with them, and the champagne flowed like water, Helena leaned against him.

"Do you think we might go for a stroll?"

"Of course, my dear. I want you to enjoy yourself. We'll go wherever you please. But, having said that, I would love to kiss you. And in telling you so, I feel that I have behaved badly and am ashamed of myself."

Charles hung his head, acting the role of contrite lover, when all he actually wanted to do was take Helena into his bed. Yet he knew he must behave himself. It would not do for rumours about his conduct to reach the ears of certain enemies — or friends.

"Then perhaps we should go to the Dark Walk," Helena answered quietly.

Judging by the muffled cries and exclamations from the feminine gender that greeted the prince's ears, to say nothing of the grunts and groans of the male visitors, the Dark Walk was obviously the place where lovers met. He turned to Helena.

"Are you *sure* you want to go down there?"

"Quite certain," she answered.

"Then may we exchange a kiss?"

"I shall be upset if we do not."

That was enough for Charles, his amorous inclinations immediately aroused. He bent his head — for Helena was quite petite — and gave her a full-blooded embrace.

"Oh!" she said, when he had eventually finished.

"What's the matter? Don't you like it?"

"I loved it."

They fell to kissing once more, the prince feeling his blood stir, his behaviour getting somewhat naughty. It was then, just as he was on the point of being indiscreet, that Cuthbert strolled past, drunk but for all that still aware of what was going on.

"Well, well," he said, more in the tones of surprise than reproof.

Charles straightened up, his hand swiftly buttoning up any fastenings that might have come undone.

"Ah, Cuthbert. I'd been wondering what happened to you. Another drink before we depart?"

"An agreeable idea."

"I thought you might think so."

Helena, meanwhile, had adjusted her hat, which had slipped down rakishly over one eye, and pulled at her skirt. Charles gave her a rueful wink and mouthed the words "I'm sorry," before setting off for the bandstand.

They said their farewells on the doorstep of her house in Duke Street.

"Goodbye, Prince Delightful," Helena whispered to Charles as she extended her hand for a farewell kiss.

He was suddenly attentive. "Why do you call me that?"

"What do you mean?"

"Prince... whatever."

"Because you look so like him."

"Who?"

"The Young Pretender. I have a statuette of him in my bedroom."

"What are you saying?"

"The truth. You can buy the likenesses in Red Lion Street. He's quite a hero of mine. You're very like him to look at, you know."

Charles laughed. "Am I? Am I really? Well, who would have thought it? Goodnight, dear girl, and when you kiss your statuette, think of me."

Cuthbert rolled out of the hackney. "Goodbye, old chap. It's been awfully nice meeting you."

"The pleasure has indeed been entirely mine," Charles answered.

And giving them a flourishing bow, he got into the hackney and disappeared into the night.

*

The rest of the visit was taken up with matters far more serious. It was by now abundantly clear to Charles that a coup was out of the question. Nevertheless, he toured the Tower of London, which he thought pitiably undefended.

More importantly he went to the church of St Clement Danes in the Strand and there renounced his Catholic faith and was received into the Protestant religion. He did this quite cynically, with his thoughts on the future, realising that the English Jacobites who supported him were, to a man, of that faith. Though he did offer up a small prayer in which he begged his mother to forgive him, remembering her dying wish that he should always remain a Catholic. Poor little undernourished soul that she had been.

So, his glorious firework of a coup d'état had fizzled out like a rain-soaked rocket. With his spirits low and his expectations completely over, Charles and John Holker took a post-chaise to Dover and crossed the next morning to Boulogne. Charles then hurried to Paris, where he caught up with Luci, paid his respects to the Duchesse d'Auguillon, then hurtled back to Luneville. The entire escapade had lasted precisely twenty-eight days.

CHAPTER SIXTEEN

Luci

It had started as an occasional letter — in elaborate code, of course — written spasmodically, whenever Charles felt like it. But after seeing her briefly on his return from London, he had stepped the correspondence up. Luci — alias Elisabeth Ferrand — kept up a continuing flow of chatter about the doings of Parisian high society. Charles, revelling in the gossip, answered with alacrity, and so their regular letter writing proceeded.

Thinking about her closely as he opened yet another missive, Charles considered that she would have made him the perfect wife — if she had had royal blood, of course. Though knowing nothing of her history, whether she be married, widowed or single, to him Luci had always sparkled with a certain freshness, a lovely wistful countenance, which appealed to him enormously. In fact, he thought, she was very like the woman he had dreamt of, the woman playing the bagpipes. Perhaps this was to be his fate. Loving a dream whilst, in fact, his real-life mistresses were nagging, bitter harpies.

Of course he had grown lonely after returning, empty-handed, from

London. Once again he had been ruled by his sexual needs and he had contacted — almost against his better judgement — the Princesse de Talmont. Whilst indulging in rampant lovemaking with his former mistress, Charles had been amused to note that Luci did not like her, calling her *une femme mechante*: a naughty woman. This was not surprising in view of the fact that the two females had known one another for quite a considerable time, both having rooms in the same convent. Why, Luci asked, did the princesse bother to visit her, when all she wanted to do was lose her temper?

Yet he could not help but feel sorry for de Talmont. Her only son — product of herself and Piggy in one of their strange sexual unions — had died at the age of fifteen. Piggy had grown even more distant and his wife had developed a mysterious illness as a result. Besides this, there was a far more compelling reason why she hesitated to see Charles. The King of France, having once imprisoned the man, was not at all keen on granting her leave of absence from the court to go and visit him. De Talmont realised that banishment from Versailles was still a distinct possibility.

Luci mentioned, in one of her many letters, that in March there was to be a masked ball in the opera house in Paris. Charles immediately wrote back that he would go if she would partner him, and was delighted when she replied with a definite yes.

He went as a Venetian gentleman, his red hair concealed by a wig of tumbling curls, his topaz eyes glinting behind a beautiful golden mask. Picking Luci up from her lodgings in the convent of St Joseph, he was delighted to see her disguised as a woman of fashion from the time of Louis XIV. She looked exceptional, her hair dressed high and elaborately, her skin radiant, her eyes glowing with pleasure behind her pretty disguise. Charles kissed her hand as he helped her into the hired chaise, suddenly bowled over by her companionship.

"Greetings, Your Highness. How good it is to see you again."

"I could say the same of you, pretty lady."

"Thank you. Tell me, what name are you travelling under tonight?"

"Silvester of Tuscany. Do you like it?"

"Quite."

"Oh. Why only *quite*?"

"Because, my dear prince, I prefer calling you by your real name. But I know that is not possible, so Silvester it shall be."

In the darkness Charles' hand stole out and gently took one of hers. It was so small, as innocent as a child's, and something about the touch of it made his heart speed up. He had the strangest feeling, one that he had not experienced since the early days of his affair with Louise, when he had been madly in love. The prince sat in total silence, wondering what it was about this young woman that he had never noticed before. Could she, who bought him books and razor blades and all the things he asked her for, be his ideal partner and gone unnoticed? And why had he never realised before just how delightful she was?

*

The evening was pure enchantment. They danced together superbly, intense feelings running between them. Charles giving her such bold glances that Luci was forced to look away to avoid the brilliance of his eyes.

"I find you exquisite, madame," he whispered.

"Please don't say that."

"Why not?"

"Because it might ruin our future friendship."

"How could it? Luci, I can never marry you because of who I am, but that could not stop me loving you. And that is what is happening. I feel certain of it."

Eyes like amber — lively and full of light — gazed at him from behind her mask.

"But, sir, you still love de Talmont. And she would make a bitter enemy of me indeed."

The prince paused, thinking carefully about his words before he said them.

"I have loved several women in my life, Luci. I am a man, after all. But I had yet to meet the woman who captures me utterly even without going to bed with her. That was until about an hour ago, when everything began to change. As for de Talmont, do not fear her. Rather, feel pity for her present situation."

Luci nodded. "How nicely put. Now can I tell you something without that royal head of yours growing even larger?"

"You may."

"Why do you think that I bother to buy you everything that you ask for? Why do you think that I chase after your wretched razor blades? Why should I warn you that certain books are not worth reading?"

Charles shook his head.

"Because I like you greatly," Luci continued. "And I have done ever since you first lurked behind my apartment, listening to everyone within talking about you — and enjoying every minute of it."

Now it was his turn to laugh. "Oh, my sweet girl, if only I had known."

"Would it have made any difference?"

"Probably not. I am sometime ruled by my baser instincts and cannot think straight."

Luci struck him gently with the feathers of her fan. "I do not wish to know such things. Shall we change the subject?" But she smiled as she said, "Now, shall we go and get some refreshment?"

"Indeed, my beautiful lady. May I offer you my arm?"

And they were enjoying themselves, laughing and glancing into each other's eyes, when Charles felt, rather than saw, somebody loom up behind him. He knew by her perfume that it was his mistress.

"So," said de Talmont. "I did not realise that you were in Paris, sir. And clearly having a wonderful time in the company of my great friend." She put out a couple of claws and pinched Luci's cheek. Too hard.

The prince bowed. "Nor did I realise that you would be at the ball, madame."

"Obviously. And how are you, my dear fellow? Quite recovered, I see."

"From what, madame?"

"From whatever plagued you when last we met."

"I do not recall my being ill, but if I was I apologise. I hope your health is fully restored, princesse."

De Talmont looked stricken. "From the death of my son, do you mean? The answer is that time heals all things but that is a wound that will never be healed. I mourn him to this day."

Charles felt suddenly ashamed, realising that he had spoken tactlessly and also feeling two-faced, bursting with love as he was for his new companion.

"I apologise for my lack of delicacy, Madame. My remark was ill advised."

"As are many things you do, you wretched man. And as for you my so-called friend, you are more than welcome to the attentions of this rogue. Good evening." And with that she swept away.

Charles turned to Luci. "I don't think that I am as nasty as that person she has just described. Am I?"

"If you were, you wouldn't read *Tom Jones*, now would you?"

A whimsical smile played round Charles' mouth. "I asked you to get me that book because someone I used to know is named in it."

"And who might that be?"

"She was called Jeannie Cameron."

Luci smiled. "I think the author called her Jennie."

Charles wondered as he danced, how he could possibly have not noticed Luci long since. Perhaps her very gentleness, her very simplicity, had blinded him to the fact that underneath these rather quiet qualities beat one of the finest hearts in France. He knew for certain that she was the woman he had dreamed about. For the first time ever in his life he wished that he were not a prince of the blood and that he could settle down with her and raise a brood of sons as thoughtful and kind as she was, and daughters with his capriciously charming nature.

Standing at the edge of the ballroom, glaring at him through a mask which did not become her, silent and hateful, loomed de Talmont. The prince realised with a shock that he was looking at an old and withered woman. Gone was the amoral social creature that had whirled her way into his life. In her place stood a bitter old hag, too full of opium to realise what she had become. It was not going to be easy to get away from her, he realised that, but somehow he would manage it because all he wanted, indeed all he would ever want, was to lie in Luci's bed and see her lovely sleeping face beside his and hear her whisper his name as she slept.

At midnight everyone present was ordered to reveal their features and unmask. But the prince resisted, standing in the arched entrance with Luci beside him and bowing to the crowd, many of whom were staring fixedly at him, one or two cheering and applauding. Afterwards, in the carriage, he giggled like a schoolboy.

"Did you hear them, Luci?"

"Of course I did. You run the most terrible risks, you know."

"But I can't resist it. And how exactly am I risking anything? None of them would ever report me to the police."

"But suppose there had been a policeman at the ball?"

"Well, I would say jolly good luck to him. At least he would know how to be light on his feet."

"Really, you can be quite intolerable at times. Please be serious."

"Why? Why should I be serious when I am alone in a coach with the most delightful woman it has ever been my good fortune to meet. And whom I am about to kiss."

And before she could say another word, Charles swept her into a thoroughly delightful embrace. And later when they had got into her bed, he did so again. Very gently, for there was to be nothing rough about this love making, he kissed her body from neck to toe and felt her quiver in response.

"You're shaking," he said. "My darling, are you nervous?"

"Yes, I am — a little."

"But why?"

"Be gentle with me."

An idea flashed through his mind. "It's not your first time, is it?"

"Yes. Yes, it is. And I know you will think me a silly chit of a thing for having waited this long."

Charles raised his head, supporting himself on one elbow.

"I could never think anything so unkind about you, dear heart. But tell me, why did you?"

"I don't really know, other than for the fact that I have not been as close to anyone before."

"Are you saying that you love me?"

"Oh yes, my dear person. With all my heart."

It was too much for Charles, experienced man of the world that he was. This quiet, sweet girl truly cared for him. Momentarily, thoughts of Louise — carnal little beast — and the Princesse de Talmont — amoral and wicked — shot through his mind. Then he bent his head and whispered in Luci's ear.

"I will always cherish you, you know that. In fact I give you a solemn pledge that, should you want me to, I will love you until the end of my days."

For answer Luci drew him down to kiss her. And so it was that very gently, neither roughly nor thoughtlessly, Charles Edward pledged himself by uniting his body with hers.

Afterwards, unusually for him, he lay awake, watching the shadows of the moon flit over that perfect face, as Luci lay cuddled in his arms. Occasionally she gave a little cough and the prince would stare at her anxiously, as if it were a child that he held so close. But she still slept peacefully and eventually, as dawn broke, he laid her back on the pillows and crossed to the window to see the new day.

It was as sharp and clear as any late March morning. The gusty winds of that violent start to the month had died away to chilly little breezes. Along the street the trees were in full bud, though as yet still colourless, while an abandoned bucket rattled and groaned as it blew along the gutter. Despite the bleakness of the outlook, Charles knew that he had at last achieved his high point. A decent woman with no attachments had fallen in love with him, the days of his cheap affairs were over. He was horribly aware that he could never marry Luci, his destiny lay with some unknown daughter of a noble house. But despite that, he would love her all the days of his life.

"Good morning, my prince," came a quiet voice from the bed.

"Good morning, my queen," he answered, and turning, he ran to the bed and the protection of her loving self.

*

It was inevitable that he was going to see de Talmont again. She had journeyed to her chateau just outside Luneville, to which hiding place he had returned after tearing himself away from Luci. With no feeling for the woman other than mild dislike, the prince accepted an invitation to dine, determined that on this occasion he would break with her for good.

He was quite horrified by what he saw. Not only had she aged horrendously, all her sins being written on her face, as the saying goes, but she was in a viperish mood, running down Luci Ferrand constantly. She clearly had no idea whatsoever that she was talking about the woman with whom Charles was deeply in love.

"Of course you are entitled to your opinion, madame, but I am afraid that I do not agree with it."

"She is a bitch of the first order, Charles. The letters she writes to me are so pointedly polite. You should see them."

"I should like to, very much." De Talmont glared at him as the prince changed the subject. "And how is Piggy?"

"I haven't seen him in weeks. I expect he is up to his own devices somewhere. I left everything behind in order to come to you, my dear. You have no idea what I have sacrificed. My reputation, my honour, almost my life. I bought this chateau so that we could live together in it. And the journey to get here made me terribly ill."

She stared at him with what she hoped was a glimmer of her old allure and was rewarded by seeing him frowning.

"Perhaps you should have stayed home."

"Don't tease me. We shall have supper and laugh together, just like the old days"

Charles drew away. "Alas, that will not be possible. I have another commitment."

"What?" De Talmont might be down, but she was not yet out of the picture.

"A royal secret. Now, thank you so much for the invitation but I really must take my leave of you."

"I think you are very rude, sir."

"And I think, madame, that you are probably right."

Then he saw that she was weeping, rivulets of tears running down her cheeks and ruining her makeup.

"I wish you wouldn't do that. I am not worth it, you know."

"Oh but you are, you are, my sweet king. You are worth every minute of every hour I spend thinking about you."

It was sounding horribly like Louise, and Charles felt a moment's panic.

"Look, if I stay tonight, will that stop you crying?"

De Talmont rushed round the table like a newly-fired bullet and flung herself on the floor beside him.

"Yes, yes, king of my heart. To feel your naked body pressed against mine. Oh bliss eternal!"

Charles stood up. "I'm afraid I must go. I am indisposed."

The princesse staggered to her feet as custom decreed. "Indisposed, sir?"

"Yes. Ask no further questions, madame. It is a subject that I do not wish to discuss. Now if you will be kind enough to show me to my quarters."

Charles left early the next morning — having slept peacefully all night behind a locked door. His affair with de Talmont was finished, done.

He had at long last met his dream woman, the love of his entire life. From now on he would make as many secret visits to Paris as possible. This, together with his dreams of overthrowing the Hanoverians, were all that would occupy the rest of his life.

CHAPTER SEVENTEEN

Luci, the Adored

It was during the night that Luci was seized by a terrible coughing fit. Charles, sleeping with his head on her breast, was quite literally shaken awake. Deeply worried, he sat up and looked at her face. She was sweating and her skin had lost its usual bloom. He was on his feet and fetching her a glass of water almost before he had time to think.

"Sweetheart, are you all right? Shall I call a doctor?"

She waved a hand in front of her mouth. "No, no. I'm fine. It's just a bad cold, that's all."

"But darling, you're so pale."

"I often am. It's nothing. Come back to bed."

And so he did, holding her in his arms and rocking her gently until she went back to sleep. He loved her with all his heart, matters of state of secondary importance to him — well, almost. He had written to a trusted colleague that his head had been completely turned, that he — the prince — was beside himself and dying of love for his new and beautiful friend. He meant every word. Charles was in love for the very first time.

To continue seeing Luci, the prince made many trips to Paris, always in varying disguises. He stayed in her apartment, much to the consternation of Madame de Vasse, who always referred to Luci as her sister and had — or so the prince thought — an almost mannish love for her. Her proximity, in a nearby room, had not been too pleasing either.

But Charles, enjoying adopting characters of different kinds, slinking around Paris dressed as a lackey, visiting bookshops and peering short-sightedly through a broken pince-nez, creeping through the public gardens in the guise of a Dominican friar, was also hatching a new scheme. This one the most daring to date. To kidnap the entire Hanoverian family in one fell swoop. Of course there were other Jacobite conspirators as well, the whole affair being named the Elibank Plot.

Whenever Charles was in Paris — which was frequently — he would attend meetings of his fellow plotters, on these occasions disguised as a student at the university. Sitting back in a lace shop, sipping a coffee and talking earnestly with his allies and friends, he relished life as he had never done before.

The final occasion on which he had seen the Princesse de Talmont had been ghastly. She had been green in the face and puking, narrowly missing his new pair of leather shoes as she threw up on the floor. Charles, who despite all the hardships he had to endure in his early youth still had a certain fastidiousness, was horrified.

"I am leaving, madame. And I mean for good."

She sank to her knees, her face betraying all the signs of opium addiction.

"After all I have done for you, you ungrateful wretch."

"That is all in the past. Now we must be moving on. Be good enough to return my portrait to Waters, my banker, if you would."

"But if I do that he will know we are no longer together."

"Well, it will only be the truth. Our relationship is at an end. Goodbye, madame. I do hope your health recovers quickly."

For answer, the wretched woman vomited once more. Charles, picking his way out with care, did not look back but made his exit through a mass of gaping servants.

The princesse, however, then stooped to her lowest level and began to pester Luci with spite-filled letters. She had guessed from seeing them together at the ball that there was something going on. However, in every other instance they had been discreet. In the note which the prince had sent to a friend there had been no hint of the identity of the woman concerned. Yet de Talmont had leapt immediately to the right conclusion — and she let fly.

It was autumn and the trees were turning the colour of Luci's hair as she sat before the window, the letter in her hand. She had been out of town while Charles had been about his affairs in other places, and also to hide from him the fact that she had again been unwell. Her persistent cough and pain when breathing were starting to worry her and she had consulted Dr Leguil, son of the country physician who had looked after all of her family. The younger man had taken over his father's practice when the old doctor retired. Now, he regarded her with a serious expression.

"Your cough, ma'am, how long have you had it?"

"Quite a while now. It seems to go and I feel better, and then it comes back again. It is most irritating."

"And do you have any other symptoms?"

"Symptoms? What do you mean exactly?"

"Does it hurt when you cough? Do you spit up any blood?"

Luci hesitated while the physician waited in polite silence.

"I did once, but that was probably from my teeth."

Dr Leguil nodded but said nothing. Then he produced from his bag two wooden tubes which he proceeded to screw together.

"May I listen to your chest, Mamzelle Ferrand?"

"Yes, of course."

He produced a silk handkerchief with a flourish, put this between Luci's shoulders, placed the wooden tube on the top and then bent his ear to it. She gazed in amazement.

"Your father never had anything like this."

"Shush," was his only answer.

Luci obeyed meekly. Eventually the examination was over and she waited for the verdict silently.

"I would not advise, ma'am, that you spend any more time in Paris. Over-crowded and filthy places are the breeding ground for disease. You will be better off remaining here, in the freshness of the countryside."

"That aside, do I have anything seriously wrong with me?"

"Possibly. I will return in a month and listen again. Meanwhile I would advise you to rest, to eat well and to take gentle exercise in the pure air. If you return to the city you will be courting disaster. I can send you round a sleeping draught that should reduce your night-time coughing fits."

"Thank you, doctor. You have been helpful."

After he had gone, Luci stood in silence, staring out of the window, then picked up the letter and read the opening lines.

The obstinacy of your taste for the country in such vile weather, mademoiselle, is only equalled by the obstinacy of your harshness toward myself.

What an old bitch the woman is, Luci considered. If only she knew how horribly ill I feel sometimes in town. But then Luci thought of her sweet lover and how much he enjoyed being in the capital. Of his kindness to her, of their love one for the other, of the beauty of nights snuggling in the warmth of his body, of the rapturous joy of feeling him within her. She knew then that even if it put the death sentence on her she would continue to go to Paris as long as she had enough breath left.

*

He was in Ghent, looking for a permanent house, somewhere where he and Luci could live and be happy, though admittedly she was not uppermost in his mind at this particular moment. The skeins of the Elibank Plot — the one in which the entire English Royal family was to be kidnapped while Charles mounted a coup d'état — were growing enormous. Lady Primrose, still a feisty campaigner, had arrived in Paris to learn what part she should undertake. And it was while the prince was arranging to meet her in the capital that another piece of information came his way. It would seem that Clementina — whose favours he had enjoyed while fighting in Scotland — had also, mysteriously, come to France.

"Don't trust her, sir." Goring, his equerry, was speaking.

"Why ever not?"

"She's a spy. You don't think it is mere coincidence that she's arrived at a time like this? She's over here to find out what you are planning and report all back to the Hanovers."

"Oh come, come. She's just an ordinary girl. There's nothing suspect about her whatsoever."

"Begging your pardon, Highness, but her sister is a bedchamber woman to the dowager princess of Wales, poor Prince Frederick's widow. The connection speaks for itself."

"Really? I know nothing of this at all. I am quite intrigued. I think I'll send for her."

"I beg you not to do that, sir. It would be a great mistake. You know that someone spies on us and reports back all we do. I think it could be the lady herself."

"What an intriguing thought."

But Charles was like a cat with a bird. He could not leave the subject alone. The idea that the passive girl who he had made love to, frequently, recklessly and — to be honest — a trifle ruthlessly, intrigued him. To be honest, she would have been the last person on earth that he would have suspected of having a dark and secretive side. But he was determined to find out if she had.

He sent money to Dunkirk for her to come to Paris, despite the mutterings of his followers. Meanwhile he settled on a house and immediately set off for the French capital to meet Anne Primrose. But first there was someone who he truly adored waiting to be seen.

"Sweetheart, how are you? Oh darling, I have missed you." He held Luci at arm's length, looking at her closely. "You've lost weight, my love."

"Yes, I have a little. Nothing to worry about."

"But you're positively *thin*. You're sure you are quite well?"

"Certain. And tell me how you are. It's been several weeks and I'm convinced you have a great deal to catch me up with."

"Yes I have indeed. Come on. Let's go out. Put your hat on. I want to be seen with the best-looking woman in Paris."

The prince was in a smart disguise for once. With a military uniform denoting that he was an officer in the Italian army, he presented a tall and resplendent figure. He had dyed his eyebrows and had somehow managed to darken his eyelashes as well, so that his topaz eyes glowed in ebony surroundings. So it was a good-looking couple that strolled along the boulevards. Charles remembered the days before he was expelled from France and used to be cheered in the streets.

He slipped his arm round her waist, feeling her bones protruding.

"Come on, sweetheart. I'm going to buy you a truly good meal and watch you eat it. You are getting too thin and I intend to do something about it."

She laughed in the sunshine, tilting her head back and looking deeply into his eyes.

"I think you are the most marvellous man."

"Me?" Charles tapped his chest. "I don't think so. I have sinned along with the worst of them."

"What man hasn't? No, I'm talking about the inner, secret you. You are as brave as a lion and mule-like in your determination. You gave your word to those men of Scotland that you would come back to them and you have spent every waking moment since plotting and scheming how to do it."

The prince slanted his gaze at her. "Well, there have been one or two moments when I haven't."

She chuckled and nudged him slightly. "And thank God for that! Otherwise you would have been too much of a paragon, and no woman in her right mind would have looked at you."

Charles stopped dead, staring into her face, remembering every little curve and line, every shadow and light that filled her lilting, lovely eyes.

"Luci, promise me that you will stay with me always. That you will be by my side whatever the future holds for me. It is true that I have a great destiny that has yet to be fulfilled but I believe that I cannot achieve it without a woman behind me. A woman that I love and cherish above all other."

"But, my dear, I can never marry you."

Charles shuffled his feet. "No, I'm afraid you can't. I must marry for position. But, darling, you can be my adored mistress with your own household and it is to you I will come every night. Well, most nights anyway."

Luci gave a peal of laughter, such a joyful sound that passers-by turned their heads and smiled.

"Oh, Your Highness, you would have to have the constitution of an ox — or should I say a ram?"

"Why? My great uncle Charles had a wife and countless mistresses."

"To say nothing of all the little bastards who ended up founding the British peerage."

"God bless 'em."

Her face changed. "On a serious note, I promise to devote myself entirely to you for every moment I have left."

Charles looked at her suspiciously. "Why do you say that? You're not ill, are you?"

"No," lied Luci, and shook her neat head.

But it was too glorious a day for melancholy thoughts. Sunshine turned all the main walkways of Paris into avenues of light and joy, where children bowled hoops and fiddlers tuned up and those who felt like it burst into song, Charles included. His pleasant, light baritone voice rang out with the words of 'Give me a lass with a lump of grass,' a Scottish ballad. Luci listened and loved him, the prince sang and loved life. And afterwards, when the sun had begun to set, they walked back, arms tightly woven about each other, to Luci's apartment — and there they fell to lovemaking by the light of the moon.

*

The interview with Lady Primrose was conducted amongst a group of fellow plotters who discussed the intricacies of the Elibank affair with varying degrees of enthusiasm, Charles sitting silently, for once, and listening to the others. But his mind had been elsewhere. What was all this that he was hearing about Clementina, he wondered. Nobody of his household seemed to have a good word for her. He determined to get the truth by whatever means necessary. But when it came to it he found Clementina so boring that his brilliant plan for quizzing her without giving the game away, came to nothing.

*

They met in the private apartment of the Comtesse de Vasse. Luci had left for her country house and so her possessive friend had made the arrangements. Charles — years of good breeding ingrained — rose to his feet as the door opened and a mouse-like creature walked in. He stared in frank amazement. Was this really the woman to whom he had made abandoned love in Scotland? He must have been blind or desperate? Probably the latter.

He extended a reluctant hand and Clementina sank to the floor in a tremendously deep curtsey before him. The prince started to grin and then turned the look to a gracious smile.

"Your Royal Highness," she said, and gave the hand a brief, dry kiss.

Her voice was small and muted, like a little girl's. Charles could not recall that it had been as irritating as he now found it. Still, he managed to look urbane and kindly as she rose — just a fraction unsteadily — to her feet.

"Miss Walkinshaw, pray be seated."

She sat down primly in a chair opposite his, her eyes firmly fixed on the floor.

"It has been a long time since we last saw each other."

"Indeed it has, sir."

"And what have you been doing with yourself? Keeping busy?"

She looked up and gave him a wan smile. "Most of my family have now departed and so I came to France to visit a sick aunt."

The prince looked blank. "Really? How interesting. Where did they go to?"

"Who?"

"Your departed family."

"They went into the arms of the Almighty, sir."

"Oh, I see. I'm sorry to hear that. Tell me, are you still interested in the affairs of state or have you turned to more feminine pursuits these days?"

At last she looked up, her dark chocolate-coloured eyes gazing into his. She was quite a fine-looking woman in a truly dull way. It flashed through Charles' mind that with a little artifice, she could make herself desirable. Then he thought how he and she had been very naughty in Scotland and could not help but smile at their youthful frolics.

"I wish I had something amusing to say, sir. I remember how you used to enjoy fun and laughter and I see you smiled just now."

"Did I? There wasn't much to laugh about, as I recall."

"Oh, yes there was. We used to have some good times, you and I. We danced and made merry."

Oh dear, Charles thought, she's talking about our sex life. He took the bull by the horns.

"Yes, we did, Clementina. And I am most grateful for the part you played in lifting my sagging spirits. But all that is in the past. I want you to consider this as a professional meeting only."

"Of course. It shall be as you wish, Highness."

Charles sat silently, trying to read her face. She was either one of the cleverest spies he had ever come across — and he had come across quite a few, even before he went to Scotland. Alternatively, she could be perfectly innocent. He decided to proceed carefully with his plan and watch the unfolding of events.

"Very well. I am wondering, Miss Walkinshaw — or should I address you by your Christian name? — whether you would do me a service."

"The answer is yes to both questions, sir."

"There is much afoot at the moment, the result of which will be felt in both England and Scotland. It would be good to know I had a reliable agent who could report developments back to me."

She stared at him, mouth gaping slightly. "Are you asking me to spy for you?"

"I would rather it was for the house of Stuart than that of Hanover," Charles answered blandly.

Her face did not alter. She was either a sublime actress or an innocent creature. Her intentions were a total enigma.

"My family has always served the Stuarts, sir, as well you know."

"But times change, Clementina. A sad fact, but a true one."

"Nothing will alter my deepest feelings, Highness."

Hoping that there was no double meaning in that remark, Charles stood up, indicating that the interview was at an end. Clementina also rose, curtseying once more.

"Will one of your people contact me, sir?"

"You can be assured of it, madam. Good day to you."

And giving a little nod of his head he left her, still bent double in a curtsey, and sauntered out of the room.

*

He was on the point of leaving Paris for Ghent — a beautiful town recently handed back to the Austrians by the French — when there came a rapid knock on his door. Charles, who was busy packing up his things and in a hurry, opened it to see his equerry, Sir Henry Goring, standing with a piece of paper clutched in his hand.

"A letter for you, sir. The messenger said it was extremely urgent."

"I'll read it when I've finished packing."

"I think it should be now, sir."

"Oh, very well."

The prince peered at the signature, HE Leguil, doctor of medicine. Then with a lurch of his heart, he scanned the contents.

Please come at once. Mademoiselle Ferrand is dangerously ill. If you wish to see her alive I would treat this matter with the utmost urgency and journey to Chantilly immediately.

Charles made an instant decision, something that had saved his life many times in Scotland.

"Henry, hire two horses quickly. We're leaving for Chantilly now."

"But..."

"No buts. Choose two swift beasts. We must make the place before nightfall."

*

Getting out of Paris, even disguised as an Italian officer, was always tricky, and today Charles was fidgeting with irritation as the two men wound their way through the dark and smelly streets. Finally, they left the city behind them and rode as quickly as their horses could take them towards the charming medieval town of Chantilly. All the way there the prince was fighting back tears of disbelief, preparing himself for a battle with the man of medicine, half convincing himself that the man was a charlatan. But when he finally arrived outside the small but charming house, leaping off his mount as if he were ten years younger, his heart plunged.

Curtains were closed and the place already looked as if the inhabitants were in mourning. Running up the steps, followed by a slowly walking Goring, Charles thundered on the knocker. A female servant answered and dropped a respectful curtsey.

"I've come to see Mademoiselle Ferrand. Is she…?"

"Yes, sir. She's upstairs. The doctor is with her."

With a million thoughts running through his mind, Charles entered the bedroom without knocking — and then stopped dead.

Luci, the love of his life, his dear one, the woman who had taught him — the naughty boy — what it was to truly love, was dying. He rushed forward but was abruptly pushed back by the medical man.

"No, monsieur," he whispered, "you must be gentle with her. She is slipping quietly out of life. Do not treat her roughly."

Charles could have answered with hauteur, but instead he felt tears spring up into his eyes.

"You are telling me that she is *dying*?" he whispered.

"Yes, sir, she has had consumption for some time."

That would explain the thinness and the fact that Luci had rouged her cheeks to hide her pallor.

"Let me speak to her. Please."

"Of course. I will step outside."

He raised her up, oh so gently, as if she were the most precious thing in the world, and at that moment felt such a pain in his heart that he knew that it might possibly break.

"Luci," he whispered. "I'm here. It's Charles. Oh, my darling."

He buried his head in the waxen neck and felt his tears mingle with her dew. She opened her eyes as if it were a great burden to do so.

"My prince. You've come. And me in such a disreputable state."

"No, my dearest sweetheart, you look beautiful. You could never be anything else."

She put up a hand, so thin, so skeletal, that he could see the bones through the skin.

"Oh Charles, I don't want to die. You almost convinced me with all your talk of becoming a beloved mistress."

"You have become more than that, my precious. To me you are my wife — and always will be, until the end of my days."

Luci sighed and closed her eyes and behind him, Charles heard Dr Leguil come back into the room. Silently, the medical man took her pulse, then turned to look at the prince, his face grim. Charles sobbed openly.

"Shush. Don't let your crying be the last thing she hears. Be a man, I beg you."

Charles gave an ironic smile. He had been the man on so many occasions during the time in Scotland when he had been on the run and had to vanish from sight, with Butcher Cumberland coming after him full blooded, searching and prying like a beastly hunting dog. But now? With the light of his life leaving him. But the doctor was right. For Luci's sake, he must rally.

Wiping his tears away, Charles put his arms round her and raised her a little.

"I'm here, darling girl. Let me stay close to you."

"Yes," she whispered. "I'll always be close by."

After that neither of them spoke and Charles held her in his arms as gently as if she were made of glass. He no longer knew what time it was or whether it be day or night, keeping his vigil as his love slowly departed this life. Eventually, Dr Leguil came and put his hand on Luci's neck, then he carefully and quietly laid her back on the bed. There was no noise in the room at all, other than for Charles' shallow breathing.

Goring appeared from nowhere and, taking the prince by the hand, led him away. Charles turned to him as they went down the staircase.

"There shall never be another woman in my life. Luci has gone and taken my heart with her."

"I understand, Highness."

"From this day forward I swear that they shall be only a necessary function. I shall never love again."

And looking at him, his equerry knew that the prince was telling him the complete and utter truth.

CHAPTER EIGHTEEN

The Return of Clementina

He had only briefly come back to Paris from Chantilly and was putting his last remaining bits and pieces into a valise in preparation for the journey to Ghent, when there came a gentle knocking at his door. Charles shouted 'Enter' and was greeted not with the sight of Henry Goring but Clementina, curtseying sedately in the entrance.

"Forgive me, Highness."

"For what?"

"For intruding like this."

"Well I'm afraid I can only spare you a minute. I am due to leave Paris in the next quarter of an hour. I only came back to collect a few things."

"I'm sorry to interrupt."

The prince turned to bid her an abrupt farewell and then realised that she was still trying to straighten up from yet another ridiculously low curtsey and put out a hand to help her. The touch of her human palm on his brought a sudden surge of tears as it occurred to him that he would never again feel Luci's light touch. He looked at the wall rather than let Clementina see that he was crying.

"What is it, your Highness? Are you ill?"

"No."

"Then what troubles you?"

"Nothing. I've got hay fever. Please leave me alone."

"Very well, sir. Forgive me for being a nuisance."

Charles realised that he was behaving badly, but was temporarily out of control. He grabbed his handkerchief and wept into it, past caring what Clementina or anybody else thought. Behind him he could detect a faint scuttling as she hastily withdrew. The next moment he heard Goring's gruff tones.

"Come on, My prince. Gather yourself together."

"I can't, Henry. I loved Mademoiselle Ferrand with all my heart."

"I know, sir. I saw that for myself. But she of all people would be advising you to leave Paris now. Please go. I beg you."

So once again the two men set off through the noisome back streets, but this time in a hired coach heading out on the road to Lille where they could cross the border and leave the country of France behind them.

*

The trouble with the Bonnie Prince was that he had lost the one true love of his life whilst still requiring a woman to have sexual relations with. Local brothels could supply his needs but were expensive and always contained the risk of infection. While Luci had been alive he had been totally content, blending his complete adoration with wonderful sexual activity. But now that he had been widowed — which was how he thought of himself — it was a different story.

His mind reluctantly turned to Clementina once more. He wrote to her offering her work in his establishment.

The suggestion went down with an outcry of horror from his intimate circle.

"You can't, sir. The woman's a spy and that's all there is to it."

"Have you proof of this?"

"It is a well-known fact in Jacobite circles. I should imagine that the only reason you haven't heard it personally is that you had a relationship with her when you were in Scotland."

"I heard the rumours but I find it hard to believe them."

Someone muttered, unseen. "Don't or won't?"

Charles was furious.

"I have listened enough! You can all go to the devil as far as I'm concerned. Miss Walkinshaw is an honest woman..."

There was a growl of laughter at this remark.

"...and I intend to send for her. Now leave, before I throw the lot of you out."

But even more trouble lay ahead when he caught up with Goring in Lens, the prince's intention being to give instructions as to which route Clementina should follow.

"I'll not go to bring that bad woman to your side, sir. You are my prince and I would rather resign than see you proceed with the plan."

"Oh be damned to you. Resign, then."

Goring did, on the spot. Charles walked away, fuming, and more determined than ever to send for the woman. But when they met again, the prince in a kindlier mood, Goring attacked once more.

"It would be inconsistent with your honour, sir, to have that woman as your companion. And if I go to fetch her I shall be no better than a pimp. And that I will never be, as long as I remain in your service."

"I thought you had already resigned. But, if not, do so now. *Immediately*, do you hear?"

So Charles was not in the best of moods when Clementina eventually arrived from Paris, looking travel-stained and somewhat weary.

"Well, madam, so you're here at last."

"Yes, Your Highness. I came as quickly as I could. What will be my duties exactly?"

Charles gave a cynical smile. "Very much as they were in Scotland, Miss Walkinshaw."

Clementina blushed. "Oh. I had thought I was to be your housekeeper."

The prince could have wept at her bluntness. She sounded like a streetwalker from the slums. A vision of Luci in all her radiance and beauty came to him and, by comparison, Clementina had all the attraction of a tired horse. At that moment he wished her back in her native land and silently berated himself for being so highly charged emotionally.

"You can be, most certainly. I shall only come and visit you when I feel the need," he answered, making things ten times worse.

"*Need*, sir?"

Was she being difficult or just plain stupid?

"To sleep with you, my dear girl. That is what we used to do, isn't it?"

"Well, yes, Highness. But I thought you were sending for me simply to keep house," she answered.

"That will be your principal job, Clementina. Though I'm afraid that I am somewhat short of funds at the moment. But I feel certain that you will be able to cope with everything."

It was difficult to say which was the more miserable of the two. Charles, mourning his lost love, or Clementina, remembering the brave young man who had made her feel a happiness that now could never be repeated. He had disappeared behind a wall of introverted silence which nothing and nobody could break down.

The great plot to kidnap the entire Hanoverian family fell apart in November. His companions immediately whispered that Clementina had secretly passed on the details, making the prince angrier than ever. It was not that he cared for Clementina — his ability to love had died with Luci — but he could not abide other people telling him what to do. He was also drinking too much, and he knew it.

One argument, however, was getting through. And it was that with Clementina in his house, he — Charles — was setting himself up for a personal attack. He had already been leapt on by villains and had only just managed to escape with his life. Further, he feared being seized by a Hanoverian snatch squad and taken to England to face Wee Georgie, that horrid little strutting dwarf, George II. And the fact that he had a woman known to the Hanoverians living with him was like putting up a flag.

Gone was the sentimental lover who used to see beauty in a flower. These days he made love in a business-like manner. Going into Clementina's room, getting on top of her, then thanking her and leaving again. He knew, deep in his heart, that he could not go on like this, that his entanglement was just a farce. So Charles began to take leaves of absence. In heavy disguise he attended a mardi gras ball in Paris, then went to Cologne where he rummaged through the bookshops and felt human for the first time since Luci died. But the Earl Marischal, with whom he had an appointment, warned him that he could be seized at any time as he walked along the banks of the Rhine, and Charles reluctantly moved on.

And then, one night when he was back home in Ghent, all his plans to ask Clementina to go home came to a shattering end.

He was sitting in the firelight, Clementina in a chair opposite his. Charles, stealing a glance at her, thought it really was time for the parting of ways. It was not that he believed the story about her being a spy — though admittedly there had been certain co-incidences — but the fact was that the poor soul bored him rigid. Luci would have been chatting, or reading, or singing a quiet happy song. But Miss Walkinshaw sat at her eternal embroidery saying nothing to anybody. That was until this night when, finally, she made a sound.

Charles lowered his paper. "Did you speak?"

"Yes. I've something to tell you, sir."

"Oh?"

Her next words were totally inaudible.

"I'm afraid I can't hear you."

"I've missed two courses, sir."

"Well, you can eat twice as much at the next meal."

"I meant my monthly flow, I've missed two. Oh don't be cross, Your Highness, but I believe I'm pregnant."

Charles leant back, stunned. He thought of his son by Louise, a child who — so he had been reliably informed — had died when but a few months old. And now, again, when he had been on the point of telling Clementina that it was all over between them, another baby.

"You are certain of this?"

"As certain as I can be without consulting a doctor."

"I see."

There was a muffled sound from opposite and Charles realised to his horror that Clementina had buried her face in her hands and was weeping.

"I knew you'd be angry," she muttered.

Everything that was decent in the prince rushed to the surface. He went to kneel beside her and put an arm round her quivering shoulders.

"There, there, my dear. I'm not cross. It's not your fault. I should have been more careful, taken precautions. Of course I'm pleased at the news."

She turned into his chest and wept bitterly. "Oh, My Prince, it's such a relief to hear you say that. I thought you would throw me out of the house."

Charles could not answer, thanking God that he had not put his thoughts into actions.

"Why should you think that? I'm not such an ogre, am I?"

"You can be when you've had too much to drink."

He shrugged the remark away. "Oh, all men are. At least I can hold an intelligent conversation."

She did not answer, instead weeping tears of relief into a small handkerchief which was already soaking wet.

"Here, take this." Charles produced a man's sensible square from his jacket pocket and gave it to her. Clementina blew her nose and the tears subsided. He looked at her, wondering what a cross between himself and this rather plain woman could possibly look like.

"So I'm going to have an heir?"

"Yes, you are."

"When?"

"October, I reckon. Though I must go to see a doctor soon. I am so happy that you are not angry with me, sir."

"Angry? No, I am… delighted."

But even as he said the words they rang as falsely in the prince's ears as though he had just told a huge lie — which, indeed, he had. If it had been poor fragile Luci who had whispered to him that she was expecting his child, he would have burst with pride and pleasure. But as it was, he had never loved Clementina — had used her when in Scotland as a girl with whom to enjoy the first, fine, free firings of youth — and now, had just been on the point of ending their relationship when she had broken the news.

A second factor that pursued the prince daily was the inexplicable loathing of her by his companions. The Jacobites, to a man, detested her, accused her of betraying the cause. No-one, but no-one, had ever asked to be introduced to her, and in private, Charles knew, they openly sneered at her. But now here she sat, like some sad whipped animal, gazing at him with a love-starved expression. Inwardly, Charles heaved a huge sigh.

*

The next seven months went slowly, Charles being kindly but distant. They slept in separate bedrooms and not once had he made his way into hers. It was as if the swelling body no longer appealed to him. Which was true, but only in the case of Clementina. When he was in love with Louise he had kissed her swelling womb, in the depths of which grew his child. And, oh with what joy he imagined the glory of Luci — the other half of him — growing larger and falling asleep in his arms, while their baby did a little dance for his pleasure. But Clementina had rather the opposite effect on him, and he had no wish to watch his child grow larger.

The presence of the prince's pregnant mistress, moreover, was like holding up a marker to indicate where he was to be found. The Earl Marischal warned him that he was not safe in any part of the Rhineland with Clementina in tow. Eventually, after much evasive action, the prince's household returned to Liege again and settled in a house there.

And it was in that house that, early in the morning of the twenty-ninth of October, Clementina went into labour and before midnight had given birth to a baby daughter, which she named

Charlotte. Charles took the child to the nearby church of Sainte Marie des Fonts, where she was immediately baptised. Then he returned, worn-out, and went on a drinking bout that lasted until the small hours of the following day.

He had at long last discovered why the Jacobites hated Clementina so much. She was writing to an ex-lover, no doubt moaning about the prince's behaviour to her. His name, Colonel John O'Sullivan, an Irishman who had joined the Young Pretender in Scotland and on whom the prince had bestowed great affection and loyalty.

It had all been revealed to the prince while she had been groaning in labour and had asked one of the midwives to send for her 'dear O'Sullivan'. Charles had been thunderstruck and had then gone downstairs, had a large brandy and worked it out for himself. It had been O'Sullivan he had contacted for Clementina's address in France whilst he — Charles — had still been in Paris. That was what had caused all the dislike — and Charles had been too blind to see it for himself.

But there was a problem with what to do about it. Clementina was slowly recovering from the birth, and the baby itself — poor little piece of nothing — was too small to send into the wicked world. For the time being, the prince's hands were tied. But he exploded angrily in a letter to Goring dated the twelfth of November 1753.

'She told me she had friends that would maintain her, so that, after such a declaration, and other impertinencies, makes me abandon her. I hereby desire you to find out who her friends are, that she may be delivered into their hands. Daniel is charged to conduct her to Paris.'

Charles also wrote a note to his valet de chambre. 'A marque to be put on the child, if I part with it. I am pushed to ye last point, and so won't be cajoled anymore.'

However, something very strange was about to happen to the Bonnie Prince. It was the moment when he fell in love with his daughter, and knew that she was definitely his. It was an event that was engraved on his memory for ever.

They had been visiting Paris in yet another desperate attempt to escape the murder squads that were out looking for him. Clementina had gone shopping, the child had been left in the care of servants, Charles was writing his interminable letters. Looking up, he had seen the handle of his study door turn. He had watched, his hand to his sword, as very slowly it had swung open. And there, standing in the doorway, its tiny face flushed with the effort of pushing the handle, stood a little blonde girl, all eyes and smiles, staring up at him.

Charles had got out of his chair and hurried towards her as she lurched forward, her small legs working so hard at their new-found skill of walking.

"Come on, come here. Come to…" He hesitated over the next word but managed to say 'Papa'. She had echoed him, "Papa," and given him a milk-toothed smile.

He had swept her up in his arms and looked deeply into her face and the likeness to himself had been there for the whole world to see. His heart had missed a beat.

"My goodness, you are indeed my daughter and a very pretty one at that. I think I shall call you Pouponne in future. Shall that be our secret? What do you think? Eh, my beautiful?"

She laughed, clapping her tiny hands together. Charles tickled her chin.

"Do you know what it means, sweetheart? Well, I'll tell you. Baby doll. You are my baby doll, ma petite pouponne."

She laughed all the more, then quite suddenly stopped and, leaning forward, gave the prince a kiss on the cheek. He smiled broadly, totally smitten. From that moment on, he gave his daughter his adoration and his soul. Clementina would remain in residence as long as Pouponne wanted her.

*

Five years of intense feeling followed. Pure and glorious pleasure when he was alone with Pouponne. Wicked and malevolent thoughts when he came face to face with Clementina. When he was drunk he shouted at her and gave her the occasional clout. When he was hand-in-hand with Pouponne, exclaiming over the wild flowers they found and the little creatures that scuttled away when human eyes descended on them, he felt a band of joy surround his heart. Never had father and child shared such a pure and blameless love. But Clementina's presence was beginning to wear Charles to a shadow, and more and more the idea of running away with Pouponne and leaving Miss Walkinshaw to her own devices began to grip every waking hour.

And now, after living with Clementina in this state of hatred, he was approaching the end of his tether. Alcohol had come to mean a great deal to him — he knew that he could almost be termed a drunk — but still found it hard to give up. His life, with no plots and plans, constantly on the look-out for life-threatening gangs, was empty, hopeless, dejected and disappointing. The only thing that gave him constant pleasure was Pouponne. The little smiles, her childish chatter, the way her face lit up when she saw him. The fact that she ran into his arms to receive his loving kisses. She was his only joy.

And then, one night in 1760 while they lived in a small village in France and Charles had been out, a tremendous surprise occurred. Clementina had stolen away with Charlotte, leaving behind a note stating that her principal reason for leaving him was the fear of losing her life at his hands.

The prince became mottled with fury. He did not care two tuppenny damns for Clementina, but to lose his beloved child, his only consolation for a dreary pointless life, was too much to bear. He was grief-stricken.

He wrote to his contact, the Abbé John Gordon, in Paris. 'I shall be in the greatest affliction until I get back the child, which was my only comfort in my misfortunes.'

The Abbé duly apprehended the missing woman as she was getting off the Paris coach. He found her lodgings and told her Charles' terms. The child was to be returned to the prince's care immediately. Clementina smiled, asked him for money and then vanished silently the next morning. Who knew where?

The prince was beside himself with grief. The house was empty, no childish chatter coming from upstairs, no tiny shoes pattering down the landing, no little kisses smothering his cheek. In his head he could hear her saying, "I love you, dear Papa," and he brought his fist thundering down onto the wooden table as tears started to pour.

But this was getting him nowhere. What he needed was a plan of action. Sitting down and resisting the temptation to pour himself a drink, Charles wrote a detailed list of all the people — friends and foe — who could possibly be sheltering Clementina and his beloved Pouponne. He then sent his valet, John Stewart, to Paris to search for them.

That night he had a vivid dream. He dreamt that he was rudely shaken by his brother Henry, someone Charles had not spoken to for years. But it was not a grown-up that shook him vigorously by the shoulder; it was the small boy that Henry had been.

"You smug-faced little worm, what are you doing in my bedroom?"

"Come to see how you're getting on without your precious Pouponne, that's what."

"I'll tell you something, beastly boy. I cannot live without her. She is the apple of my eye and I shall never know happiness until she comes back to me."

"Well, you might have to wait a long time."

"Why? What do you know? Come on, tell me."

Henry jumped off the bed and ran round it, sticking out his tongue. "I know things that you don't, so there."

Charles, who had also changed into a boy, leaped after him and caught one of Henry's ears which he twisted maliciously.

"Stop it! You're hurting! I won't tell you anything until you let go."

"What do you know, you little stinker?"

"I know where they're hiding out."

"You do?" said Charles, frankly astonished.

"Yes, because I'm the good boy and I know all Papa's secrets."

"What do you mean? What has Papa got to do with it?"

"You don't talk to him anymore, do you? Just like you don't talk to me. Think you're above us just because you went and had a fight with the Scots."

"I didn't fight them. They were on my side."

Henry thumbed his nose. "You know what I mean. Trust you to be difficult."

The dream was becoming unpleasant, reminding Charles of his actual boyhood.

"Go away," he shouted. "Leave me in peace to find my Pouponne."

"Shan't," Henry answered.

Charles punched him, but only hit the air as he woke up sweating.

The day was overhung by the nightmare and, almost as if it was expected, a note arrived by messenger from one of the women lookouts to whom Charles had written. It said that Clementina and Pouponne were definitely still in Paris.

"But where? In which place?" Charles screamed aloud.

And then came the final deadly blow. A letter arrived from King James III — Charles' father, with whom he had had no dealings in an age — saying that Clementina had put herself under his protection and this he had granted her. As for the child, Charlotte, she had been sent to a convent to be educated — and that was that.

James had thrust in the dagger and turned and re-turned it in the wound. The letter fell to the floor and Charles stared at the ceiling for hour upon hour. He would neither eat nor drink until Pouponne was restored to him. Neither would he forgive his father. Now there was nothing left to live for. It had all been taken away. From this moment on he would live in a house of whispers.

CHAPTER NINETEEN

Anne Webb

Tales of the prince's tragic breakdown soon reached Paris. The Jacobites, living in both England and France, blamed Clementina with one voice.

"Never could abide the woman. Knew damn well that she was spying for the other side. Pox on her that she could bring the prince so low."

"I remember him in Scotland. The youngest and fairest of warriors, so full of hope and glory. That it should have ended like this."

"Aye, you're right. I witnessed his entry into Edinburgh, it was unforgettable. He rode in on a gallant white horse and the women shouted for him. There's not one who wouldn't have gone to bed with him that night. And there was not a man in Scotland who would not have fought for Charlie. My God, but they were stirring times."

"So what exactly is the matter with His Highness now?"

"He is suffering from a total breakdown of all his faculties, madam."

"Why? Does anyone know?"

"I believe it is because his daughter was taken from him. He turned into such a bundle of nerves that at first he would eat and drink nothing.

Then eventually when he was too faint to walk, his doctor came and told him that he was killing himself and what good would that be when he found his Pouponne again? That stirred him into life once more, but nowadays he drinks enough for three men and eats most sparingly."

The woman who had spoken earlier made a tutting sound and said, "If I went to see him, do you think he would receive me?"

The men chuckled. "Much would depend on his mood but it might be worth a try, madam."

"I once cured a brother of mine of acute alcoholism. I thought I might attempt the same with the prince."

"Then good luck to you, Lady Webb. I'll write him a preparatory note. Not that it will do any good, mind. He never answers any correspondence these days."

"But he might read it. Besides, I feel ready for an adventure. I shall go uninvited."

*

The truth was that the great spirit of the Young Pretender was completely shattered. His sexual flings aside, he had loved only one woman in his life — Luci, who had died so pitiably young — and the rest of all the great well of emotion that bubbled beneath his rather charming exterior had been bestowed on that lovable scrap, Pouponne. The day that he had picked her up and looked closely into her face had been his undoing. He had loved her with a force that had frightened him and by taking her away, Clementina had delivered him a blow from which he could never recover. Unless, by some miracle, she might be returned to him.

Meanwhile, Charles lived in a pit of darkness and despair. He kept the shutters closed and the curtains drawn. The entire day was devoted to drinking, starting with a double brandy before he even got out of bed. So he was surprised one day whilst consuming his 'breakfast', when a servant came in.

"Forgive me for disturbing you, Highness, but a lady has called to see you."

"What?"

"A lady Jacobite, sir. She gave me her card."

Charles peered at it. "What does it say?"

"Anne, Lady Webb, and an address in London."

"And she's here?"

"Yes, outside in the hall."

"Damnation. What does she want?"

"I don't know. She didn't say."

"Oh, I suppose I'd better see the wretched creature. Offer her a drink or something. I'll have to have a shave, curse it."

Not only did the prince remove the red fuzz that had been growing on his face unchecked for some time, but he fetched from the back of his clothes press a striking suit in midnight blue silk. Its folds hung on him. He had sworn that he would eat nothing until Pouponne was returned to him. But though he had been forced to give that up when a medical man stated bluntly that he was starving himself to death, he was drinking far more than he ate, with the usual deleterious consequences.

Peering into a mirror in the bright light of day, he thought that he looked all of his forty-one years. He wished then that he could turn the clock back to when he was the Young Pretender, Scotland's Bonnie Prince. That had been the best and worst of times in one. But such magic was beyond his capabilities. Instead he must go and see this woman and find out what she wanted.

She was pretty in a rather striking way; dark brown hair swept up round her face and the length of it plaited and falling over one shoulder. Her eyes were a vivid hazel shade, deep set and clear. The face quite pointed and pixie-like. When she smiled — which she was doing now — she displayed small teeth. Charles drew himself up and held out his hand for the customary kiss. Did he imagine it or did she bite him slightly? Whether she did or didn't, he felt a rush of pleasure leap in his tired and miserable loins.

"Oh Your Highness, what an honour it is to meet you at last. I have wished for this moment ever since I was a girl and now, finally, my dream has come true," she gushed.

"You flatter me indeed, madam. I was thinking today that I looked rather worn out."

"There is a certain sadness in your eyes, sir, but that would be explained by the loss of your pretty daughter."

"You know all about that, do you?" Charles sighed. "Yes, she was taken from me two years ago."

"Well, I have news for you, sir. I glimpsed her only the other day."

"You did?" Charles sat down, indicating that the woman should do likewise. "Where?"

"In an art gallery. The sisters had taken their pupils on an educational visit and I saw Pouponne amongst them."

"You are sure it was her?"

"Quite definitely. Her picture was widely distributed at the time of her kidnapping. For that is how we Jacobites regard the incident, Highness. Charlotte was kidnapped by that wretched woman. How *dare* she take a child of royal blood?"

"Indeed, indeed. But tell me, how was Charlotte looking? Was she pale and miserable?"

"To be quite honest with you, sir, she was giggling with another girl when I saw her."

"Really? At what?"

Lady Webb gave a delicious, crystal-clear laugh. "A nude Greek statue. Male, sir. Need I say more?"

For the first time in two years the prince put his head back and let out a bellow that shook the house.

"Oh my God, she takes after me in more than looks."

"I didn't know that male statues had that effect on *you*, sir," squeaked Anne Webb, tears coursing from her eyes.

The prince fell around in his chair, shrieking with laughter, clutching his sides, weeping with mirth. A servant, nervously putting his head round the door, saw the couple convulsed and withdrew again quickly.

"He's laughing, he's actually *laughing*."

"Thank God," said Charles' valet de chambre. "May this magical woman stay for the rest of her life."

It was as if Anne Webb did indeed hold some strange enchantment, for once the prince had reassured himself that all was well with Pouponne, he felt as if a tremendous hole in his chest had been stitched back together. The child was having a good — too good! — education. She looked bonny and well and he could not ask for more. Except that he wished his father, King James, would allow him access to her. But none of these thoughts were in his mind as he looked down the length of the dining table and saw a pretty, pert face looking back at him.

"How long can you stay, Lady Webb?"

"A week, sir, if that would be convenient. And I do wish that you would call me by my given name of Anne."

"And to return the compliment may I ask you to address me as Charles?"

"Oh no, Your Highness, that would be going too far. *My prince* is as much familiarity as I would allow myself."

Charles grinned. "Very well then, Anne. You must do as you please."

He did not drink as much as usual, wanting to stay fully aware of the ripple and flow of her clear-cut conversation. She was sharp as a toothpick and now that he had laughed again, after two years of miserable silence, he was enjoying himself enormously. His loins, which had remained relatively quiet during his long harsh mourning for Pouponne, were now quite definitely active again. He began to make a few tentative enquiries.

"Tell me about your husband. Is he an elderly man?"

"Not particularly, sir. However I do have one relation who will be of great interest to your royal self."

"And who might that be?"

"The Earl of Derwentwater. If you will remember, he came out for your father in the uprising of 1715. He died a martyr's death, I fear."

"Of course. A very great man. I am honoured to meet one of his clan."

"The honour is entirely mine, my prince. Remember that my family is willing to serve you in any way you choose."

This had to be the remark that Charles had been hoping for.

"Do I take it correctly that would include yourself in that, Lady Webb?"

Her crystal eyes were dancing in the candlelight.

"Of course, Highness. I am entirely at your command."

"Then may I join you when you withdraw?"

"Certainly, sir."

As soon as she left the room, Charles bolted for his own quarters where he attacked his teeth with a fearsome--looking brush and gargled madly with a rosewater mouthwash.

"By God," he muttered to his reflection, "I'm not used to this. Village girls are one thing, but a lady of quality is an entirely different kettle of fish."

However, telling himself that he had not lost an iota of his charm, he made his way a few minutes later into the pink salon into which Lady Webb had been ushered by a bowing servant. She was fast asleep on the sofa, her breathing rather stertorous, her dark hair spread on a cushion. She looked very small and somewhat innocent.

Charles sat down in a chair opposite and watched her sleep, sipping a brandy, and thinking that he had no right to disturb such sweetness. She had made him laugh, had restored his humanity, made him realise that Pouponne was well and happy. After a while he got up and quietly left the room, leaving the sleeping beauty to enjoy her rest undisturbed.

Over the next few days the pair of them grew close in every way. Though nothing could ever replace Luci in the prince's affection, Anne Webb became a woman in whose company he could happily have spent the rest of his life. He stopped drinking quite so heavily, went out for long walks and even longer rides, laughed and joked and giggled. They went to bed together with enormous ease and comfort, each giving to the other a sense of well-being. Lady Webb's husband was not mentioned again. That is, until the day she left.

"Must you really go, Anne? I shall be lonely without you."

"I am afraid so, Your Highness. I must return to my poor old husband. It is my duty to do so. Just as it is my duty to stop your enormous consumption of alcohol."

"I do wish you would let that subject drop."

"If I don't, it will be you who will be doing the dropping, sir."

"How dare you speak to me in this manner?"

"I dare because I care for you, Your Highness."

Charles let out a deep sigh. "Why do women have to nag all the time?"

"Because you are a beautiful and wonderful man. A great and good man. A man much sinned against. And I would hate to see that man kill himself because fate has turned against him."

"I suppose that when you are gone, you will write nasty things to me."

"Not if you take care of yourself."

"But how will you know?"

"Oh, I shall find out, never fear."

She turned away and when she looked at him again, Charles saw that her eyes were brilliant with tears.

"You really worry about me, don't you?" he exclaimed, not truly believing it even while he said the words.

"Yes," she answered quietly. "I really, really do."

And with that she gave a deep and reverential curtsey and stepped into the awaiting coach. The prince watched until it had drawn out of sight and then turned back into the chateau, sighing heavily. He knew that what Anne said was true. He was drinking too much and disliked the effect it was having on him. He relied on its first warming comfort to get through the day and then, when he was sodden with it, hated himself for being so dependent. He needed a woman like Anne Webb to take charge of his life. But even more than that he needed the company of Pouponne.

As predicted, the first letter from Lady Webb was full of the subject.

I have knowledge enough to know that your preservation is a miracle of divine providence. You think you have, and it is true, a very good constitution but you don't eat enough to support it. The quantity of wine you drink continually heats your blood to such a degree that the least inflammation would carry you off in a few hours.

"Oh damn the blasted woman," muttered the prince, but nevertheless put down the glass of wine he had been about to consume and wandered instead into the garden. "But she's right," he continued the conversation with himself. "I must make some effort. I must go hunting and riding like I used to. I must cut down on the booze. For Pouponne's sake, it shall be done."

And by some enormous effort of an iron will, Charles got back to something resembling a normal life and was seen out and about, taking the air and looking vastly improved in health.

He kept up this regime for three whole years and then, one cold December night, in the year 1764, just when he was about to retire, something completely unexpected happened.

He was dressed casually in a crimson satin gown with a rather dashing cap on his head, sitting by the fire with a stray cat that had wandered in from somewhere asleep at his feet, when he heard a carriage rumble up the driveway and stop outside. He had no idea who could be calling at this hour of the evening and, reluctantly getting up from his chair, crossed to the door of his salon and peered out.

The hall was dark, lit only by a few candles, and Charles could not see anyone, though he could hear the distant sound of voices in the background. Then suddenly he heard a burst of laughter and saw a figure approaching through the gloom. For a minute he thought it was the Walkinshaw woman and his heart sank into his boots. Then he heard a voice calling, "Where are you, my Bonnie Prince?"

"Anne!" he shouted and dashed into the passageway and picked her up off her feet. "You've come back, you little devil! How did you get in? I told Goring to ban you from the house. But where have you been these past few years?"

"My husband has been very unwell, alas. But seriously, did you ban me?"

"Yes. I thought you would nag me about my drinking. However, I don't think Goring took it to heart. Well, obviously he didn't because here you are and I've never been more pleased to see anyone."

They kissed with the familiarity of old friends.

"I do hope, my prince, that you were not sitting drinking brandy."

Charles shuffled his slippered feet. "I was just having a nightcap to keep out the cold."

"It is indeed a bitter night. But you will have someone to warm your bed tonight."

"You little rogue," he said, and playfully smacked her bottom.

Slipping off her fur lined cloak, she took a chair opposite his on the other side of the great fireplace.

"I have some wonderful news, Charles."

"Which is?"

"Your brother Henry…"

"What about him?"

"He is eager to be reconciled with you, but is too nervous to write to you direct."

The prince leant back in his seat. "That devil from hell. He has been a thorn in my side ever since he was born."

"You were jealous of him," Anne Webb stated forthrightly.

Charles frowned, never enjoying criticism but taking it from this amazing woman who had somehow wheedled her way into his life and turned it around.

"Yes, I was. He was such a sweet-looking baby and Papa loved him like the infant Jesus. Little snot."

"That is hardly the way to describe a cardinal of Rome."

"No, it isn't. But I shall never forgive him or my father for taking in that wretched Walkinshaw woman and denying me the company of my own daughter."

Anne took a sip of her brandy. "Highness, listen to me. Your brother is a cardinal — whether you like it or whether you do not — and did what he thought was the right thing at the time. You cannot go on holding a grudge for ever. He wants you to be his friend again and I see no reason why you should not accept his offer. There, I've said what I came to say and now I suppose you will dislike me for the rest of your life."

Charles did not answer, staring into the fire, a morose expression on his face. Eventually he spoke.

"I could never dislike you, Lady Webb. You always speak your mind — and for that I admire you. If someone else had been as forthright I would have had them removed from my company. So let us for the time being change the subject. Please, stay a while with me and I will give you my answer before you leave."

Anne smiled in the shadows. She knew she had won the day. She also knew that to remark on it would be fatal. So she simply said, "You are looking well, my prince."

"Am I?" He glanced up. "Damned if I feel it. Do you know I shall be forty-four on New Year's Eve?"

Now was the time for some kindness. "You are coming into your prime, Highness. They say that a man is at his most powerful between the ages of forty-five and sixty."

"Really? I can't say that I agree."

"Well, you won't know until you try."

The strange cat, fast asleep at the prince's feet a moment before, suddenly came to life and walked majestically from the room.

"Is that yours?" asked Anne. "I thought you were a dog lover."

"Having been a stray myself," Charles answered thoughtfully, "I now give shelter to anything that asks for it. Dogs, cats, all God's creatures — they are one and the same to me."

"And your brother? Is he not a stray in this world too?"

"And am I not the greatest stray of all? I had a purpose once, years ago, when I was in my sky blue youth. I was to be the saviour of Scotland. I ended up hunted, sleeping rough, covered with lice, bitten half to death by midges. So that was the end of my sweet dream. Did you know that twice I had to don the garb of a female in order to escape?"

Anne threw back her head with laughter. "Did you? Did you really dress as a woman? I never knew that."

"Indeed I did. I wanted to carry a pistol beneath my skirts for protection but Miss Flora Macdonald would not let me. She said that I might be searched. I answered that if I was examined *that* closely, I would soon be revealed for what I truly was. She did not laugh."

"Where were you going?"

"Over the sea to the Isle of Skye."

"It all sounds very romantic."

"It does when I recount the story — but in fact, it was terrifying."

"Yes," Anne answered thoughtfully, "it must have been."

In fact, she considered, the Bonnie Prince's life must have been one long frustration, so it was small wonder that he had turned to womanising, to drinking too much, to loving his small daughter who was snatched away from him by Clementina.

"It must have been the last straw," she said aloud.

"What?" he answered.

"When Miss Walkinshaw left and took Pouponne with her."

"Clementina was not all that she seemed," he answered shortly. "And I would rather not add anything to that statement, if it is all the same to you Lady Webb."

Anne gracefully bowed her head and turned the conversation to other matters. Soon, she felt certain, Charles and Henry — the cardinal duke — would be reunited and then, hopefully, the Bonnie Prince could know some happiness once again.

CHAPTER TWENTY

Henry and Charlotte

It was bitterly cold. The snow blew at a slant, east to west, filling the driveway, covering the hedges, the trees glistening with a million droplets from a chandelier of ice. The animals had long since been herded into shelters except for one poor sheep that had run away and now raised its voice in a pathetic mewl as it slowly froze to death. Everywhere, as far as the eye could see, was a glinting, blinding, tapestry of various shades of creamy white.

A cavalcade of coaches was making its way up the drive, the breath of the plumed horses pulling the leading conveyance shimmering in the air above their heads. They came to a halt at the front door of the Château de Carlsbourg, in the small town of Bouillon. Prince Charles Edward Stuart was at long last leaving, at long last in contact with his brother Henry, at long last putting behind him all the misery and loss of equilibrium caused by the disappearance of his only living child. His personal effects were going to Rome, he was going to Paris for private reasons, among these to lay flowers at Luci's grave. Then he would proceed to the papal city, to join Henry.

The bitter weather had gripped France as well; Paris was employing snow sweepers in every street except for those filthy lanes where the people of good breeding would never dare venture. Chantilly, that sweet little town where Luci had been laid to rest, was frozen solid. Charles slithered and slid in the graveyard and eventually fell to his knees — not intentionally — before her sad, small headstone. He gazed at it, saying nothing, not even weeping, for a long time before he spoke.

"Luci, my darling, I am sorry to have left you so long alone. A great deal has happened to me in those intervening years. I wish you had met my Pouponne, my lovely little girl. I hear she is quite big now and that she looks very much like me. But you should have been her mother, sweetheart. Then, how differently things would have turned out."

He cried then, silently, tears slipping down the side of his nose. Meanwhile the cold penetrated his legs and feet, where he knelt in the snow, and it was the faithful John Stewart, who had been with the prince since Scotland and who had gone in search of the missing Pouponne when Clementina had first walked out, who finally raised him.

"Come along, Your Highness, you can do no more good here. Luci will hear you wherever you are."

And putting his arm round his royal master's waist, he led him out of the graveyard and into the waiting coach and back to the icy city of Paris.

*

He could hardly believe it. His father, James — to whom he had not spoken or written a word since the debacle over Clementina and Pouponne — died on the second day of his journey from Paris to Rome. Charles was notified of the death at Urbino, given a hastily scribbled note from his brother. It took a long time for it to sink in that he was no longer the Bonnie Prince but now King Charles III. In the eyes of the Scots at least, though the Pope in Rome was making a terrific to-do about it. Whatever people thought, Charles knew the truth and entered the coach with a certain amount of pride.

The rest of the journey was frightful. The roads were practically impassable, there was a terrible accident, his vehicle actually overturning and crashing to a halt right by a steep precipice. Several people were hurt but Charles crawled out uninjured. Andrew Lumisden, a Scottish Jacobite who had fought in the '45, met him two changing posts beyond Florence and was shocked to see that he was suffering with swollen legs and feet from sitting so long in one position. He kissed Charles' hand.

"Your Majesty," he said.

The former prince stared at him. "You are the first person to call me that. Thank you."

Lumisden bowed low. "I have known you since you were a boy, sir. You were one of the most courageous young lads I have ever seen. And you have had your amount of suffering as well. Now you have come into your own so I will say it again. God bless Your Majesty."

Charles extended his hand and the Scotsman kissed it. Shortly afterwards, he got into another coach and continued his nightmare journey, over roads glistening with snow and ice, towards the papal city. Finally on the twenty-third of January 1766, Charles spotted the outskirts of the place he had last clapped eyes on twenty-two years ago.

When he entered the Piazza San Apostoli a small crowd began to cheer and shout 'Viva il re!' Charles turned to Lachlan Mackintosh, who had commanded a regiment in the '45.

"D'you hear that, Lachlan? They're greeting me. I think it's marvellous."

Mackintosh — who had more than a sneaking suspicion that the claque had been organised by Charles' brother Henry — merely nodded his head and smiled.

For Charles, entering the Palazzo Muti again after all the years away, came as something of a terrible shock. For there, once he had got past the phalanx of bowing servants and walked into the receiving room, was the brother he had both loved and hated for nearly every moment of his life. At first, Charles was blinded by the flash of scarlet that greeted his eyes. Then Henry Benedict was on his feet and inclining his head, with its vivid red skull cap.

"My dear brother," he said, his voice deeper and quieter than Charles remembered it.

The prince could not answer, too overcome with an emotion that was difficult to analyse. Instead he burst into tears, overwhelmed by the moment, all the mixed feelings welling up inside him. Surprisingly, Henry wept too, the deep brown eyes — a shade darker than his brother's — full of tears. Thus they stood, arms round each other, neither saying a word.

"It's been a long time, brother," Charles managed to gasp out at last.

"Too long," answered Henry from deep inside the folds of the prince's coat. "Far too long. But know, my very dear chap, that I have always loved you and will continue to do so for all that remains of my life."

Charles was too overcome to answer, despising himself for the years of hatred and jealousy that he had been spitefully levelling against this good, kind man. Eventually, he pulled away from their close embrace and stared deeply into Henry's face.

It had altered considerably and his brother was no longer the youthful creature who had haunted his imagination. The round, chubby visage had grown longer, more pointed about the chin. The eyes, which had once looked at Charles so mockingly, were now velvety in their benevolence. Yet there was a certain toughness behind them. A look which the prince recognised in himself. The hair, what Charles could see of it, was dark under its full-bottomed wig. But the eyebrows, nose and mouth were exactly like those of Charles. He felt that it would be easy enough to masquerade one as the other.

"I've missed you," said Henry. "I felt quite broken by the fact that my brother no longer wanted me."

"I *did* want you," Charles answered slowly. "It was just that I was so upset by the loss of Pouponne that I could no longer think properly."

"Do you hear from the child at all?"

"Nothing, not a word."

"And how old is she now?"

Charles looked slightly uncomfortable. "She must be about eleven. The Walkinshaw woman wrote to me at the time of her birthday."

"What did she want?"

"She was pleading for Charlotte's recognition."

"And?"

"I don't know. I haven't made up my mind. But tell me something, Henry. Am I really regarded as Charles III here in Rome? A small crowd cheered me in. But does the Pope recognise me as such?"

A strange expression flitted across Henry's features. "Not yet, I fear. I am going to see him tomorrow to explain the situation fully."

"Does anyone believe that I am the king?"

"Oh yes, sir," answered Henry, sinking down on one knee, his magnificent gown rustling. "May I be the first to kiss your hand?"

"Yes," the prince replied, his heart leaping with joy, "and you may kiss me on the cheek as well."

And he seized the cardinal duke in a boyish hug and held him tightly, just as he had all those years ago.

*

His legs and feet were terribly swollen after all the hours of travelling so, having settled himself in at his childhood home, Charles took to his bed to get them back to normal. He was quite proud of his legs and Anne Webb's warning about too much alcohol making them dropsical was always in the back of his mind. So, much as he loved the bottle, he tried to keep the amounts in moderation.

As soon as the limbs were back to normal he was out and about, walking in the Corso, fully masked, which was fun. He went to the opera, and parties. Furthermore, he started travelling, hunting, going rustic in the country, having lovely long dinners with his brother, playing the cello — at which he was very good — and developing a growing fondness for Cyprus wines.

Meanwhile the Pope — a rather nasty little man — refused outright to allow Charles to take the title of king and, furthermore, insisted on the prince kneeling and kissing his toe — not a pleasant pastime. Then, to add insult to injury, he had kept him on the floor for a full fifteen minutes. Inwardly, Charles seethed at the indignity. But there was nothing he could do. Clement XIII was a puffed up pontiff and his word was final.

Afterwards, Charles questioned Henry closely but there was no action his brother could take. It was an impossible situation and both of them knew it. Angrily, the prince left for his country retreat and though he had sworn to himself that he wouldn't, he hit the bottle again quite hard. Once again, drink was becoming a serious problem for the man, not young enough now to recover next day.

Still it took away his feelings of utter rejection, of being a total failure in every aspect of his life. Scotland had been a complete defeat; his first child — poor little boy — was claimed by another man and then died in infancy; his love affair with de Talmont had turned to hatred; his beloved Pouponne had been snatched away from him. But above all these bitter and terrible losses had been the death of dear, faithful and kind Luci. His one love, taken in all her youth and beauty by consumption. It was small wonder that his hand went out for the drink bottle and as the warmth hit his stomach, he felt better. Still there was one thing that would revive his spirits. To see his little Pouponne again. Charles picked up his cello and as he drew the bow across the strings, he thought of her and dreamed a little.

*

It was her fifteenth birthday and for a special treat her mother, Clementina, was taking her out for tea. Out from the convent where she boarded and studied, out into the wonderful city of Paris, out to where people lived and breathed and enjoyed being alive.

Life had not really been very exciting since they had left her papa. Even thinking about him now made Charlotte go a little moist in the eye. To this day she had strong memories of him. After all, she had been six when her mother whisked her away for reasons that she couldn't fully understand. He had been such fun to play with, so affectionate towards her. However, Charlotte found it difficult to comprehend why he never replied to her letters. She had been writing to him since she was eleven and answers never came. But this was not the moment to think about it. Instead, she turned to the mirror.

A serious person stared back. A person with waist-length brown hair, greenish eyes and a face that her mother had told her was 'very Stuart'. If 'Stuart' meant a long nose, thought Charlotte, it was definitely true. She turned sideways and decided that perhaps her profile was her best feature. Sighing, she pinched her cheeks to give them a little colour and left the small cubicle, which passed for her bedroom, in one of the convent's quiet passageways.

Clementina was waiting for her downstairs, looking defeated, an expression which clouded her face until she smiled. This she did on seeing her daughter.

"You're growing tall, dearest."

"Like my father."

Clementina sighed. "Yes, he was very long in the body."

"Is it bad for a female to be so?"

"No, as long as you don't tower over your suitors."

"I promise I won't."

Clementina smiled and slipped her arm through her daughter's. The one good thing that had come out of her relationship with the Bonnie Prince, in her opinion anyway.

They made their way through the crowded streets until they came to the Café Procope, founded in the late 1600s, where they sat down at an elegant little table for two and ordered tea and gateaux. Charlotte gazed about her, loving the luxury and splendour, in total contrast to the bleakness of the convent. Much as she enjoyed her education — her agile mind willingly absorbing the various subjects taught — she wished that she dwelt in more luxurious surroundings.

Realising that someone was looking at her, Charlotte lowered her gaze, then glanced quickly up again. It was a man dressed in black clothes, his eyes the colour of the evening sky, his lips curving into a smile despite his attempt to look serious. She was smiling before she realised what she was doing and quickly switched her attention back to her mother. Even though Charlotte was apparently studiously studying the menu, she knew that the stranger was continuing to stare at her. She could feel his glance, then heard his light baritone voice as he spoke to a waiter.

"May I see the wine list, please?"

"Certainly, Monsieur de Rohan."

So he was known in this charming café. Obviously a man of substance. From under her lashes Charlotte stole another glance. He was dashingly handsome and though he wore a short tie-wig, the girl could see a hint of dark hair beneath. This together with his delightful smile was enough to make her heart leap. He knew perfectly well that she was looking at him though he kept his gaze firmly fixed on the list that the waiter had handed him.

And then he did the most wonderful thing. He stood up and bowed to Clementina.

"Forgive me, madame, but I feel that we have met somewhere. Is it possible? Ferdinand de Rohan, at your service."

He bowed again. Clementina looked puzzled.

"I do not believe so, monsieur."

"But surely I cannot be mistaken? Perhaps I saw you at one of my mother's little gatherings. She is the Princesse de Rohan. She regularly hosts soirées."

"I do not believe that I am acquainted with the lady, though I am flattered, of course, that you should think so."

Everything hung in the balance and Charlotte felt that she had one toe poised on the brink of life. Then the wheel of fortune clicked a notch and Clementina spoke.

"Would you care to join us, monsieur? I don't think I have had the pleasure of meeting your mother, though I should very much enjoy doing so."

"Then you shall, madame. I will speak to her tonight." He shot Charlotte a look, his eyes alight with triumph. In fact one eyelid shot down and up again, very briefly but very definitely. She could not help smiling at him as if they were conspirators in a well-rehearsed scenario. She was fifteen years old and already half-way in love.

"This is my daughter, Charlotte."

"The pleasure is entirely mine," he said, and gave another, even deeper, bow before gravely kissing her hand.

The waiter, appearing as if he had been instructed, produced another chair and listened as Ferdinand whispered instructions to him.

"Will you join me in a glass of champagne, madame?"

"I do not drink, monsieur, having seen the effect it had upon certain erstwhile friends."

Charlotte spoke up. "May I have a glass, Mama?"

"No. I should think not indeed."

Ferdinand said, "Oh please, madame. Just on this one occasion. If you would be kind enough to permit."

"Very well. But just a small glass, Charlotte."

Ferdinand brightened. "A beautiful name for a beautiful daughter. Is she named for you, madame?"

"No, for her father," Clementina answered abruptly.

Charlotte was on the point of telling him who her father was but was silenced by a piercing look from her mother.

"He must have been very charming," Ferdinand replied — and once more gave that rapid sideways look at the object of his attention.

*

The very next day, Clementina received an invitation addressed to the Countess Alberstroff, as she now styled herself.

"It's to a soirée at the home of the Princesse de Rohan," she exclaimed aloud as she broke the seal. "And you have been invited as well!"

"Oh please, Mama, let me go. I know I am young but I must start soon mingling in society. Otherwise I will grow up into a regular lumpkin."

Clementina looked severe, an expression she would never have adopted in her daisy youth when she had fallen madly in love with the Bonnie Prince.. And, very vaguely, she remembered the feelings that she had had then.

"Oh, very well. But I think I had better get you a new dress. Your old one is rather shabby."

Charlotte flew at her, smothering her with kisses and words of love and Clementina recalled how once — so very long ago — Prince Charles had done just the same to her and she would have granted him the world had it been hers to give.

*

So, looking as attractive as she possibly could, Charlotte set out for her first grown-up party, longing to see where Ferdinand lived and to talk to his brothers and sisters and be accepted by them. But when she got there she first had to be received by a rather austere and somewhat unfriendly and very upright lady who regarded her through a hand-held lorgnette.

"And you are?"

"Charlotte Stuart, ma'am."

"With the Countess *Alberstroff*? Why do you have a different name?"

"Because Stuart is my father's name. The Countess is my mama. They have separated."

"I see."

The next minute, Ferdinand appeared from nowhere, and in a very boisterous mood saying, "These are the delightful people with whom I became acquainted recently, mother dear."

The princess turned the lorgnette on her son. "Really? Well, well."

Charlotte felt a sense of injustice rising in her.

"My father is…" she started to say — and then she thought better of it. She knew that Charles had been truly brave, that he had loved and played with her as if there were no such thing as time for bed, that she — in return — had adored the very ground he walked on. But Charlotte also knew that he and Mama had had a terrible falling out and that these days Clementina had adopted both a ridiculous title and a silly name. So she swallowed her words, dropped a deep and royal curtsey, and said, "I am honoured to have been invited, Your Highness."

A hand at her elbow helped her as she straightened up and a voice whispered in her ear, "Delighted you could come. You have made the evening bright, my dear."

She looked at Ferdinand and thought him quite the most handsome of young men.

"And you have made it joyful by your very presence, sir," she answered.

He grinned at her. He had that delightful way of appearing solemn and then suddenly breaking into a smile that lifted the heart. Charlotte knew at that moment — come what may — that she would love him deeply until the day she died.

"Let me find a place where we can talk quietly," he said. "There are certain things I have to say to you."

"You're not angry with me, are you?"

Ferdinand looked at her in genuine surprise. "Good heavens, no. Whatever gave you that idea?"

"I don't know. A childhood memory perhaps."

"Why should that be? It wasn't an unhappy time was it?"

"It was a great deal happier when my father was there."

"Do you no longer see him?"

"He and Mama fell out and she ran away from him. He used to call me his Pouponne."

A sudden tear glistened in Charlotte's eye and Ferdinand wiped it away with his finger.

"Your dew," he said quietly.

"I'm sorry."

"You must have loved him very much."

"I did. He was just so wonderful to be with. That is when one could get close to him, of course."

"What do you mean?"

"Well he was often surrounded by his advisers and gentlemen."

"Why? Was he somebody important?"

"He was — still is — Charles Edward Stuart."

There was an audible gasp, then Ferdinand said, "You don't mean the hero of Scotland?"

"Yes, I do. He is my papa."

Inwardly Charlotte glowed with satisfaction at the look on her companion's face.

"Then I am honoured to be in your company, Miss Stuart."

"Oh please, call me Charlotte. I really do prefer it."

That they should become a couple was destiny. It was as if they had always known one another, could only be truly happy in each other's company, were the two halves of a whole. They spent that evening laughing, talking, giving one another admiring glances. Towards the end of it Ferdinand whispered, "I must see you alone."

"I am a pupil at a convent school."

"But surely you get time off?"

"We do, but it is strictly monitored."

"Don't worry. I'll think of a way round it."

*

On her next free Saturday afternoon Charlotte received a note, apparently from her mother, asking her to go straight to a tea garden as it was not convenient to pick her up at school. Not sure whether it was genuine or not, she made her way there only to see Ferdinand, smiling his lovely smile, rising from his chair and bowing. She blushed with pleasure, her heart telling her that she would love him always.

"My dear girl," he said. "You look exquisite in that little dress. I am so proud to be in your company."

"And I yours."

After the ordering of their tea and various delectable gateaux had been brought to the table, Ferdinand took one of her hands by the wrist.

"There are several things I have to tell you about myself, some of which you are not going to like."

Charlotte nodded but did not speak, her mouth full of cake.

"First of all, I am considerably older than you are, fifteen years older, to be precise. Secondly I am the youngest son of a family who, by tradition, send their junior sons into the church."

He paused and Charlotte gazed at him, not liking what she was hearing at all.

"Have you nothing to say?"

"No. Please continue."

"The fact is, dearest darling Charlotte — pretty Pouponne — that I can't offer you anything but my undying love. I cannot marry you,

I will be bound by the regulations of the church never to wed. I fear I am too old for you, in fact I believe I am a complete wretch who is trifling with your affections."

Charlotte briefly put her hand on his. "But you are not trifling with me, are you?"

"No, my dear. But the fact is that the king himself is going to grant me permission to become an archbishop. My family want it so much, you see. As for me, I intend to live as normal a life as is possible in the circumstances."

"Are you saying you want me to become your mistress?"

Ferdinand put his head back and laughed long and cheerfully.

"When you are a bit older, yes. Meanwhile, can we just continue courting?"

"I'd like that very much," Charlotte answered — and taking his hand, held it close to her.

CHAPTER TWENTY-ONE

Charles and Charlotte

The prince was singing in the bath, cleaning his chest hair vigorously with a long-handled soapy brush, looking down at his body and thinking it was not in bad shape considering all the punishment it had taken in his forty-nine years on the planet. In short, he was feeling better than he had done in years.

The reason was perfectly simple. He had gone to Viterbo to take the health-giving waters, had eaten a sensible diet, cut down his drinking and put himself into the hands of a good doctor, following the man's advice to the letter. Furthermore, there was an excellent social scene, a good opera season, exciting and enjoyable company. For the first time in an age, Charles had stopped thinking about the past and turned his mind to the future. And the principle thought was marriage. He would soon be in his fifties and the need to have a legitimate heir to the Stuart dynasty was starting to bother him. His dear sweet Pouponne was a bastard and therefore could not succeed.

The only fly in the ointment was Charles' need to be recognised as king by the Pope. The old one had died and a new man had taken his place. But as the prince's brother had pointed out, there were difficulties. Yet when Charles had met the new pontiff he had been treated with every courtesy, the Pope — Clement XIV — insisting on standing throughout the entire interview. He had told Charles that though he personally would like nothing more than to restore his full title, there were terrible complications in the way. By the time the meeting was at an end, the prince had realised that it was a hopeless task. In future he would appear in Roman society as Baron Renfrew. And why that pseudonym, Charles — who had thought it up — had no idea.

*

Charlotte often wrote to him, sending her love, enquiring about his health, saying what a struggle it was to make ends meet. He never replied because she still lived with Clementina, for whom Charles now had an implacable hatred. So many Jacobites had told him that not only had she had a lover but that she was also a Hanoverian spy, that he had come to believe it.

Ferdinand had reluctantly taken his place in the church but wrote to Charlotte daily, even if it was only to scrawl 'I love you' on a piece of paper. Their meetings were occasional but wonderfully romantic and soon after her seventeenth birthday, Ferdinand had taken her virginity away in a small Parisian hotel to which he had travelled incognito. Like her father, Charlotte adored making love, yet she feared pregnancy. But Ferdinand was careful and always came to their rendezvous armed with sheaths made of a sheep's gut and tied with blue ribbons at the top.

"What would your cardinals say if they could see you?" she had asked as Ferdinand was putting one on.

"God be praised, I would imagine."

"You are so naughty, do you know that?"

"As are you, Miss Stuart," he answered as he slid deliciously within her.

And there the conversation had turned into shouts of delight, of pleasure, of ecstasy, until they both shot up on a fountain of sweet sensation and afterwards fell asleep.

*

Charles had at long last found a princess willing to marry him. He knew that he would never love her in the least, all that emotion being taken up by his perfect woman, his darling Luci, who had been snatched from him by cruel death. However, the important thing was to sire an heir. The girl was eighteen and her name was Louise of Stolberg. She was also — unbeknown to anyone — shrewd and had her eye on the main chance.

An offer to become the future Queen of England appealed to her. The interminable ins and outs of the marriage contracts being drawn up, the marriage portion to be settled, the pin money to be decided upon, and so on and so forth, took their time. Eventually though, a proxy ceremony was performed in Paris, using a stand-in bride, while Louise set out for Italy. When she eventually arrived, after spending nineteen hours in the coach, she put on a reverential smile as she stepped out of the conveyance and took Charles' hand.

She was disappointed. She had heard much of his daring and his wild good looks but all she saw was a middle-aged man who had at some time hit the bottle too hard. Still, he had pleasing eyes and a nice smile and his figure was good, she thought, as she curtsied deep.

Charles, however, was entranced. Here was prettiness — a round face, fine red lips, a high — slightly large — bust, and dark blue lustrous eyes with a glitter in their very centre. But her beauty was of the superficial kind, alas. On looking twice, the prince decided that he could not expect much in the way of intellectual stimulation. But, sadly, he was not in the first flush of youth and the poor child was not to know that he had given his heart years ago and could never do so again.

The wedding ceremony took place in the private chapel of the palace of Compagnoni Marefoschi. Charles dressed to the inch, his bride looking equally splendid. Her mother, very oddly — or so the prince considered — had insisted on immediate consummation, so he led Louise to the bridal chamber quite promptly after the formalities and there set to it.

It was very far from his best performance and Louise had simply closed her eyes and accepted fate, which left him feeling sad. But still she was young yet — a mere twenty, the marriage plans having taken two years to reach conclusion.

The next day had been better when the crowds shouted, 'Viva il re,' and a grand reception given by the couple for the benefit of the local dignitaries did not end until three in the morning. Shortly afterwards the newly-weds set off for Rome with eighteen post horses, Louise sitting very upright and expecting to be greeted as queen at every stop they made.

*

"Oh, it's too much," shrieked Clementina, throwing the note she had received into the air.

"What?" said her daughter, slightly dazed, only having briefly returned from a sojourn in Paris with Ferdinand.

"It's your father, my girl. He has married some empty-headed vessel, some chit from the house of Stolberg. And, hear this, she is only one year older than you are!"

"Oh dear God," answered Charlotte, sitting down on her bed.

"And there's more besides. He bestowed an extra five thousand pin money on her when she gave him a sickly smile. Would you believe it?"

"Oh Papa, Papa, have you gone out of your mind?"

"Yes, I think he has. And to think of the poverty that we live in. It's an utter disgrace."

Charlotte stood up. "Let us go and see him."

"What? Have you gone crazy as well?"

"No, Mama, I am perfectly serious. I think we should travel to Rome and put our case quite clearly. After all I am his heir, legitimate or no."

Clementina stared at her daughter, who seemed, suddenly, to have grown in strength.

"Can we afford it?"

"Yes, we can. I shall borrow the money if necessary. I think it is high time that we paid my father a visit."

And with that, Charlotte turned to the portmanteau which she had not fully unpacked and started to place things back in it.

*

Louise was bitterly disappointed by her arrival in Rome. She had expected crowds lining the streets, cheers and shouts and hats thrown high, flowers scattered before the carriage, children raised in adult arms so that they could take a peek at the king and queen. Instead, the conveyance had trundled through the streets with not one member of the public even so much as glancing in its direction.

The arrival at the Palazzo Muti had been better; personal servants had bowed low, flunkeys even lower, and lackeys had positively prostrated themselves upon the ground. Within these walls she was treated like a queen but by the rest of the Roman population — with the exception of Charles' brother, of course — almost with disregard.

She hated Roman society. It was not enthusiastic enough to satisfy the pretensions of a self-loving, conceited, manipulative, silly little girl who had thought that she was marrying the heir to the English throne. For what reason, she considered thunderously, had she made the sacrifice of giving herself to an older bridegroom? It was like having a jug of icy water tipped down her spine.

Fortunately, there was one saving grace. The cardinal duke Henry liked her and had given her delightful gifts; a court dress of lace and gold thread and a beautiful box made of gold, on which was picked out Henry's portrait in diamonds. But as for the title by which she was known — Baroness Renfrew — why, it was laughable, it sounded like a character in a second-rate opera.

*

What was so horrible to contemplate was the Bonnie Prince's refusal to see her. Charlotte had always imagined that when she turned up on his doorstep, as it were, he would melt and receive her with the love that once he had so patently shown her. But an order had been issued by Charles himself, for Clementina Walkinshaw to leave Rome at once and go back to France. And that included her daughter as well. Privately, when Clementina had gone out, Charlotte had wept bitter tears. The trouble was that deep down within her — and she could not make it go away however badly she was treated by him — she would never, could never, forget what a wonderful father he had been.

She could still, if she closed her eyes tightly, imagine his arms around her and the way he would amusingly make the noise of a wheel rotating while smothering her cheek with kisses. She had loved him with all her heart — and now she didn't know what to think. It was as if he had cut her dead in public, in the street. When her mother had been given the ultimatum to leave Rome immediately without Charles even seeing his former mistress and his daughter, Charlotte had advised her to stay. But now, faced by this stone wall of implacable dislike, they had no alternative but to leave and retrace their steps. The one concession that had been granted them was permission to change their dwelling place from Meaux to Paris. Hollow victory indeed.

*

Charles was sitting in his study, staring pensively at a book that he was not reading. His mind was full of the past, visions that brought him both happiness and tristesse. He thought of the child he had once loved to distraction, pictured her retracing her steps from Rome, getting more depressed with every change of coach and country. Those wonderful tawny eyes of hers filling with tears. If she had been alone he would have seen her, embraced her, given her a welcome. But no; she was under the petticoats of the vicious woman he had taken into his life, had impregnated to his horror, and then adored the resulting child with all his heart.

From the other room he could hear the sound of high-pitched giggling. Louise was entertaining some young traveller or other. She was getting quite a sweet reputation amongst the gallant young men who called at the palace and were made welcome, yet he trusted her implicitly. It was a pity that she had not become pregnant, though. Charles desperately needed a legitimate heir, but so far, there was no sign of the longed-for event. With a sigh that was suddenly much deeper, much more intense than he would have wished, the prince turned back to his book.

CHAPTER TWENTY-TWO

Louise Again

It had been difficult deciding which character to play as a wife. Should she be stately and gracious, every inch a queen? Small hopes of that ever happening! Should she be demure, the little wifelet, pawing his chest for presents? Should she be a will-o-the-wisp, a mystical magical creature, one that would keep her husband guessing until the end of his days? Or should she try to be a combination of the lot? It was a difficult conundrum for somebody born without a massive amount of intellect.

During that horrible coach journey, which had taken hour upon hour, she had pondered the question but not found an answer. She had known one thing, however, the moment she saw him. There was no question of her falling in love with her husband and having to forget all about which role she would take as she entered the crazy world of high passion.

He was far too old to raise a spark of interest in her youthful heart. She had taken one look at Charles Edward Stuart and decided to be, temporarily, submissive, dewy-eyed and willing. And after that, when she was proclaimed queen of all England — which was his wife's title by right — to wait and see what was best. She hadn't even liked him particularly, thinking him rather boring and stuffy. She had wanted beauty and passion, lithe hips, seductive glances and delicious kisses. Instead, she had got an old man with a sad, secretive smile and a world-weary manner.

Louise had noticed, from the first moment she had walked into the Palazzo Muti, that one of the lackeys bent double before her had, as he straightened up, given her the most appreciative of glances. Those dark brown Italian eyes had widened in pure admiration and she had not been able to resist giving a little toss of her head to show that she was aware. But she had forgotten about him in the first few days of being queenly. Fawning servants, flunkeys bowing in corridors, finely cooked meals, and finally — triumph of triumphs — a visit from the cardinal duke bearing fantastic presents.

After that, things had gone a little flat. She had found out the name of the amorous lackey — Bernardo Rotolo — and taken to flirting with him, just a tiny bit. Gossip had got back to her aged husband who had dismissed it as ridiculous rumour. She had known then that as long as she gave Charles kisses and cuddles, he would look no further. He was perfectly happy in his library, surrounded by his books, a bottle of wine and a glass on a small table beside him.

They sometimes went out for day trips, during which Charles wore the blue ribbon of the garter, drawing obvious attention to the couple. Most people bowed, some with a deprecating smile, and Louise could not get enough of it. She made a stately progress, glancing to right and left with an elegant posture, showing the world that she was born to greatness; even if it was a little tardy in coming.

The theatre was almost a nightly pilgrimage. Frankly, Louise was bored to tears by the whole business. She didn't like opera and thought ballet not much better. Charles, on the other hand, was an opera buff and followed every performance avidly. Louise enjoyed watching the number of men who focussed their opera glasses on her and acknowledged their bows and waves with a slightly cool inclination of her head.

Occasionally, Charles would give a dinner party or a ball and it was at one of these that Louise met her first love. Thomas Coke, heir to the Earl of Leicester, was a young Englishman doing the grand tour. They fell passionately in love, but though he begged her to have intercourse with him, she refused.

"Thomas, no! Please remove your hands from my attire. I cannot go to bed with you! Oh darling, don't kiss me like that. You know it makes me weak."

"Louise, you are torturing me. I want you so desperately. Don't touch me down there. I will explode!"

"Then do so, beloved. As long as it is not in me."

"Why, do you still have relations with your husband?"

"Yes, yes. If a child should be born resembling *you*, I think he would go mad."

They did everything but have sex, for Louise was still trying to produce an heir by her husband, and wanted no lover putting any doubts in Charles' mind as to who was the father. Amongst her string of suitors she earned the soubriquet Queen of Hearts, telling her many admirers that she believed in loving companionship, but dared not go no further than that.

Yet as the months went by there was no sign of the longed-for pregnancy and Louise began to wonder why she bothered with her husband any more. She had married to become a queen, and all she had ended up with was a sham little court in the Palazzo Muti, where visitors treated her with the dignity that would have been appropriate if she had in fact been of royal blood, but in the big world beyond nobody looked twice at her. As for Charles, she was frankly bored to tears with him. She needed romance, passion, adoration, constant reassurance. Instead, he called her 'my dear' and kissed her only when they had what passed for sex.

Her new passion in life was a Swiss, and terribly amusing. His name was Karl Victor von Bonstetten and he delighted the fellow guests at a dinner party by carving meat terribly badly. But with her he remained aloof, deliberately turning his head away so that all she could see was his glorious profile. But this kind of behaviour was a ploy, done deliberately to attract women — which it did.

"Oh Karl, my dear, shall we play a hand at cards?"

"If that is what Your Majesty would like."

"There is something I would like *more*."

"Oh, and what might that be?"

"To get to know you better."

"If Your Majesty would explain a little…"

Louise had stamped her foot. "You really are so irritating."

"If I have done anything to offend Your Majesty, then I humbly apologise."

"Oh be quiet and give me a kiss."

And in this way had begun another serious, but unconsummated, affair.

The prince, meanwhile, was approaching the new King of France — Louis XV having died suddenly — for the pension they had promised him on the occasion of his marriage. As usual he was getting nowhere and Louise intervened, thinking it her queenly duty to do so. The French announced that as she had acted with the greatest diplomacy and been reasonable into the bargain, they would award her a small personal pension of 60,000 francs a year.

Charles could have wept with despair. His marriage was breaking down, his wife seemed unable to conceive and she had been granted a pension which should, by rights, be his. He decided that to move to

Tuscany would be less expensive than Rome and would also occupy the mind of Louise, giving her something else to concern herself with as there was, as yet, no child forthcoming.

The ill-matched couple set forth for Siena, then went on to Pisa to take the waters. Louise loved the place. Strutting forth daily like a little bird of paradise, she rapidly became the talk of the town and was surrounded by admirers of all ages.

"Good morning, Your Majesty."

An inclination of her pretty, brainless head.

"Nice to see you looking so well, Majesty…"

A faint twitch of the lips and a momentary pause.

"May I say, Your Majesty, that you are the prettiest queen I have ever had the good fortune to see."

This warranted a halt and the sweetest of sweet smiles.

"You may say so if it pleases you, sir."

Another florid bow from the gallant. Louise walked on, thinking *if only one of them could become a lover in the true sense of the word.* She was dying for lack of romance, she wanted youth and strength and beauty, and all she had was a middle-aged husband who was thinking of his glorious past and not casting his eyes in her direction.

They moved on to Florence. It was wonderful, buzzing with life — particularly life that was male and young and handsome — and Louise became an overnight sensation. Charles was for moving on, Louise was longing to stay. Temporarily, the role of delectable kitten was the one that she decided to play.

"Oh my sweetest husband," she purred, stropping round him. "Has anyone told you recently that you look gorgeous when you are asleep?"

He stared at her. "Nobody. Besides, very few people see me in that condition."

"Well, I do. Sometimes I just creep into your apartment and stare at you."

"For heaven's sake, why?"

"Because I love your little cuddly face, especially when you snore."

"What!" Charles exclaimed.

"It makes me just want to hug you and kiss you and sit on your lap and love you."

As the prince was already seated, Louise launched herself at him full tilt and finally perched on his knees. Charles winced very slightly.

"Oh my darling," she crooned on, "how happy I am. I think my joy has been brought about by living in this beautiful city. It is so alive and vibrant — oh, that was such a big word for me to say. What do you think, my love?"

"Well, I must say they put on some good operas."

Charles had engaged boxes in both theatres and was enjoying his visits to them enormously.

"There you are. You are as happy as I am here. Oh please, little consort of mine, do let us stay."

The prince capitulated, he was contented enough and Louise, with her court of admirers, was very contented too. Charles liked the boys well enough. All young and strong and up for anything, as he had once been. He was particularly drawn to those who sat paying reverent attention when he talked of the glory and horrors of the '45. He decided to himself that Louise ran a little court of medieval knights, all chivalrous, whose pure intentions were beyond questioning, and who, to a man, adored her platonically.

Meanwhile, Charles had tried repeatedly to get the new Pope, Pius VI, to recognise him as King of England, but the whole affair had ended in utter humiliation for the prince. Yet this brought about what Louise had been silently hoping for. It was time to buy a permanent home in Florence. And she had found the very place, the Palazzo Guadagni. As well as having a spacious entrance hall and suites of beautifully decorated rooms, it also had a large garden behind. Everything in her life was going well — with the exception of one thing. She wanted above all to meet the perfect man. And one day she did.

He was an Italian stallion. His name Vittorio Alfieri, his title count. He was tall, thin, with a mass of bright red hair and huge expressive eyes, which rolled with relish in Louise's direction. He was an accomplished seducer, through and through. His first affair had been when he was aged seventeen and he hadn't stopped from that moment on. He took one look at Louise, found out that she boasted the title Queen of England and that her husband was now something of a physical wreck, and decided to make his play.

Once invited, Alfieri came regularly to the palazzo — but as for getting Louise into bed, that was an entirely different matter. The most they could manage for two whole years was to hold hands and exchange kisses while Charles sat lightly dozing in another room. Alfieri, in a constant state of arousal, muttered loving words into her ear, while Louise, on fire with passion, tentatively put out a hand to feel his hardness. At the same time his fingers crawled into her lap and straight between her thighs. But further than that they did not dare go, because of the noise which satisfaction would make. The would-be lovers gave themselves the nicknames of Psipsia and Psipsio and wove themselves into a romantic, fairy-tale fantasy which would end when Charles shuffled off this mortal coil and they could walk into a sunset accompanied by the sob of violin strings.

The prince, meanwhile, had sought the help of a French doctor and carried out most of the physician's stipulations with the exception of giving up alcohol. He walked in the streets — a pastime that Louise, who had to accompany him, detested because it was too hot. He ate little and slept a lot, particularly at the opera where a couch had been installed in his box. Sometimes he had to dash from this when one of his crippling stomach pains beset him, in order to vomit in the public passageway. Not the done thing at the opera at all.

In 1778 Alfieri began to make serious moves to support Louise in the event of her leaving her husband, for the couple had finally consummated their love. While Charles slept after lunch they had gone to a box room in a remote part of the palazzo and bolted the door. And there, on the small unmade bed within, had reached the heights of ecstatic bliss, muffling their shouts of pleasure with one of Alfieri's scarves brought specifically for the purpose… but not quite as effectively as they would have wished. Eventually, as with all secrets of that kind, it was discovered and reported back to Charles. He began to organise a network of servants to act as spies.

Things came to a head on St Andrew's Night, the thirtieth of November, in 1780. The prince shouted at Louise that she had been constantly unfaithful with Alfieri whom he — Charles — had received as an honoured guest in his house.

"You have betrayed me, you little whore. On today, of all days."

Louise froze, the many roles she played for once run dry.

"You, sir, are impotent. What do you expect me to do? I am still a young woman," she retorted when her brain had cleared a little.

"Tonight I drank to Scotland, the country to which I promise to return one day. And all the time while I was toasting that wonderful place you and your lover were fucking in a corner somewhere. What vile situation have I come to?"

"You married me when I was scarce more than a child. You have only yourself to blame."

"Enough, woman. If you open your mouth again I swear before God that I will strike you so hard your teeth will fly across the room."

Louise took a step away from him, stumbled and fell across the bed. In a second Charles was on top of her, pulling at the flap in his breeches. But his erection had been damaged by drink and nothing but a sad and wizened member appeared. With a howl of despair he stumbled from the room, leaving Louise alone in the candlelight.

*

It was Alfieri, of course, who came up with the master scheme. If Louise were to run away from the palazzo, then she would be caught and brought back by force. Better by far to escape while Prince Charles was with her. It was a plot of genius, the work that only an Italian dramatist could have conceived.

Nine days after the attack, which by now Louise had exaggerated to being beaten round the head, having her hair torn out and an attempt made to strangle her, the trap was set. On the ninth of December Madame Orlandini, a wealthy Jacobite widow, came to breakfast. During the course of the meal she mentioned, oh so casually, that she was going on to see the needlework of the little white nuns.

"Would you like to join us, Your Majesty?"

Charles looked up from his study of the newspaper. "Yes, why not? It will do me good to stretch my legs."

"I would love to see it," put in Louise.

The meal finished, the three of them entered the carriage which took them the short drive to the convent. There was a young man standing near the entrance, whom Charles very vaguely recognised.

"It's Signor Geoghegan, isn't it?"

"Oh good morning to you, Count. How nice to see you up and about at this early hour," the man answered in a delightful Irish accent.

"Yes, it is a bit early," Charles answered cheerfully, quite used to being called count as the Count of Albany was another pseudonym. Meanwhile, the two women had ascended the convent steps, rung the bell, and were immediately admitted. The prince followed more slowly and banged the closed door with his stick. After a long interval a nun appeared at the grille in the entrance.

"Yes?"

"Can you please let me in. I am with the two ladies who have just entered."

"Are you the Count of Albany?"

"Yes, I am."

"Then the answer is no. The countess is within, seeking sanctuary from her brutal husband. This the mother superior has granted. Good day to you."

The grille slammed shut. When Charles turned, the young man had vanished and he stood all by himself in the harsh sunlight. Further attempts to see Louise were obviously futile. He despondently got into the carriage and returned to the palazzo, once more alone.

CHAPTER TWENTY-THREE

Pouponne

She hadn't cried at first, when Mama had put her long coat on her and pushed her rather swiftly into a carriage. She had thought they were going on an outing, though Mama had a very set look on her face for someone due to go on a pleasure trip. But when the carriage took off and she had realised that it was going to drive a long way away, she had turned to her mother.

"Where are we going, Mama?"

"To Paris, darling. We shall have to catch another coach to get there. But you will like it. There are lots of shops and things to do."

"Will Papa be coming?"

"No, I don't think so. He will be busy at home."

"Oh."

The penny had dropped when the Abbé John Gordon stood waiting as the Paris coach came up to its terminal.

"Madame, I do hope you realise the full consequence of your actions."

Six-year-old Charlotte had been all ears.

"I do indeed, Monsieur Abbé."

"The child, of course, will have to be sent back to the prince."

Clementina had looked at the cobbles and Charlotte knew that her mother was about to tell a lie.

"Of course, sir. When I receive His Highness' instructions, I will, naturally, comply."

But she hadn't. As soon as dawn broke the next day, Clementina had taken the child and gone to other lodgings. Then Charlotte had known that she was truly separated from her lovely, wonderful, playful, adorable father and she had howled long and loud, driving poor Clementina to distraction. Eventually though she had given in and accepted the situation, though her spirit had not been broken so much as badly damaged.

After that it had been one long, dreary round of miserable convent rooms until, one day in a tea room in Paris, she had set eyes on Ferdinand and known love of another kind. As she had grown older she had supposed — in times of quiet reflection, of which there were far too many — that because he was so much more mature than she was, perhaps she had chosen a father figure. But who would be seduced at seventeen so subtly by anyone paternal? No, it was real love and it filled her with a deep and lasting zest for living.

The fact that they could only see each other occasionally, though terribly frustrating, added a certain piquancy to their relationship. Ferdinand would escape from the archbishop's palace, dress himself all in black and behave like an ordinary man about town, which in reality was exactly what he should have been. He did not like being a cleric and resented the fact that his family had pushed him into it in return for a considerable income, which they had pocketed. But now his absences were being noted by the other clerics and he was on his way to see his beloved Charlotte to ask her to move nearer to him.

"But, sweetheart, I can't leave mother."

"Why not? You are nineteen now. Most older women have daughters married and gone at that age. Your mama will surely get used to the idea."

"You know perfectly well that she relies upon me solely for companionship. Oh Ferdy, darling, please be reasonable."

"No, you be reasonable with me. You know perfectly well that if I had not been thrust into the church by my avaricious family we would be a married couple by now. Furthermore, it is getting more and more difficult to slip away to Paris without being noticed. After all, I *am* the archbishop."

Charlotte had done the worst possible thing and erupted in peals of laughter. Ferdinand had shot her the blackest look imaginable, picked up his valise and stalked out of the room. After the initial shock was over she had looked out of the window to see him getting into a hackney coach. She had heard nothing from him since and it had nearly killed her.

Now three years had passed, during which she had grown more and more bitter. So much so that she had applied to become a canoness — a lay member of a religious order who lived in a convent and accepted the duties of a nun. She had had strict instructions from her father — who, no doubt, was holding her in reserve in case of political need — neither to marry or take holy orders. She could make no move and felt utterly bereft. Her mother's small pension from her uncle, the cardinal duke, had been halved. Charlotte had applied for one but had been turned down. She had no dowry, no lover and no hope.

So it was that on an April evening, sharp with showers and smelling of early lilac blossom, she reluctantly took out the one decent dress she had left and grudgingly applied a few cosmetics to her face, which was too startlingly like that of the Bonnie Prince ever to be a true beauty, but which held all the attractiveness that he possessed. She had been invited to a dinner and reception by Lord Elcho, as much out of curiosity as anything else, she presumed. Sighing and feeling completely bowed down by the machinations of a cruel fate, Charlotte reluctantly stepped into the fiacre that Lord Elcho had kindly sent to fetch her.

As soon as she walked into the magnificent receiving room she saw Ferdinand and her heart sank down to her feet. He looked young and somehow dwarfed by the magnificent red finery that bedecked him. Displaying a tremendous composure that she did not feel for an instant, Charlotte walked forward and gave a small curtsey to her host and hostess. Lady Elcho extended her hand.

"My dear Miss Stuart, how very nice to see you."

Lord Elcho was bowing. He had been out with her father during the '45 and had escaped to France after the rout at Culloden.

"How are you these days, my dear Charlotte?"

But before she could answer there was the swish of silk on the tiled floor and out of the corner of her eye she could see the brilliance of scarlet. Ferdinand, in the full dress of an archbishop, had come to stand beside her. She ignored him.

"Very well thank you, my lord."

"Good, good. Delighted to hear it." And with that the Elchos turned away to greet their next guests.

Her former lover spoke and Charlotte could detect the merest tremor in his voice.

"Good evening, Miss Stuart. Ferdinand de Rohan. Do you remember me?"

"Of course I do," she answered, turning away.

"And I remember too. In fact I've never forgotten. Oh my dear girl, it is so wonderful to see you again."

She gazed at him and was shocked to see that his eyes were glinting with unshed tears. In that moment Charlotte Stuart fell in love with him even more deeply than she had done before.

"I've missed you," he said, and she knew that he was speaking the truth and that he was trembling slightly.

"And I've missed you, too."

"I've also learnt something — and this is what it is. That my life is completely and utterly empty without your company. Charlotte, will you come back to me and forgive me for my foolish and childish behaviour?"

She felt her life turning on a mere word, a single word that would rescue her for ever from eternal loneliness.

"Yes," she said. "I would like that very much."

Now he wept in earnest, tears running down his cheeks, his whole face crumpled with relief.

"Oh darling, I love you so much. I've a plan for our future."

They could not touch one another, nor do a thing but smile as if they were engaged in normal conversation.

"What is it?"

"I am going to lease a house in the rue St. Jacques — where you live with your mother — so that I can be near you. And I am going to acquire a country home, big enough to house the lot of us."

In the firmament a star danced as Charlotte's future unrolled before her like a glittering carpet.

"Can we go outside for a breath of air, Archbishop? My cheeks have grown somewhat warm."

"Certainly, my child. Allow me to open the garden door for you."

They stepped out into the grounds and strolled till they were out of the sight of the house, then they both sped into the shrubbery and disappeared from view, the Archbishop's scarlet robe swishing over the dew-damped grass as he welcomed his beloved back into his life.

After their reconciliation, Ferdinand and Charlotte indulged themselves in an even closer relationship, sharing a bed together whenever possible and enjoying happy sun-filled days when they would roam the countryside, that is when his clerical duties allowed. He, of course, like all males, became careless about contraceptive protection and eventually Charlotte missed her monthly flow.

"Ferdinand, I believe that I might be pregnant."

He turned to her, dressed in full canonicals and looking very stately as a result. For a moment he did not smile and then he grinned broadly.

"Sweetheart, this is the most wonderful news. Are you sure?"

She smiled wryly. "A bastard gives birth to another bastard. Yes, I'm fairly certain."

Ferdinand seized her firmly by the shoulders and sat her down on the edge of the bed they sometimes secretly shared in the archbishop's palace.

"Listen, my girl, there is no such thing as a bastard in the eyes of God, only in the eyes of society. You and your mother have fared very badly in the world, but only because your father took such a violent dislike to Clementina. In other cases, those born of unmarried parents have done extremely well for themselves."

"Yes, that's true enough."

"It is I, not you, who would be cast out of society if ever this birth — or any subsequent — should become public knowledge. It is I who was forced to take a vow of chastity — one which I have totally disregarded. And why do I do all this? Because, sweet Charlotte, I love you and always will. Rest assured, my dearest, that I will nurture this child with all my heart."

And so he did, when a girl was born in June 1779. She was named Marie-Victoire and she was hidden away most discreetly in his country house at Anthony, a few miles south of Paris. As is so often the case, Charlotte became pregnant for the second time quite rapidly. Once again the birth took place in the greatest secrecy, and another little girl joined her older sister. The Archbishop baptised her privately — as he had done Marie-Victoire — and this child he named Charlotte-Maximilienne-Amelie, after her mother. The much-put-upon Clementina nursed and cherished them when Charlotte went to Paris to make a nonchalant appearance.

Meanwhile, Charlotte continued to write to Charles, hoping against hope that one day he might answer her. Then his new Paris agent took up the same refrain. And finally the Moor — whom the prince had taken recently into his service — made a strange remark.

"If you fear this girl so much, master, it will give her power over you."

Charles stared at him but remained silent — and in that silence a thought was born.

*

Pregnant again and sick as a dog. Why, after all the care they had taken to keep the family to their two daughters — who were now five and four respectively — had they slipped up once more? Charlotte had douched herself afterwards, sending hot water upwards, Ferdinand had tied on one of his beautifully made condoms and fastened an elegant blue bow at the top. Yet despite their great care to prevent another child, one was on the way. It was November 1783, and poor Charlotte was having a hideous pregnancy.

Despite feeling awful, she had continued her dreary routine of sending letters to 'Cher Papa', only for them to be presumably torn to shreds and discarded. Why she did it was quite unclear to Ferdinand.

"Tell the old beast to go to hell. He's been ignoring you for years. It is perfectly obvious to everyone except yourself that he wants nothing further to do with you."

"But once he used to love me. I know it. He was far sweeter to me than Mama."

"So you have told me — a thousand times. I'm sorry to say this, my dear, but you are just wasting time and effort."

Yet despite all this, despite her pregnancy, despite a persistent pain from her liver, Charlotte continued to write.

Then, in 1784, two extraordinary things happened. In May she gave birth to a boy, much to the delight of Ferdinand — though it left her feeling rather weak and somewhat worried about the pain in her side.

Then there was a public announcement that shook everyone in Europe — to say nothing of Scotland — as it passed round at whirlwind speed. Prince Charles Edward Stuart was at long last recognising Charlotte as his legitimate daughter and heiress. This entitled her to be known henceforth as the Duchess of Albany. To crown it all, he wrote directly to Charlotte and asked her to come with great speed to Florence.

She became short of breath when Ferdinand — who was dealing with her correspondence while she recovered — rushed into the room to tell her and would have leapt up onto the bed had she not been feeling so drained by the recent birth and the swelling in her side.

"Go to him at once? But how can I? I've only just given birth."

"But, darling, you will have to go as soon as you have resumed normal duties. You have been waiting for this moment for most of your life. You *cannot* pass it by now."

"But the baby? The girls? What will happen to them?"

"I will still be their father, even if only in secret. They shall live in great comfort. And your mother can take over your obligations."

She was too full of the depression that comes with just having had a baby to answer. Instead, she burst into a storm of weeping. Ferdinand, who loved her so much, finally sat on the bed and gently took her in his arms.

"Hush, my darling. He has never forgotten you, that much is obvious. He still thinks of his precious child, his little Pouponne."

"Do you really believe that? After all these years?"

"Yes, and now — at long last — he wishes to do you honour."

"Oh Papa, you have left it too late," Charlotte answered, and wept afresh.

CHAPTER TWENTY-FOUR

Charles and Pouponne

Coming into the room immediately from the brilliant light of a Florentine day she could see nothing, temporarily blinded. The smell of stuffiness and decay was the first thing to startle her, so much so that she took a couple of steps backward, bumping into a cabinet as she did so. Then out of the gloom a voice, slightly tremulous and quivering somewhat, said, "Pouponne?"

Oh God, how time rolled back. She was six years old, the prince was on his hands and knees, blindfolded, while she crawled away from him, giggling and joyful, the happiest little girl in the world.

"Where are you, Papa? Where have you been?" she asked.

"Never far away, my dear. Never far away."

The next minute she found herself kneeling at Charles' feet, where he sat in his wing-back chair. Tentatively, a long-fingered hand reached out and stroked her hair.

Charlotte could not help but notice that the smell of him was different. Where once his bodily scent had been youthful, vigorous, very much that of a young man who took a lot of exercise, now it was musty, almost stale. It was as if he did not go out much into the freshness of the air. But his voice had not changed. It still had that lovely, lyrical tone that had come down over the years and charmed so many people; the Seven Men of Glenmoriston, Louise de Rohan, Madame de Talmont, to name but a few. And not forgetting, of course, Charlotte's own mother, Clementina Walkinshaw, currently nurturing the Bonnie Prince's oh-so-secret grandchildren.

"Sweet daughter, please rise. I want to look at you. Ring the bell on the little table and Marco will come and draw back the curtains."

Charlotte got to her feet and did as instructed. Almost immediately a man, black as an Arabian night, a scarlet turban on his head, came in silently and drew the drapery from the window, then stood and awaited further instruction. Charlotte smiled at him and he bowed deeply. Charles had bought him in a slave market, standing apart from the others with an air of great majesty about him.

The prince stood up and his daughter surveyed him. He who had once been so bonny, who had had women standing in their dozens just to catch a glimpse of him, who had wooed ladies of quality and broken hearts with impunity, still had an indefinable air about him. It was nothing tangible, nothing that one could point at and comment on, but something of the young chevalier was definitely still there.

For no reason that she could understand, Charlotte's eyes filled with tears. Her memory of him had always been that of a beautiful being, her delightful parent, and now to see an old man stand before her was almost more than she could bear. But he was holding his arms out and looking at her with those vivid eyes of his only somewhat dimmed. Charlotte dropped a reverential curtsey to the man of the past, followed by another — more dignified — to the present prince.

Charles had been expecting a grown-up version of his beloved little daughter but in that he was to be disappointed. She was tall, had a good figure, but as she had grown older her face had come to resemble his more and more, losing the sweet and innocent roundness of childhood. But she could have been sired by no-one else. He smiled at her fondly.

"You look like me," he said, rather foolishly.

"So I believe, Papa."

"Come here, my girl, and kiss me, my true heir in every sense."

*

Almost as soon as she arrived in Florence, Charlotte had decided on two things. One was to maintain a regular coded correspondence with Clementina. Her three children Marie-Victoire, Charlotte and the baby — another Charles Edward — she code-named 'the flowers in her garden' and constantly enquired about their welfare. The second was to get her father out and about, exercising and breathing fresh air. Knowing that he loved opera as greatly as ever, Charlotte decided that they should go to Lucca to see a highly-praised work. However their journey was interrupted by the prince having a seizure on the way. Marco, the Moorish servant whom Charlotte had come to both like and admire, held the prince in his arms while he twitched and convulsed, then quietly let go of him and walked a few steps away when Charles recovered.

"Why did you not stay with His Highness?" Charlotte asked him.

"Perhaps he would not like to have been embraced by a man of my race, Your Grace," had come the answer before Marco bowed deeply and withdrew to a discreet distance.

So, disturbed by her papa's sudden health problems but deciding to continue the journey, Charlotte proceeded on to the opera, then back to Florence and to her own personal dilemma. As a mother — and a new one at that — she was torn to shreds. As a daughter — long overdue in recognition — she felt it her duty to care for her father in his declining years.

Dear God, what a predicament. Added to which was her growing anxiety about her own wellbeing. The pain in her side was becoming more frequent and she found that the only person she could talk to without artifice or pretention was the Moor, Marco.

"I just wish that I could get my uncle — the Cardinal Duke — on my side. His support would mean so much to me. I really feel that I cannot cope with the prince's poor health on my own."

"Madam, you must write to him again. He is presumably annoyed because the Pope has recognised you as the Duchess of Albany whereas he has not. A man is never so unhappy as he is with his own people."

Charlotte chuckled, thinking to herself that it seemed like months since she had laughed aloud and long. Last time had been when Ferdinand was playing the fool in front of Marie-Victoire and had fallen backwards over a log, his archbishop's robe descending over his head, displaying a great deal of naked thigh and other personal things as he did so. She and her daughter had rolled about in mirth.

Now she said, "You speak the truth, Marco. I imagine that this is what his cool behaviour is all about."

"There is something else, madam."

"And what might that be?"

"The Bonnie Prince …"

The Moor always used this form of speech when referring to her father.

"Yes?"

"His divorced wife, who by Allah's good faith and justice I have never met, is not yet out of the picture."

"What are you saying?"

"That Louise of Stolberg is corresponding with the cardinal duke, sweetness and light pouring forth from her every word — may Allah not smile upon a wicked woman. She pretends that she is finished with the fraudulent Alfieri for ever more."

"How do you know all this?"

The Moor did not answer but rolled his beautiful eyes in the direction of the ceiling and laid a long finger on the side of his supple nose.

"You are not going to tell me," Charlotte observed.

Marco smiled a dark smile and shook his head slowly.

But despite this news Charles was happy at last, his heart full of the joy of finally living with his beloved Pouponne. He made very grand announcements about her to which not many people listened. The Duchess of Albany was his legitimate heir and as such should be recognised by everyone, he proclaimed. On St Andrew's night he invested her with the Order of St Andrew, and proudly declared to all present that his dearly beloved daughter would succeed him as Queen Charlotte when it was his turn to depart this life. Afterwards, she had spoken softly to Marco.

"That will never happen, you know that as well as I."

"They say that the dreams of old men are the very thing that allow them to die content."

Charlotte sighed. "I know, I know. I will never disillusion him. By the way, any news of the despicable Louise?"

"She is quiet, which does not bode well."

"A complete whore if ever there was one. Anyway, the excitement of legalising me seems quite to have worn the prince out. I think we should visit Pisa soon to take the waters, which might comfort him. You will accompany us, of course."

"To be in your company is the kiss of Allah."

They set off and indeed the prince rallied slightly, and though he was content to doze away the evenings, Charlotte found herself tasting the high life. The Pisan nobility opened their doors to the royal pair and the balls, receptions and parties abounded. To crown her happiness — if any woman could be truly happy when parted from her children — the cardinal duke finally wrote to her and told her that he now accepted her both as his niece and as the Duchess of Albany.

She met him, brimming over with smiles and affection, when she and Charles made another tour of Tuscany later in the year. It was October 1785, and the moment she set eyes on Henry Stuart, Charlotte knew that he was going to be a true friend. After the kissing and hugging and the vows of kinship between the brothers was over, she finally managed to get her new-found uncle on his own. Charlotte gave a reverential curtsey before she spoke.

"I am honoured to meet you, Your Grace."

"My dearest niece. It is I who do the honouring."

"May I speak to your frankly?"

"Of course, dear girl."

"My beloved papa is not well, sir."

"No, indeed. I am very much struck by the change in him."

"How do you think I should proceed, uncle? May I call you that? It would not be too forward of me?"

"My sweet niece, it would most definitely be not. Let me say now that I think my brother looks quite frail. I truly think that if he could stand the journey it would be better to bring him to Rome where I can assist you in caring for him."

"But will he want to go? The city of Florence has been good to him."

"But too full of memories of that wanton who dared to marry him. She has been writing to me, declaring her innocence and saying that she has dispensed for ever with her lover, the appalling Alfieri. She wanted funds, naturally."

"Oh Uncle, I hope you did not give them to her."

The cardinal duke looked somewhat ashamed and changed the subject.

"Tell me, does my brother still go out?"

"Oh yes, indeed he does. We attend the theatre and the opera regularly, indeed the Grand Duke of Tuscany has had the Stuart boxes redecorated; the box — where we sit to watch the plays — in yellow and the one in the Opera House crimson damask. But gout has made Papa's legs swell up and nowadays he is carried everywhere by chair."

"Gout? How much does he drink?"

"Very little, sir, and that is the truth. I have been quite strict on that score."

"Well done, my dear. He has indeed found a treasure in you. But the burden of care is too great for one person. If we can move him back to Rome then I can ease it."

Surprisingly when Charlotte mentioned Rome to the prince, he gave her a strange smile.

"Back to the Palazzo Muti, eh? So I shall die in the house in which I was born."

"You must not talk of such things, Papa. There is a lot of good living left to do."

"Do you know something, my daughter?"

"What might that be?"

"That I would really like to die in Scotland. In that glorious land of roaring peaks and glassy lochs. That's where I left my soul, do you see?"

"I think that it might be rather an ambitious journey."

"My God, girl. I just wish you could see it for yourself. See it through my eyes as I did so long ago."

"Perhaps I will, one day."

"Then you will have to travel incognito. There'll be a price on your head from those wily Hanoverians. D'you know, if I had continued on at Derby and not listened to that whining bastard Murray, I could have taken London. Wee Georgie was ready to run and take his beastly brood with him. I would be King of England, and it was just the devil's bad chance that made me give in to that odious creature."

"What happened to him?"

Charles made a sound of utter contempt. "The bastard arrived in Paris, asked to see me. I told him to go to hell, that I never wanted to see him again. That he had betrayed me at Derby and his evil schemes had ruined my life. I told him to leave the place fast. After that he wandered all over the continent and eventually died in Holland. I did not dignify his grave by pissing on it."

Charlotte knelt at her father's feet and put her arms round him.

"I expect that they love you still, those that knew you in those great and glorious days."

"I doubt it, my dear. Though it is sweet of you to say so."

"I think, darling Papa, that in that you are wrong. I think that one day you will become a legend in Scotland of what you hoped to achieve and how badly you were treated."

"You do?"

"I do indeed."

*

On 1 December 1785, the prince left Florence for ever. By now he was not the only sick one in the party. The pain in Charlotte's side had grown worse and she feared that something unthinkable might be the cause. As well as to her invalid father, her thoughts strayed constantly to the three motherless children being brought up by their grandmother and the man she had loved all her adult life, Ferdinand de Rohan.

Charles stood up to the journey well, sitting for twelve hours a day in a coach without grumbling. The Cardinal Duke came to meet them at Viterbo and stayed with them for the rest of the journey to Rome. Charles' face as he entered the Palazzo Muti was a study. He had been born here and now he supposed that this was the place where he would die. Life's extraordinary encircling claw had him firmly in its grip.

That night, as the Moorish Marco was hanging up his clothes, handed to him by one of the two valets who helped the prince undress, Charles said loudly, "I suppose this damn place will claim me as well. It was where my beloved mother died, you know."

Marco muttered, "Allah believes that one should return to the place of one's ancestors to pass from this life."

"What was that?" asked Charles, cupping his ear.

The Moor bowed before him and repeated what he had just said.

"Really? Is that a fact? Well you can tell Allah from me that I never liked this wretched palace and I don't suppose that I ever will. But I am going to make the last few months of my time here worth every minute. Theatre, operas, concerts, chamber music, balls, parties — I shall be at every one of 'em. I am going out in style."

"I will inform Allah of your wishes Bonnie Prince, never you fear."

Later, Marco saw Charlotte, sitting alone, sipping a glass of brandy before she retired to bed.

"The prince has a message for Allah, Highness."

She did not laugh, instead she looked at him and he could tell by the exhaustion in her eyes that she was far more ill than she would openly admit.

"Madam, is there anything I can do for you?"

"No, Marco, no. As I am sure you know already, being a master of ancient knowledge, I am sicker than I want anyone to realise. It is to my father that I am going to devote all the time I have left, and I am going to make his passing from this life as joyful as possible."

"He shall live to the hilt, then? As he wishes."

"To the hilt." And she raised her glass before downing the contents.

*

And so Charlotte's promise was fulfilled. That summer they left Rome's overpowering streets for the quiet town of Albano — where Charles' father King James III had lived apart from his wife — and here they enjoyed an active social life, while the little theatre stayed open for them after the season had officially ended. Charlotte gave musical parties which Charles attended, beaming with happiness.

"I love you, my dear daughter. Be sure of that. Is there anything I can do to make you truly glad?"

"You have already done so by acknowledging me, Papa."

"But is there any one thing that would make you completely overjoyed? And, if so, what is it?"

"That you should write to my Mama. Just a note. It would make her so pleased."

And so Charles sent for paper and ink and did the unthinkable. He wrote to Clementina — his enemy — and wished her well. He signed it, *I am and shall be your good friend, Charles R.*

Now there was nothing left to do but enjoy as best he could all the pleasures that life could throw at him. A task which the grand old man pursued to the best of his ability.

CHAPTER TWENTY-FIVE

The Bonnie Prince

They had all gone now. His women, his friends, his loves, his hates. Above any of them, of course, was Luci, who had bought him books, razor blades, anything and everything, and who had given him all the love that he had ever needed. But added to her were the clinging, clutching Louise, the cruel, tantalising de Talmont, the many girls he had taken to bed and whose names he had never known. The list was endless.

Everyone who had been out with him in the '45, with one exception, had died. Every Jacobite officer, plus the Seven men of Moidart, all were rotting in their graves. As for his enemies, suffice it to say that Lord George Murray — he who had ordered that the prince retreat at Derby and who Charles had hated implacably ever since — had met his end. The prince had survived everyone, he had lived beyond his time.

After a summer spent in Albano he had come back to the Palazzo Muti, and as he had staggered through its portals — one leg terribly swollen with dropsy — he had gazed at them with a kind of resignation.

"So you'll have your way," he had muttered. "I shall die within your confines."

After that he had taken to lying on his couch and life had passed him by in a kind of dream. Sometimes his sleeping mind had played tricks on him, and he had thought people from the past had come into his room and stared at him. Then he had woken to see the kindly face of his beloved daughter Pouponne smiling at him, sometimes still a child, sometimes as a mature woman.

"Go back to sleep, Papa," she would say, and he would close his eyes and drift off once more.

Then one night — he had known it was night because he was lying in his bed — the dream had become vividly real. So clear, in fact, that he had twitched back the coverlet and put a tentative foot on the floor. The dropsy, gout, and all the other painful problems that had beset his legs in the recent months, were for once lying dormant. Looking round to make sure that a servant was not watching, Charles made his way to the door.

He opened it and peered out. The Palazzo Muti was either in deep shadow or he was having a vision. Because instead of a long candlelit corridor he could see that he was sleeping in a humble abode with a narrow passageway. He simply couldn't understand what was happening, but nonetheless made his way downstairs to the front door and flung it open. Outside, etched stark and vivid against the light of an argent moon, towered the looming peaks of Scotland.

The prince realised then that he was taking part in a vivid dream in which he had been granted his longed-for wish; to return to the land of his youthful triumph and tragedy, to hear again the sound of the pipes, to sniff once more the pure air that blew fresh from the snow-covered peaks. He felt younger too; tall, broad-shouldered and ready for anything the world could throw at him. A daisy-white horse tethered nearby looked up and breathed down its nose in recognition. He went and patted it appreciatively. A stable boy came up.

"Do you want him saddled up, Mo Prionnsa?"

"If you would, please."

It was the ride of his life. He cantered through a poppy-red dawn onto a beach where the crystal foam dashed the feet of his galloping white mount. Then on past sleeping villages tucked into the side of massive mountains, the colour of indigo. The sun came up over a glen that was terrifying in its majesty, three mighty peaks rearing up on all sides, barren and grim. The dawn picked out their grey and relentless escarpments — killing grounds for mortal men.

But in the distance the prince could hear a faint hum, that grew in strength the closer he got. He realised then that he was decked out in immense finery, that he was the golden child the people wanted, that two men were riding beside him, one to the left, the other to the right. That he was reliving the entrance into Edinburgh. With a mighty roar the noise reached its peak and burst into a thousand cheering shouts.

"It's the Bonnie Prince. The Bonnie Prince Charlie. He's come to us. Huzzah! Hooray! He's here at last!"

The streets were very bright, unusually so. The Bonnie Prince blinked at the brilliance. Yet even though he was afraid, he felt compelled to go towards it. It surrounded him. The roar of the crowd was ebbing away. He was on foot and alone.

*

"He's dying, Your Grace. Hold him tightly. He is making the final journey."

"Oh Papa, don't leave me. It is your loving Pouponne."

"He is fulfilling his destiny, my sweet lady. He is going into immortality. I beg you not to hold him back," whispered Marco the Moor.

And then there was a sudden silence as very quietly the Bonnie Prince's breathing ebbed away and ceased.

*

He was bathed in radiance now. Walking on slowly towards a glittering, gleaming light in which stood Luci, smiling and beckoning. He hurried towards her, not afraid, not old, once again the man who had come to save Scotland.

And in this manner, the Bonnie Prince made his way out of the world of men, and into the beating heart of Scottish legend. A place in which he will remain and be loved forever more, in the land of shining lochs and fiercesome hills.

HISTORICAL NOTE

In fictionalising the life of the Young Pretender I came across the usual number of difficulties. Differing schools of thought, for one. For example, Charles could never have a satisfactory relationship with women because of his mother, one biographer thought. It is true that she was an anorexic religious maniac but quite how that was going to affect Charles for the rest of his days I fail to see. Indeed, he had a robust and reasonably fulfilled sex life and thanks to the research done by Professor Bongie in the Royal Archives at Windsor — where the professor was faced with a jumbled correspondence which initially almost frightened him away — we know the prince had a son by his girlfriend, Louise, Princesse de Rohan, Duchesse de Montbazon. This was foisted on to her husband, Jules de Rohan, who accepted that the child was his because Louise was sleeping with him at the same time as the prince, much to the latter's annoyance. Louise was one of the most hysterical, sex-obsessed, clinging little creatures that I have ever come across in all my researches.

A quick word about those Windsor letters before I move on. Professor Bongie was on the point of not examining the papers when he first saw them in the Royal Library. But as he read one or two of the notes he was gripped by a sense of intrigue and suspense. They were written in French and were from Louise to the prince, sparing no details of what a highly-charged sexual liaison they were having. Furthermore, of the difficulties they encountered with the network of spies and lookouts organised by Louise's mother-in-law, the Princesse de Guéméné, who disliked the pretender greatly. All praise to the professor for unearthing such a well-hidden love affair.

Many may blame Charles for his apparent cold-heartedness at the end of the relationship. But equally, those who have fought against the web of lies and self-deception, to say nothing of emotional blackmail, that a thwarted lover can come up with, will understand exactly how he felt.

Now to his children. As I have said, the boy that Louise gave birth to was brought up as the son of Jules, her husband. He died at the age of five months. The hawkish mother-in-law knew of his parentage, of course, and so did Louise's father. Is it possible that Jules guessed? I imagine that he did. The parents may have kept silent but there is always servants' tittle-tattle and gossip — and servants were involved in trying to keep the prince away from Louise. Jules must have heard some whisper and put two and two together.

The second child was the much-adored Charlotte, the baby of Clementina Walkinshaw. That Charles worshipped this little girl is abundantly clear. When Clementina ran away, taking the child with her, the prince had a complete nervous breakdown. Many years later he was reunited with her. Any hope of a legitimate heir had now faded away and so, against all odds, he pronounced Charlotte legitimate, creating her the Duchess of Albany. Yet nobody knew, except the woman herself, that she was terminally ill with cancer of the liver. She resided with the Bonnie Prince and nursed him — despite being in agonising pain — and outlived him by only a few months, dying on the seventeenth of November 1789. She left behind her three highly secret children.

Their father was Ferdinand de Rohan, a younger brother of Jules, husband of Louise — the lover of Charles Stuart and mother of his infant son. The Rohan family were in the habit of selling their younger sons into the clergy in return for a goodly amount of future monetary reward. Ferdinand's brother, Louis, became a cardinal and was arrested by Louis XVI for his part in the Affair of the Queen's Necklace, and thrown into the Bastille. Ferdinand rose in the church to the rank of Archbishop of Bordeaux and later of Cambrai.

It was such common practice in those days to offer one's younger boys into the church that the fact that Charlotte had three children by the Archbishop of Bordeaux was not considered likely to give the Pope a coronary, however people nowadays would shout, 'How shocking!' It was normal behaviour for the young men concerned to live perfectly ordinary lives. Which they did!

The first child was Marie Victoire Adelaide, born in 1779, the second, another girl, Charlotte Maximilienne Amelie, was born a year later. The third and last was a son, Charles Edward, who arrived in 1784. The fate of these grandchildren of the Bonnie Prince has been frequently disputed. A Polish author, Peter Pininski, has gone to great lengths to prove that he is descended from Marie Victoire and thus is the last surviving Stuart. Personally, I do not believe this, particularly the role played by Jules de Rohan — Louise's husband — in the cover up.

It seems that when the girl was born, obviously in greatest secrecy, Ferdinand asked his eldest brother, Jules, to help out, to pretend the child was his and so it is Jules's name that appears on the actual baptism record. But let us not forget that it was Jules's wife — the sexy Louise — who betrayed him with the Bonny Prince in his own house while he was away at war. He must have discovered this after he returned. I simply do not believe that the gossip never reached his ears. Would a man who had been cuckolded by the Bonnie Prince stoop to assist in this plot? I don't think so.

What I think is far more likely is that Thomas Coutts, the banker and person of note in the eighteenth century, who was related to the family of Clementina — the prince's former mistress and the children's grandmother, obliged out of necessity to bring the children up — went to visit them in Paris, took the two girls under his wing and went back with them to England, where they vanished discreetly into polite Georgian society.

The fate of the boy is better documented. He led a most extraordinary life, calling himself Count Roehenstart, going from country to country, always in pursuit of funds. Strangely he died in Scotland, in Dunkeld in Perthshire. The cause of death was a coaching accident. He told so many exaggerated stories about himself during his lifetime that nobody believed a word he said. But eventually the facts were sorted out by historian George Sherburn and it was proved that he was indeed the grandson of Charles Edward Stuart.

In her will, Charlotte did not mention any of her children by name. She left the bulk of her money to her mother, Clementina Walkinshaw, with the words 'and any of her necessitous relatives'. She also left a further amount to a faithful servant — 'the Moor'.

www.ingramcontent.com/pod-product-compliance
Lightning Source LLC
Chambersburg PA
CBHW031122210626
46816CB00016B/1763

* 9 7 8 1 8 3 9 0 1 1 6 1 0 *